THE FORGIVING QUILT

a novel by
Ann Hazelwood

American Quilter's Society
www.AmericanQuilter.com

The American Quilter's Society or AQS is dedicated to quilting excellence. AQS promotes the triumphs of today's quilter, while remaining dedicated to the quilting tradition. We believes in the promotion of this art and craft through AQS Publishing and AQS QuiltWeek®.

Director of Publications: KIMBERLY HOLLAND TETREV
Content Editor: CAITLIN TETREV
Assistant Editor: ADRIANA FITCH
Project Editor: SARAH BOZONE
Graphic Design: CHRIS GILBERT
Cover Design: MICHAEL BUCKINGHAM

Additional copies of this book may be ordered from the American Quilter's Society, PO Box 3290, Paducah, KY 42002-3290, or online at www.ShopAQS.com.

Text and designs © 2016 Ann Hazelwood
Artwork © 2016 American Quilter's Society

Library of Congress Cataloging-in-Publication Data

Names: Hazelwood, Ann Watkins, author.
Title: The forgiving quilt : a novel / by Ann Hazelwood.
Description: Paducah, KY : American Quilter's Society, [2016] | "2015 |
  Series: East Perry County series ; 1
Identifiers: LCCN 2015043272 (print) | LCCN 2015047510 (ebook) | ISBN
  9781604604047 (softcover) | ISBN 9781604603293 (ebook) | ISBN
  9781604603293 ()
Subjects: LCSH: Widows--Fiction. | Self-realization in women--Fiction.
Classification: LCC PS3608.A98846 F67 2016 (print) | LCC PS3608.
A98846
  (ebook) | DDC 813/.6--dc23
LC record available at http://lccn.loc.gov/2015043272

Dedication

I dedicate this novel to my deceased parents, Esther and G.L. (Fritz) Meyr as well as my siblings, Shirley, Betty, Marilyn, and Louis.

My fond memories and appreciation for family history are treasured gifts I hope to share with all of you. Enjoy!

A WARM THANK YOU!
(THE FORGIVING QUILT)

Writing about the charming communities in East Perry County, could not have happened without the generosity of the following people.

Pat Rappa, Pearline and Larry Degenhardt, Nancy Hadler, Carla Jordon, Imogene Unger, Dee McGuade, Audrey Kennedy, Carol Marten, Joan Brown, Eileen Petzoldt and my many relatives and friends, who were born and raised in these communities.

A big thank you as well to all the residents, businesses and museums, who continue to preserve this county for future generations.

CHAPTER 1

"There is no way I'm buying another quilt, Maggie," I said walking away from her in the aisle of Murphy's Antique Mall.

"Kate, look at this amazing price, and it appears to be in really good condition," Maggie persisted.

"You know I'm trying to get rid of things right now," I argued. "No matter where I move, I'll never have the room to keep the quilts I have! If you like it so much, you buy it!"

"I just might, and you'll be sorry when I show it off at the Beach Quilters Monday night," she teased.

"Hey, if you want to stop at the Golden Bakery for coffee, you better hurry up," I warned. We've been here over an hour!"

"Okay, okay, just let me finish this row," she said as she folded up the quilt in her arms. "You're really not going to buy anything?"

"I'm not even tempted, Maggie, so I'll meet you at the front door," I said in frustration.

I loved spending time with Maggie, as she truly was my best friend, but she was the kind of shopper who could drive you crazy as she had to look at each and every item. I, on the other hand, could skim over the merchandise as I walked down the aisle and know at first glance whether I was interested or not. Adding more things to my life right now was bad timing. I could shop with the best of them but my life had just been turned upside down. It was time to downsize!

As I waited for Maggie, I watched buyers purchasing everything from jewelry to benches. Watching the excitement on their faces reminded me of when I had started collecting antiques and quilts during the weekend of the Blueberry Festival.

The Blueberry Festival, in my home town of South Haven, Michigan, brought in thousands of tourists who came every year to enjoy every facet of blueberries imaginable.

"Thanks for waiting," Maggie said as she finally joined me. "Can you carry one of my packages for me? We'd better stop at the car before we go to the bakery. You're not in a hurry are you?"

I took a deep breath, trying to be polite. "I suppose not. These crowds though have a way of wearing you out," I explained. "I'm not sure today's activity has been a good use of my time."

"We've never missed this annual festival, Kate," Maggie said with some impatience brewing. "We both just turned fifty, girlfriend. I hope we can continue our tradition till we're ninety." I laughed. "By the way, I have another cool condo to tell you about!"

We put the packages in her car before heading for coffee.

We squeezed into one of the last empty tables in the corner

of the Golden Bakery. With the August heat, I changed my mind from a hot cup of coffee, to a nice, large glass of frosty ice tea. Maggie insisted we share a piece of their famous cheesecake. Baking was something I loved to do but never did, so when I got around good pastries, I was in heaven. Every time I was here I would think if I could find another way to make pastries. Having baked goods in the house was one of the many luxuries I was not allowed without a lecture from my now deceased husband. He was a health nut who made me turn into a closet eater. I savored my first bite and tried to identify its ingredients.

"So what are you going to do if your house sells quickly?" Maggie asked, breaking the silence from our first bites.

"I'll never get a buyer with the ridiculous price my realtor is asking," I answered between bites. "I do have a buyer for the beach house in Florida, so I'm happy to cross it off my list! Luckily, the next door neighbor wants to buy it."

"That's great!" Maggie responded as she waved hello to a friend she recognized. "Do you have to go to Florida soon?"

"I don't have to go there at all, which is great," I said gratefully. "They're taking the place as is, furniture and all. They'll just end up renting it to their relatives and friends."

"I don't know how you are handling all this, Kate," Maggie said shaking her head in disbelief. "Clay has only been gone a month or so, and you're making all these decisions. Don't they say when you're grieving, you shouldn't be making hasty decisions? You have just had a major, unexpected shock in your life!"

"I want it all over and done with," I stated putting down my napkin. "Clay's car accident was his own fault from his relentless drinking. His recklessness not only took his life, but now Jack and I are paying the price for it. It makes me angrier and angrier when I think about it. He thought he could control everything he touched but he couldn't control himself when it came down to it."

Maggie shook her head in sympathy. "You're reacting a bit harshly," she continued. "I know your house is too big for you. I understand how you would want a change. A nice condo with no upkeep would allow you to travel and do what you want. It's a shame however, since you just got your home decorated the way you wanted. It's absolutely beautiful. It should sell right away, with all you have done."

"It's just a house, Maggie. It was never a home." I said sadly. Maggie looked at me strangely. "I can give it up in a flash. It has too many bad memories." I could tell Maggie was at a loss for words.

"Okay, okay," she said patting my hand. "I just wanted to tell you about a condo Mark's friend is selling. He bought it when he came to South Haven, and now he's getting married. It's like brand new and located in the Meadows. You know you rarely see anything for sale in that gated community. You don't want to wait long to look at it, if you're interested."

"I can't right now, Maggie," I explained. "I have too many other things to do right now.

"Okay, but if it slips away to someone else, don't say I didn't tell you so!" she warned.

"You mean like the log cabin quilt I just passed up?" I said teasing her back.

We sat there for another half hour sharing our latest thoughts and concerns like we had our whole lives growing up together in South Haven. We both shared June birthdays, just two days apart, so we always celebrated together. Neither of us finished college, but I studied Interior Design and Maggie had studied accounting. Maggie was a social butterfly which influenced me as well. Her father finally made her drop out since she wasn't attending classes. Fortunately, she married Mark at an early age and he could afford for her to be a housewife. It suited her just fine. When I married Clay, she couldn't understand why I still felt I wanted a career. Clay didn't understand it either, which was certainly a bone of contention in our marriage. He wanted a trophy wife to enhance his career. He thought I should just concentrate on being Jack's mother and enjoy the country club life, we were privileged to have.

CHAPTER 2

After I left Maggie, I drove home deep in thought. What did women like Maggie and me do when we were no longer kept women and our children were grown? Surely there had to be more than redecorating our houses, charity lunches, quilt gatherings, and fundraisers. Maggie and I were so alike, yet looked totally different. Maggie changed her hair color often because she was terrified of a gray hair showing up. I, on the other hand, had been blonde all my life, so if there were a few gray hairs, they blended in beautifully with my natural color. Maggie was taller than me. We both hated dieting and only admitted it to each other if we cheated. We both knew we married too young, but all our friends seemed to accept engagement rings around the same time. We each had one child. Clay and I had Jack, and Maggie and Mark had a daughter, Jill.

Jack was creating a life of his own in Manhattan with a

successful Ad Agency. He was single and loving every minute of it. Maggie and I often wished her daughter and my son would marry someday. We thought Jack and Jill went together in more ways than one! It was fun to imagine!

Clay and I were very proud of Jack, as he seemed to be well grounded with a heart of gold. If we were lucky, he'd pay a visit to South Haven two times a year. I did worry how Clay's accident might impact him in the future.

My Beach Quilting friends were dear to me and were very diverse in ages and interests. Thank goodness Maggie asked me to join years ago. They didn't care how rich or poor I was, and their personal attention to me after Clay's accident was something I will never forget. It was also an outlet for me to release some of my creative juices, since professional decorating wasn't happening. I loved the therapy quilting provided to me. I loved feeling and buying fabric, as I envisioned many uses for its color and design. I was getting better and better with my skills, taking a class now and then at Cornelia's Quilt Shop.

Maggie made contemporary quilts. The bolder and more colorful they were, the better. She did have a weakness for antique quilts, especially crazy quilts, because of all the embellishments. She loved the latest and greatest machines and gadgets, where I gravitated to hand work. We were each other's greatest fans, which gave us both the confidence we needed. Maggie had the good fortune to display a lot of her quilts in her home. Clay never wanted someone's old quilt hanging in a house of his, so I knew better than try to display them. If it wasn't new or expensive, he didn't consider it worthy. I begged for him to compliment my quilting now and then, but he hardly would take notice, or respond. I was sure he didn't want his friends to know I was a quilter.

Clay's heritage was German and his family succeeded in the lumber business through several generations. Since Clay's father John died, Clay had been President of Meyr Lumber Company. Now with Clay gone, his brother James took over as President. Both brothers were spoiled growing up, with an extravagant lifestyle the business had provided the family. They occasionally disagreed on matters, but nothing serious enough to affect the business. James was married to Sandra, who loved being a trophy wife. We never saw each other unless it was a business related function. She was in her glory since James was now President. There was no doubt they were also grooming one of their two sons to take over when James would be ready to retire. I really didn't care anymore, as my exit sign was flashing in hopes of leading me to a different life.

Immediately after Clay's fatal accident, the Meyr Lumber board of directors offered me a fair settlement. I knew James thought it to be too generous, but he was out numbered on the board and he didn't want to appear insensitive. I tried to think of our son Jack's interest as I settled the matter. I had to give Clay credit for having a will and investing wisely.

When I arrived home, I stayed in my car, deep in thought. I was thinking about what I had and didn't have as my life was changing. What did I want in my new life? Right now, I didn't have a clue!

Carla, our cleaning woman, was a dear friend and had been with us many years. She witnessed many tribulations in our household and her affection was always there, whenever needed. She was ten years older than me, but despite our different ages and lifestyles, we were very close. She was like family. We paid her well, at my insistence, as I knew she had financial difficulties. We would make fun of Clay's quirky demands of neatness and control. She had become a beginner quilter, so I was happy to give her some of the fabric I kept accumulating.

Our neighbors were spread far apart and I had no friends among them. We were living in the most prestigious part of South Haven, Michigan. In the 1780's, pioneers built sawmills here. With its location on Lake Michigan, they could ship to ports in Chicago and Milwaukee. Some of the early steamers were built here in South Haven as well. In no time, schools, businesses, hotels, and homes developed, which also attracted tourism. When the lumber business declined, it freed up land to grow peaches, apples, and blueberries. Blueberries became the town's signature and attracted attention far and wide. Every organization, business, and church embraced the blueberry symbol for advertising and fundraising. The Beach Quilters made a blueberry themed quilt each year, to raffle off for some charity, during the August Blueberry Festival.

I prided myself in making the best blueberry muffins in the state and would win any contest, if entered. Despite my love for baking, there weren't any takers in Clay's healthy kitchen, so I gave away most everything I baked. I owned shelves of cook books and loved picking out recipes I wanted to try or change. Jack loved my chocolate chip cookies, and on occasion, Clay would weaken and enjoy only one. Now and then, I'd send Jack a box of cookies to New York, which pleased him very much.

CHAPTER 3

As I walked in the house, my cell phone rang. It was Maggie.

"You were so anxious to get home, I forget to ask if you were going to the Rotary's "Wine and Dine" event this weekend," Maggie said with excitement. "It might do you good to get out."

"No, I may not be in town," I answered. "Remember, I told you I had many things to take care of. It's a long story, but Clay's Dad acquired some property in Missouri. Clay inherited it after his father's death, and now it's in my lap. I have never been there, but I'm anxious to get it on the market to sell. I thought I might drive there this weekend to get it listed."

"You've got to be kidding me," Maggie said with exacerbation in her voice. "You never mentioned this before."

"Well, there was no reason to," I explained. "I think Clay

and James may have gone there a time or two. It's located in a very, very small town. I think Clay's, Dad may have gone there to hunt or fish, but I really don't know the story. It does have a house I'm told, with a fair number of acres. The sooner I mark it off my list, the better. I'm not up to the Rotary event anyway. I don't know how to respond to people anymore. I'm tired of hearing them say they're sorry. I can't tell if people are genuine in their sympathy for me, or if they just miss Clay's business connections." I could hear Maggie sigh as if she were tired of my pity talk.

"So you're just going to pick up and go just like that?" Maggie asked sarcastically. "What town is it?"

"It's called Borna," I stated. "I do have a realtor's name from there. I already called him and he said he'd meet me there when I'm ready."

"Borna? I never heard of it!" Maggie announced suspiciously.

"On the internet it said it only has two hundred and forty some people so I don't suppose you have heard of it," I casually said. "It's in the eastern part of Perry County in Missouri. I just hope I don't drive through it, I'm praying my GPS will pick it up!"

"So you're okay going alone?" she asked with wonder in her voice.

"Sure; why not?" I responded. "I have nothing else to do right now, and I think the day's drive and getting away from here will do me some good."

"Okay, Miss Independent Lady," Maggie teased. "Keep me informed as you go. If I wasn't on the Rotary's planning committee, I'd insist on going with you."

"I know, but thanks anyway. With me deciding to go

alone, I can leave at any moment," I confessed. "Try to have fun without me. Mark's going, right?"

"I suppose. We haven't talked about it," she said disappointed. "By the way, I stopped at the Farmer's Market after I left you," she said changing the subject. "It was packed but since I was parked nearby, I went ahead and bought some things. It was fabulous as always. Every time I go, they've added more artists."

"I don't need anything, remember?" I reminded her. "It is the best market around for sure! I love all the unique displays of course. Was the guy there who makes all those different kinds of bread?"

"Yes, and I bought some like always," she bragged. "I knew you'd be sorry, you didn't go!" I laughed and agreed she was right. She lucked out today, getting the bargain quilt and the fresh, homemade bread!

After a somewhat lengthy conversation, we hung up saying "love you" to each other as always. We shared everything and truly loved each other. I kept thinking about the bread I missed out on. This particular baker had a small German bakery some miles out of South Haven, and his breads were to die for. You had to get there early, or he would be sold out every time. South Haven's Farmer's Market did not only have produce vendors, but local artists as well. It was not like me to miss it this morning, but my mind was certainly elsewhere!

I went to pour myself another glass of ice tea to cool down and sit out on the sunporch where I had the number of the realtor in Borna. I sat down, kicked off my sandals and laid my head back on the cushioned seat. Was I acting too quickly with everything? I knew to vent my anger which I felt entitled to. Clay's accident could have been avoided, and he nearly killed someone else in the process. As a forsaken widow, I thought I was supposed to be crying all the time, but instead I felt anger. Tears would only come when I saw what it had done to Jack. He looked up to his father, and it was sad to know their relationship had ended.

I decided to relax for the evening and call the realtor in the morning. Somehow I felt this was not a good time for me to make plans. Clay's dog Rocky kept coming by me for attention. He was lost without Clay. Thank goodness Carla had taken an interest in him. I got up to let Rocky out and filled his bowl with his favorite dog food. I suppose I did have a purpose here, as I looked around the large empty house. I'd take a shower and find a book to take my mind off of things. Sleep would be sure to come, if I imagined another time and place.

CHAPTER 4

Hours later, I walked into our master bedroom to change for bed thinking once again about the last night Clay and I shared our bed. We each had our own bedroom, where we dressed and kept our clothes, but we still knew the value of keeping our relationship as personal as we could. I walked into Clay's room, which had been left exactly as it was the day he died. I looked at his oversized closet with his clothes hanging exactly spaced. They would all have to go. I pushed the hangers altogether, knowing if he were watching, he'd go ballistic. Shoes were perfectly lined up in color order. His tie inventory was huge, and yet they all looked alike! After a phone call to Jack to see if he wanted anything, I'd be making a call to Goodwill to come and get everything. On the dresser lay some of his personal things which were given to me after the accident. There were hundred dollar bills in his money clip, plus his wallet and watch. I needed to cancel his memberships, I reminded myself, but those kinds of actions made it all so final.

Clay was buried wearing his wedding ring. I removed mine from my finger after the funeral. I was no longer married. I was a widow. How suddenly life could change in a minute of carelessness. Clay had some nice, expensive accessories. Nothing I saw enticed me to keep anything as a remembrance. There was a pocket watch Clay had inherited from his father, and I had already put it in Jack's hands. When I think back, Clay was definitely his father's favorite, which I knew James had to be aware of. Perhaps it had to do with Clay being the older of the two, but Clay indicated James was just not as responsible.

There lay his cell phone as if it were waiting for someone to put in their pocket or make a call. I couldn't help but wonder who Clay's last phone message was from. As I scanned the numbers, I didn't recognize any of them, besides my own. Sometimes he would call to let me know his schedule, but no frivolous calls to just check in on me. Most of the calls were to either tell me he'd be late or if something had to be cancelled. I was not listed as one of his calls on the last day of his life. One number appeared frequently, so I assumed it was work related. Out of curiosity, I decided to click on his voice mails. His last call was from the store in Douglas, confirming his appointment. The next was a woman's voice which said, "Hi babe, sorry I had to change our plans at the last minute, but I had no choice. Give me a call. Love you!"

"What was this? I repeated it back to make sure I heard it correctly. Babe? Who would be telling Clay she loved him? Despite wanting to throw up right there on the bedroom carpet, I scrolled to hear if there were any more voice mails from her. Sure enough, another said, "Great weekend babe. I'll see what I can do about the Hamptons. Love you!"

I sat on the side of the bed to get a grip on what I was hearing. I guess I was really as stupid as Clay thought I was most of the time. This had to be an ongoing affair and with all the travel Clay did, I was totally ignoring it all. I never dreamed he was insensitive enough to have an affair. I thought he wanted everything perfect! Would he really be so stupid as to take a chance with a love affair?

I had to find out who she was. I didn't recognize her voice, so it couldn't be any of my friends, thank goodness. I stood up to copy down the number from the phone. So Clay had it all, he must have thought. How long had this been going on? Now he has nothing and no one. Who did he think of when he faced his sudden death? Why wasn't I enough, as the perfect wife? I noticed the last voice mail from her was on the day he had the accident. Was he upset she had to change their plans and he had too many drinks? When did she learn of his accident and how? Was she at the funeral? These were so many questions making me weak and crazy. Who else knew about this affair?

I walked back into our bedroom and knew I would never sleep in our bed ever again. I walked into the kitchen to pour myself a glass of wine. Did I want to call Maggie? Did I dare share this with anyone? My hands were shaking, almost spilling the wine. I took my full glass out onto the sunporch, searching for fresh air. I took in deep breaths to avoid total panic. I sat on the lounge seat and laid back to talk to the only person who was listening to me. Please God help me digest and get through this, I prayed. No one must know what I know. At least, not yet!

CHAPTER 5

Around two o'clock in the morning, I awoke in the darkness of the sunporch. The discovery of Clay's affair came rushing back in my mind. It wasn't just a nightmare, and I needed to get a grip and get over it. I realized I still had his phone in my hand so I went to my bedroom and placed it in my dresser drawer. I hoped he could see that I knew about his affair.

Even though it was the middle of the night, I decided to shower as if I could scrub away the bitter resentment I was feeling. I wanted to scream out and call him names. I couldn't imagine ever forgiving him. Any happy memories of our marriage seemed to disappear instantly.

Carla would be in today. I'd have her make the phone calls to bag and collect Clay's things. The sooner, the better! It might even give her as much pleasure, as it did me, to have his things out of the house.

I put on some coffee and decided I would make that phone call to the realtor in Missouri as soon as the sun came up. It now was more important than ever to cross it off my list. Now that I had a plan, I suddenly had an appetite. I went to the freezer and pulled out a white iced jelly roll saved from the Golden Bakery. I was hoping it had a thousand calories. I deserved each and every one of them. From now on I wouldn't feel guilty about eating or doing whatever I wanted. No going to the gym today to work out. I may never go back to the place where Clay gave me a membership every year. I held the gooey pastry up in my hand, as if to show Clay what I was eating. After I warmed up and devoured my sugar high and one cup of coffee, I decided to call the number of the woman known as "babe." I retrieved the cell phone from my dresser drawer and clicked on the number. If nothing else, it was going to freak her out to get a call from a dead man. After three rings, a sleepy voice said, "Yes?" I took a deep breath and stupidly said, "With whom am I speaking?" Her response was a quick hang up. What was I expecting? Did I think she was going to say who she was or say, "Yes, it's babe. What's up?"

I suddenly heard Carla come in the house, calling out to me. I quickly put the phone back in my dresser drawer and went to greet her.

"You're here earlier than usual Carla," I said with a grin. I was actually glad to see her.

"Speak for yourself, Miss Kate," Carla said with sarcasm. "What has you up so early, today?"

"Oh, lots of things, plus I wasn't sleeping so well," I explained. "I decided it's time we get rid of Clay's clothes and things. I have Goodwill's number on the desk and wondered if you would call them today and ask if they can take the things as is, or if they have to be boxed or bagged." She looked at me strangely. "I also will be going out of town over the weekend to list the property in Missouri, so I'll be arranging those plans today. There isn't really much cleaning to do, so do you mind taking care of that?"

"Why of course not, but are you sure you are ready for all of this?" Carla asked with concern. "Don't you think you should give this a little more time?"

"Oh no, it's time," I confirmed. "Folks have told me I would know when it's time, and it's time! Just concentrate on the clothing and shoes. Keep his accessories in a box. I'll have Jack take a look at them the next time he comes home." She knew I was dead serious.

"Okay honey," she said sadly. "How is our Mr. Jack, anyway?"

"He's fine and very, very busy, which has to be helpful for him," I reported. "He used his vacation time for the funeral, so I don't know when I'll get to see him again."

"Now let me know when you leave, ya hear? I'll be sure to check on the house every day," she offered. "You can't be too careful they say, after someone's death. Some folks watch the obituaries and funeral dates thinking no one will be home."

"I know, and I appreciate what you're saying," I said with gratitude. "My realtor here has only shown the house once or twice. I think the listing price is way too expensive and I'm going to tell her so. I'm anxious to get out of here."

Carla looked shocked at my attitude. "Well, you have no place to go to, so it better not sell too fast," she warned. "What's the hurry?"

"I need to move on Carla," I said, knowing she didn't

know my circumstances. "I have way too much stuff, and I want a much smaller place like a condo or one of those cute small houses on Lakewood Street."

"My yes, Miss Kate," she nodded. "You do have too much stuff! I've told you so for a long time." She laughed as she poured herself a cup of coffee. "I'll make the call shortly, and we'll get this show on the road."

"Thanks, Carla," I said smiling. "I don't know what I'd do without you."

I went to find the piece of paper with the realtor's name in Borna, Missouri. I apparently didn't have much to choose from in the region, so I hoped he had a good reputation.

"Blade here," he casually answered as if he was waiting to hear from a friend.

"This is Kathryn Meyr from South Haven, Michigan," I announced. "I talked to you briefly about a listing there in Borna. I'll be arriving this weekend to list the property on 6229 Main Street. Could you meet me there on Monday morning?"

"Why yes, ma'am," he said with a country twang. "I've been expectin' your call. I'm sorry to hear about your Mister's accident." I remained silent. "So, I'll stop by around 9:00 then, if that'll suit you ma'am. You'll find the key to the house underneath the back door mat."

"Very good," I responded. "I want to settle this as quickly as possible."

"Yes ma'am," he concluded. "I'll take care of it!"

I hung up feeling I'd taken a baby step, and I began to look forward to getting out of the house and driving into the countryside. I immediately went to my bedroom to throw a few days' worth of clothing and toiletries into my overnight bag.

I would have to find a place to stay once I was close. It was my understanding the property was pretty run down and not to expect too much. It dawned on me I should have asked this Blade guy for directions, in case my GPS didn't pick up the area. I could always call him as I got closer.

I called Maggie to let her know my plans, and told her I would email some photos once I got there. She warned me like a little child to be careful, and how sorry she was about not going with me.

"Don't you wine and dine too much with those Rotarians, okay?" I teased her. "I know how you can sometimes be!" When she laughed, it was with the warm feeling of someone who really cared for me and made me realize I still had some things to be thankful for.

I went to tell Carla I would be leaving first thing in the morning. I suggested she take Rocky home with her, but she thought it best she check on the property each day and leave him here. She told me not to worry. Later, I would ask Carla if she would take Rocky permanently. If she declined, I would make it a point to ask James if he had any interest. Jack had fun with Rocky, but never felt he had a very personal attachment to the dog. We all knew Rocky was Clay's dog. Right now, I didn't want any reminder of Clay around me.

Carla said she had made the call to Goodwill, and she would begin to get things ready for tomorrow's pick up. I decided to run a few errands, which included buying some emergency things to keep in my car. Our trips were always in Clay's SUV so I wanted to equip my car with anything I might need including a blanket from the hall closet. My new Mercedes was Clay's idea, and I would soon get rid of it when time allowed. It was certainly dependable enough for this trip.

This was going to be a little adventure to get my mind off of my adulterant, alcoholic dead husband.

When I returned home, I got out a map to visualize where I would be going. There seemed to be one small town after another in what they called East Perry. The town names were German, which comforted me. Borna was certainly an odd name. I would have to ask Blade about its origin.

I checked out Clay's bedroom, and Carla had done her job well. There were boxes and piles ready for someone to remove. How sad it all was. I had to remind myself this was all just stuff, just like our house was only a brick and mortar building. It never really was a home like the first house Clay and I had on Sulphur Street. We both seemed to be pretty happy there. Raising Jack with his school activities, plus a charity or two, kept me busy and satisfied.

Clay and his brother were competitive not only in the business, but with their personal lives as well. If one got a boat, the other had to have a bigger one. The houses were the same way. Their relationship was kept civil, for mostly business purposes, till their father suddenly passed away. James never got over Clay being next in line to run the company. Business was booming now, and I knew they were looking to expand in other states, which was why I thought Clay was traveling so much. Did James know he was seeing someone? I'm sure I would find out in time.

When I crawled into bed, my plans allowed me to relax and fall into sleep.

CHAPTER 6

The next morning, after I took care of Rocky's needs, I gave him a hug, grabbed my bag and got in my car for a long day's drive. From glancing at my map, I would be driving major highways till I arrived in the more rural part of Missouri. I wanted to put any negative thoughts of Clay out of my mind today and only think of a relaxing drive, change of scenery, and getting this transaction completed. It was times like this I wished my father were still alive. I valued his opinion, and some of his advice concerning Clay was now coming back to me. My mother died when I was a teenager, so my father and I were very close. He'd been gone for two years now, and there isn't a day I didn't think of him.

After a few hours rolled by, I needed gas and felt rather hungry. I glanced across the highway and noticed a fast food place that had hamburger written all over it. Today, I was going to indulge hoping once again Clay was looking at me in disgust.

The hamburger, accompanied by french fries and a diet coke, was pure delight. I had forgotten how much satisfaction they could provide. It was another small step to freedom and perhaps a tiny bit of revenge.

Even the relaxing drive and enjoyable meal couldn't get this other woman out of my mind. Was she from his office? Was she thinner than me? Did I know her? Was she at the funeral? I tried to think who all was there, but unfortunately, at least a hundred people came by for the visitation. Most of them were work related and I'd never seen them before. I knew I would feel better once I shared this discovery of "babe" with Maggie. Perhaps I could call her tonight.

Missouri was a state I had never been to before. The beautiful hills with sunshine reflecting on early patches of fall color pleasantly surprised me. The many cliff cuts made the roadway somewhat mysterious. So far, my GPS was on track and told me I had a good many miles to go before my destination. Getting there before dark was now my biggest concern, as well as a place to lay my head for the night. Perhaps there would be a charming bed and breakfast in the area. Why didn't I check into such a place before I left?

It was getting near dusk when I pulled off the major highway onto a well maintained county road. The curves and hills started coming one after another. I passed white painted fences, farms, churches, and houses nestled amongst the forest. It was charming for sure. Before I had to make a turn on another road, I saw a sign for Unionville up ahead with a population of 161. A charming colonial house with green shutters on small paned windows caught my eye. I wanted to check it out, but time was running short. From what I could tell, it looked vacant. Perhaps I could stop on my way out of town. This must be where all the small towns begin. I had passed a bigger sign that advertised the historic town of Dresden, so it must be more sizable and popular.

I made the turn and found myself going much slower than the rest of traffic on this rural road. Large trucks, who obviously knew where they were going, wanted to pass me. Some had signs that had East Perry Lumber written on them. To alleviate my nervousness, I pulled over on a side road to let the cars and trucks pass me by. As I continued along, I started seeing places where large areas of trees were cleared away and in the distance noticed buildings belonging to the lumber company. It didn't appear I was going to escape the lumber industry. Strangely, no one told me about any lumber company being located here. Perhaps that was the tie that Clay's father had when he purchased this property. I rolled down the window to breath in the fresh country air. The temperature was cool, but very refreshing. Hopefully, my little town of Borna would be appearing soon around one of these curves. It was interesting to see all the varieties of homes and barns. I loved barns for some reason. Many of these seemed to be well maintained. I loved the animals who wanted to greet any living soul along the fence lines. I thought about stopping to take photos on my phone, but there never seemed to be a place to pull along the roadside.

Finally, the sign I had been looking for - Borna: Population 254. Thank goodness there was still some daylight to help me see house numbers. I passed a tavern type of business with lots of pick-up trucks parked in front. This must be the place to be on a Saturday night, I assessed. Around the next curve, I saw a large brick house on the right, fairly close to the road.

Quite clearly on a stone was painted 6229. This is it! I own that brick house, I told myself. I slowly kept going down the road so I could see what else Main Street provided. There was another tavern and then a sign to the left that read Saxon Village. If I kept going straight, the road was going to lead me to the town of Dresden. Okay, this was it. I saw Borna in thirty seconds. I turned around, with no other cars coming either way, and headed back to the brick house.

I carefully pulled into a driveway putting me under a huge tree with a twisted trunk. As I looked towards the large, bulky, brick house, I saw a light on in the window most likely from the kitchen. I got out of the car and looked around the forsaken place, which could have been lovely at one time. Behind the house was a small barn like structure, with an open carport area filled with junk and a stack of wood. A nice brick patio greeted me before I went up the steps to a small wooden deck. It was obvious the patio and deck had been added in the last ten years. Before I went up the steps, I couldn't help noticing the deafening silence of the night. I held my breath as I turned the door mat over in hopes of finding the key. To my relief there it was just like Blade said. I pushed open the heavy door and the smell of old house wafted over me. I reached for the nearest light switch and found an outdated kitchen with an ancient stove and refrigerator. The empty darkness was somehow very sad. My eyes noticed heavy ornate woodwork leading me into the spacious dining room with a large bay window. My eyes were drawn to a double open doorway with pocket doors coming out from inside the wall. I found another light switch bringing my attention to the large fireplace in what was likely the living room. Odds and ends of trash were strewn about and the dust was smelly and heavy. As I came out of the living room, I found myself in a grand hallway which featured a large, wooden staircase leading to the upstairs. Even with the terrible dim light, I could see the ornateness of the staircase. Off the hallway were two smaller rooms connected to each other. Something told me I should wait till morning to explore the upstairs.

I was feeling chilly, as the house seemed colder than the outdoors. There wasn't any furniture or heat, so spending the night here would mean sleeping in my car. I started to see if I could find the thermostat when I heard a loud banging at the front door. I must have jumped a good foot or two, in fright. The center of the huge door was an oval piece of glass revealing a lady waving to me. I wasn't sure what to do. She appeared harmless. Maybe she thought I broke in.

"Hello!" she yelled.

"Can I help you?" I finally asked without opening the door. A petite, brown haired, woman stood there with a big smile.

"I'm your next door neighbor," she continued to say in a loud voice. "I didn't mean to scare you!" I took a deep breath and unlocked the double, locked door. It was much heavier than the back door. "I'm Eleanor Meers, from next door," she began. "I saw the light on over here, and knew you might be showing up some time today. I try to keep an eye out for this place."

"I'm Kathryn Meyr," I said cautiously. Either she was a very nice neighbor or a nosy one.

"How did you know I was coming?" I asked feeling calmer.

"Well, in case you haven't noticed, Borna is a small town, and Blade, your realtor, is like a little old lady in these parts.

We all look out for each other around here, you might say. It's not like we have a police station down the road." She blushed.

"He seemed to be the only realtor, so he agreed to list the place for me," I confessed.

"That's right," she nodded. "You can't get any of the larger realtors to come out this way. Blade knows everyone around here. Most folks just put a for sale sign out themselves, but if you need a realtor, Blade's all over it."

"Well, it's nice to meet you, Eleanor," I said with a smile.

"Please call me Ellie like everyone else does around here," she offered. "I live alone next door here to your right, and I own a winery down the road."

"Oh, a winery, how nice!" I trying to picture it in my mind. "Say, do you know where the thermostat might be in this house. It's really chilly in here."

"It's probably down the hall, but I don't think I'd turn it on, without having it checked first, Kathryn," she warned. She saw my disappointment. "I think you should just come next door with me and spend the night. I'll fix you something to eat and offer you a good glass of wine. How about it?"

"Oh, I couldn't impose!" I immediately responded. "You don't even know me."

"I know enough," she nodded with a smile. "I know you are a very fine lady from South Haven, Michigan. I also know, you really don't have any options on where to sleep tonight, other than your car, and I wouldn't advise it. You're probably hungry and very tired after your long, day's drive. Besides, I would enjoy the company." She made sense, and she had a very, honest look about her.

"Well, if you insist," I said, giving in to a very tempting offer.

"Please call me Kate."

"Okay Kate. Just drive your car out of your place, and drive around to the back entrance to my house next door," she instructed. "The whole town likely knows you've arrived, but I wouldn't leave your car parked here." I didn't ask what she meant by that.

I did just as she instructed and I felt pretty fortunate for her offer. Hopefully, my gut feeling about Ellie would prove to be a good move.

CHAPTER 7

I grabbed my one bag out of my car and entered Ellie's tiny house. It looked more like a quaint cottage. The warm charming atmosphere embraced me immediately as my eyes noticed her many collectibles.

"This is adorable, Ellie," I said as I put down my bag. "My love is interior design and this is right out of a magazine!"

"Well, thanks, but I didn't have much to choose from in Borna when I wanted to find a place," she revealed. "I had to redo everything, but now I'm real happy with it. It's really a one person house, but I have everything just like I want it. I feel really safe being close to the road." Oh, it all sounded so perfect to me! "Your room is off the hall down here. That's where I put anyone who comes to stay. You have a really small bath, but it all works! Freshen up if you like, while I get you something to eat. Are you a white or red wine drinker?"

"Whatever you have already opened," I said graciously.

"Please don't go to any trouble."

"I'll pour you one of my house reds from the winery," she suggested. "I think you'll like it. I bet you drink red, am I right? I'm a pretty good judge of folks and their wine."

"You're right. It sounds good!" I chuckled under my breath.

The tiny bedroom was like a doll house with nooks and crannies too cute to touch. Everything was cream or white, and my feet sank into a plush white throw rug in front of my bed. I was so tired, I could have crawled into a ball and gone to sleep on the rug. This was better than any B&B I could hope to find.

When I came out to join her, Ellie had a healthy sized ham sandwich waiting for me on the coffee table with nice large glass of red wine. She bragged about the country ham, and said she had homemade cookies if I was still hungry.

"I haven't eaten since lunch," I confessed. "I was in such a hurry to get here before dark. I didn't want to take time to eat." As I ate, I admired her darling blue and white kitchen which was the size of one our bathrooms at home. The wine was perfect, and Ellie was watching as I took my first sip.

"Do you like it?" she asked eagerly.

"Oh yes; I must remember the name of this to take home with me," I said wiping my mouth with a blue and white checked napkin.

"Welcome to Borna!" she said lifting her glass to make a toast.

"Borna!" I responded with my clink of the glass.

"Not to bring up your unfortunate situation Kate, because I know you just lost your husband recently in a terrible accident, but how is it you ended up with this property?"

"I think it's a very fair question to ask," I began to explain as I cleared my throat. "My husband's father bought this property a long time ago. I have no clue how it all happened because this property was never mentioned to me till after my husband was killed. My husband inherited it and now it's mine. They must have rented it to folks off and on from what I've heard. I think he and his brother may have been here once or twice, but I really don't have any background. I'm putting all our property up for sale, which is why I'm here.

"I know you come from South Haven, Michigan," she said smiling. "It's beautiful there on the lake and I've seen pictures of the light houses."

"Yes, it's beautiful, but a fun thing about South Haven is that it is the blueberry capitol of the world!" I bragged laughing.

"Wow, how fun is that?" Ellie responded. "I love blueberries."

"I should have brought you some!" I said. "So tell me about Borna! I am curious about the name. Do you know any of its history?"

"Fortunately, you are talking to the town's history buff," she admitted. "Most of the small villages around here are named after German people or the towns they left in the Saxony region of Germany. Borna is one of them. I've read its villagers were into landscaping and lumbering, so when they arrived here they chose to name it Borna. I'm told the rolling hills are very similar there. The town has a high percentage of Lutherans, who settled here. The first Lutheran college is not far from here in Dresden. We have a Saxon Village near here as well. It tells the history of the first settlers in this region. If you can visit there, before you head back, you would enjoy it! There is a lot of history here and folks are pretty proud of it."

"Well, it all sounds interesting," I said smiling. "I'm feeling rather at home then, as all the Meyr's are Lutheran. Clay and I were never very active at our church. Our son Jack went to the Lutheran grade school in South Haven."

"Oh, so you have a son?" Ellie asked with interest.

"Yes, Jack, who's twenty-eight and lives in Manhattan now," I shared. "I worry about him and how his father's accident will impact his future."

"How are you handling what's happened?" Ellie asked with concern.

"Oh, that is a loaded question for which I have no answer," I teased. "I take it one day at a time. It was a nice diversion to take this trip and get away for a while." She nodded like she really understood.

"So, what about you, Ellie?" I asked, wanting to get the topic away from me. "Do you have children?"

"No, I don't," she quickly stated. "I did have an early, short marriage at a very young age, but thankfully we did not have children. I am living my lifelong dream right now. I always wanted to have my own business instead of working for other people. I wanted a rural setting for the winery. The business also gives me the opportunity to meet folks from all over the country. The Red Creek Winery, which is its name, has provided me the best of both worlds. I just acquired a piece of land nearby where I want to plant grapes. I have some good workers now who can help me, when the time is right. Frankly, it's where I spend all my time, so I really don't need a big house."

"It does sound perfect for you," I said jealously. What a

fairytale, I thought.

"So what is your lifelong dream?" Ellie asked catching me off guard.

"Frankly Ellie, I didn't know I wasn't allowed to have my own dream," I said sadly. "I know that sounds strange, but I got caught up in being a model wife for my husband's career." She looked at me with sadness.

"So now what happens with no husband?" she finally asked.

"You hold on to that question Ellie, but for right now, I'm in the process of selling off this house and our other property. I'm hoping to downsize into a condo. I have a very large house right now."

"Well, I'm not going to keep you up all night," she said getting up to remove our glasses. "You have to be exhausted. We can talk more tomorrow over a good cup of coffee. I don't go to the winery till close to lunch time. If you need anything, just let me know."

"This was more than I ever dreamed, Ellie," I said shaking my head in disbelief. "Thank you so very much."

CHAPTER 8

I quickly fell asleep when my head hit the soft pillow. When I didn't wake up till morning, I knew I'd had a good night's sleep for a change. I had to reacquaint myself as to where I was in this little princess bedroom. I could smell the coffee, so knew I needed to jump into the shower and get ready for the day.

"Good morning," Ellie greeted when I joined her.

"Oh, I can't remember when I've had such a good night's sleep," I bragged as I stretched my arms.

"That's great!" she said pouring me some coffee. "Are you really hungry or will some delicious German coffee cake be sufficient for you? I have peach crumb and toasted coconut."

"Coffee cake sounds great!" I answered with my stomach growling. "Did you make this?"

"Oh, heavens no," she said shaking her head. "No one can make this German coffee cake like Helen Grebing. I buy it from her when I can. It's too time consuming. It's not as easy as it looks, and I don't have time in my life to watch dough rise for any occasion."

"Is there a recipe?" I asked taking the first bite. "Oh my, this is delicious."

"Well, I'm sure there is, but no one can master the little details that make it turn out like hers," she explained. "I don't know if she uses a recipe. That generation of good coffee cake bakers is slipping away. During the Saxon Fall Festival, they bake many of these coffee cakes in their outdoor oven!"

"Seriously, they're baked in an outdoor oven?" I asked between bites. "I would love to see that. I love to bake more than anything else. I would be curious to try her recipe. It's so rich in flavor and the texture is not like any other coffee cake." Ellie nodded in agreement.

"I'll try to check on the recipe for you," Ellie said as she tidied up her kitchen. "You could probably handle it, if you bake a lot, but I would never make it myself."

"Oh, Ellie, I better get next door to meet Blade," I said looking at my watch.

"Just leave your car here," she suggested. "You'll need to stay at least another night don't you think? I have to leave here before noon time, but I'd love to invite you to the winery tonight. We can celebrate your FOR SALE sign going up. I'll leave the house unlocked, so you can come back here anytime you want."

"Really? I asked, thinking how trustworthy she must be. "That would be great except I really didn't bring any nice clothes."

"If they're clean, you'll be fine," she teased with a laugh. "Everyone around here dresses casually. If I you need anything to wear, I can help you out there. Now if you get hungry at lunch, you can raid my refrigerator or go down the road a piece to Marv's place. He has great sandwiches and everyone there is really nice."

"You mean the tavern I passed with the pick-up trucks last night?" I asked with a smile.

"That's it," she nodded. "We don't have a lot of choices around here. Don't let all the men who hang out there bother you. Marv's girls will be glad to help you."

"Okay, thanks," I said putting on my light jacket.

I went on my way by foot and decided to walk around my house in daylight to see it better. The landscaping sure needed attention, and the leaves on some of the trees were already falling on the lawn. It was a stately house, built around the turn of the century. I figured. Dr. Paulson, who was the man whose family my father-in-law had purchased it from, was probably one of few folks in town who could afford to build a house like this. I visualized the large front porch with sturdy wicker furniture and maybe a swing at one time. Walking towards the back, I saw some stain glass windows on the side of the house by the good sized, bay window. I wonder what this house looked like after the Doctor had it built? Surely someone will want to take a look at this property right in the middle of Borna. This empty, forsaken place on Main Street has surely been an eye sore for the community.

I was ready to unlock the back door when an old, green, SUV pulled up in the drive. This must be Blade arriving.

"Well, I see you found the ole place," he yelled, getting out of the car. "I'm Blade, by the way!"

I found myself looking at a bad version of a car salesman and a cowboy. He looked about fifty, had a dark mustache, and wore a cowboy hat and boots. This good ole boy was going to be my realtor?

"Yes, I'm Kathryn Meyr," I announced, as he got closer, to shake my hand. "I got here last night. Ellie, next door, was nice enough to let me to spend the night at her place."

"Oh yeah, the wine lady's been pretty nice about keepin' an eye out here," he reported with a slur in his voice. So Ellie was known as the wine lady around here?

As we walked in the house, I was feeling somewhat awkward around him, but this wasn't South Haven, I told myself.

"Have you had a chance to take a look around this forsaken place?" Blade asked shaking his head.

"Somewhat," I answered. "I haven't been upstairs, but I think it's a pretty sturdy house despite the dirt and clutter."

"It's been vacant a good while now, Ms. Meyr," he stated with disgust. "It needs a buyer real soon, and I'm more than happy to see that happen!"

"I just bet you are!" I responded without thinking. "So what can you tell me about this place?" I headed for the staircase.

"Ah shoot, it's old, I know that much," he began. "Ole Doc. Paulson kept it real nice in those days, but when he got really sick, he sold it to someone who never came around here. So when doc died, the place died, too. Then by golly, I get this call from a new owner who said they needed to rent the place for some income. They asked if I could arrange it. Well, that didn't go so well. The renters couldn't pay much and didn't take care of it. Before long, I couldn't collect any rent at all. It ain't easy evicting folks, I can tell you that much."

Blade's description was not painting a very pretty picture of this place. He followed me up the stairs, which still continued to make me feel uncomfortable. When I looked at all the doors off the large open hallway, I couldn't believe the sizable rooms and closets. One door went to the attic, which Blade was hesitant to show me, so I thought I'd check it out later after he was gone. A large doorway with pocket doors connected the two largest bedrooms, which I thought was interesting. The hardwood floors were surprisingly in very good condition, considering the age of the house and having renters. The biggest bedroom had a fireplace, which was a nice surprise. It was open to a smaller room which was likely a sitting room years ago.

"Does the furnace work and what about the fireplaces?" I asked Blade, who shrugged his shoulders like he didn't have a clue. "Any prospective buyer is going to want to know this Blade. Will you get someone to check it out for me?"

"If you want, but you can also let the new buyer deal with all that stuff," he said lazily. "By the way, I had two different renters remark about something mysterious going on upstairs. I don't know what exactly, but it's not something we'd want to share with anyone who looks at this place."

"You mean like a ghost?" I ask blatantly. He nodded. I ignored what seemed to be nonsense and probably hearsay. "Is this the only bathroom in this house?"

"No, there's a half bath off of Doc's exam room downstairs," he reported. "That other small room to the right is where his patients waited."

"Oh, how nice!" I said picturing it all. "He knew exactly what he wanted when he built this place, didn't he?"

"I suppose ma'am," he said following me down the stairs.

"Blade, do you know of any help I could get around here, to clean up this place?" I asked as another dumb-founded look covered his face.

"Why on God's earth would you want to go to all the trouble ma'am?" he asked with a raised voice. "I sell a lot of places "as is." Let the next guy go to all the work and expense. There's a sucker born every minute, ya know!" He busted out laughing. I couldn't believe his attitude.

"I don't do things that way Blade," I said as calmly as I could. "I owe it to my Father-in-Law to do the right thing here. I want the place presentable to show, for heaven's sake. I'll do it myself if I have to. What about the yard? Can you find me a couple of young men to clean and rake up the yard and patio?"

"I don't know," he said scratching his head. "I have some fellas help me now and then."

"Where can I buy some cleaning things in this town?" I asked as I watched him squirm.

"Down the road at Harold's Hardware, in Dresden," he pointed.

"I see potential here Blade, and the more we can get for this house, the more money you'll get," I said boldly. "Making it clean and attractive will mean more dollars. Doesn't that make sense to you?"

"Yes ma'am," he said in a sour tone. "You're the boss. I'll see who I can find."

"I'll also need a dumpster or a place to put all the trash we carry out of here," I added ignoring him. He shook his head and walked out the door.

I assessed the downstairs and knew the only way to make things more presentable was to haul out any trash and give the house a good cleaning. I decided to start by making a trip to Harold's Hardware in Dresden. I was anxious to get another look at the neighboring village anyway, so off I went.

The sun was shining and I felt a sense of freedom I hadn't had for some time. Did this freedom include cleaning? When was the last time I had to clean anything? Did I even know what supplies I needed to buy? If Carla could see me now, she'd be roaring with laughter.

I drove down the road and around the corner and saw a sign for Dresden, stating the population was 352. Seeing more businesses, a school, and a bank said to me this village was perhaps more prosperous, than Borna. There was Harold's, on the right, like Blade had described. There was parking right in front of the historic building, which had a large red sign saying Harold's Hardware.

"See you later Harold!" yelled a young man coming out of the store. As I came in the door, I looked for the person he called Harold. A good sized, friendly looking man in his sixties or so stood behind the counter wearing a green carpenter's apron. This must be Harold. He smiled and nodded to me as I moved towards him. I looked about the small store and spotted the aisle with the cleaning supplies. I filled my arms with things I thought I would need for basic cleaning. Harold approached me and asked if he could help me find anything.

"No thanks, but if you can take these things to the counter, I can get the rest," responding to the offer.

"I'll be happy to," he said with a big grin. "Are you new to these parts?"

"Yes, I'm Kathryn Meyr," I replied extending my hand. "You must be Harold."

He laughed. "You're Doc Paulson's house owner, I bet," he said shaking my hand.

"That's right, but hopefully not for long," I noted. "I hope to get it on the market after I do a little cleaning up on the place."

"Ahh, such a fine place at one time," he reminisced. "Doc delivered our first born son, way back. Now he's got his own family. We sure miss having our own village doctor around here. Now we have to go to a clinic some miles away, and ya never know if you're gonna get the same doctor." That sounded unfortunate to me.

"I love these small villages," I said with a big smile. "They have so much charm and history."

"You got that right, but we've all had to share some municipal services to make ends meet," he shared. "Some folks now and then suggest we merge Dresden and Borna to save even more money, but it's very controversial so I don't think it'll ever happen!"

"Oh, my, I didn't know anything about that," I said with some concern.

"It's really all about the name change," he stated. "Folks don't like change, and if they grew up in Borna, they want it to remain Borna. Each town has its own history, so blending the two doesn't make sense to me. If we were to merge, the law says we'd have to come up with a completely different name. I can't imagine anyone agreeing to do that. How would you like someone to come along and suggest you change your name?" I smiled understanding his point.

"So have you let the city fathers know how you feel?" I asked as if it were my business. He shook his head.

"I have to do business here ma'am so I never voice my opinion on anything political like this in public," he said as he took my charge card. "I just try to understand both sides and lend them an ear if I have to."

"Well, that's too bad," I said, thinking about how I would feel. "I better get going. I have lots to clean today. It was nice to meet you Harold. Thanks for your help."

"Same to you, ma'am," he said graciously. "I'll help you carry this to your car."

"Thanks so much," I happily responded. "You'll probably be seeing me again!" He waved me goodbye as I drove away. What a dedicated, sweet, man he was.

I decided to drive down the road a bit further and came upon a sizeable Lutheran church. Next to it was a sign for the Lutheran Heritage Center and Museum. The log cabin sitting farther back from the road must be the college Ellie was telling me about. Too bad I didn't have more time to stay a few days longer so I could see all the historic sites. I turned the car around and headed back to Doc's house. Somehow calling it Doc's house seemed a better reference to my house, as I only had the title to the house.

When I pulled into the front of the house, there was Blade's SUV, and it appeared he had two young men with him. He seemed to be giving them instructions. This was a good thing. One had a rake in his hand and was heading to the front of the house.

"Oh, Blade, thank you!" I said as I got out of the car. "I picked up some cleaning supplies so I could get started in the kitchen. Please let your helpers know I will pay them well if they do a good job."

"Gotcha," he yelled out. "I told them to carry all the yard waste to the sink hole a ways down the road from here," he reported.

"Is it my sinkhole, and is that legal?" I asked innocently. He laughed and shook his head like I was some dim wit.

"I think if you, the owner says it's okay, we're good!" he said with his sleazy grin.

"Okay Blade, give me a break," I retorted. "I'm not from here and I don't know the rules. I met Harold, by the way. I like him. I better get to work."

I could tell Blade loved bossing the guys around. He was not about to pick up a stick himself, however. I looked at the grimy kitchen as I unpacked my supplies. I wasn't quite sure where to start so I opened the cabinets and started tearing out the old shelf paper. I was thinking about whether to have Blade haul off the stove and refrigerator. I sure wouldn't want them, if it were my house. As I opened each cabinet, I prayed I wouldn't find any traces of a live or dead mouse. If I did, I'd be on the road to South Haven in a flash.

When I stopped to get myself another bottle of water, it dawned on me that I hadn't thought of Clay and his "babe" for one minute today. This distraction was turning out to be a good thing for me. I also realized the visit had given me a new, sweet friend named Ellie.

CHAPTER 9

When I was down on my knees cleaning out underneath the kitchen sink, my cell phone rang. I quickly grabbed my phone out of my purse and saw it was Maggie.

"Well, thanks for getting back to me," she began her call. "We were late getting back last night or I would have called you. You're not lying on the side of the road are you?"

"Oh, I'm sorry Maggie," I said feeling badly. "When I finally got here, right before dark, things happened so quickly, I didn't think to call. Fortunately, a really sweet neighbor, who lives next door, offered to let me stay at her house for the night, or I would have had to sleep in my car. There is nothing around here like a hotel, motel, or a B&B. She's single and owns a winery close by. In fact, she's invited me to go there this evening. How about that? Her little house is adorable so I'll be staying there again tonight."

"Well, well, aren't you the trusting tourist!" Maggie teased.

"I guess you did luck out there, but what's your old house like? Don't forget, you said you'd send me a picture."

"Oh, I will; I just haven't had a chance," I explained. "This place is a real mess, Maggie. I have to get it in better condition before I put a sign out. I can't let people see it in this condition.

"So who's going to clean it for you?" she innocently asked.

"It appears it's going to be me," I confessed. "When you called, I was on the floor, cleaning out under the sink. I had to go buy cleaning supplies before I could do anything. Blade, the realtor did manage to get a couple of young men to clean up the yard. It's going to take me a few days here, I'm afraid. I'll keep in touch."

"I can't believe I'm hearing all this!" Maggie said sarcastically. "You my friend, getting dirty and on your hands and knees? I'd like a photo of that, too if you don't mind! By the way, what are you going to wear to the winery tonight, Miss cleaning lady?"

"A clean pair of jeans, I guess," I said laughing. "Ellie said it would be fine. It's called Red Creek Winery. Isn't the name just charming?"

"It is, and just go for it girl. You deserve a little fun after all that work," Maggie said giving into my crazy plans. "Be careful now. You don't really know those people. By the way, thanks for asking about the "wine and dine" last night."

"I'm sorry," I said feeling guilty. "Was it fun and did they raise a lot of money?"

"It did about the same as always," she said matter of factly. "Folks asked about you, of course. James and Sandra were there like always. When I told them you went to Borna, James gave me a sour look. He asked what the trip was all about, but I changed the subject and walked away."

"Good! Clay didn't leave the Borna property to James, that's what's up!" I stated clearly. "This is just another thing for him to get jealous about. I'm so glad I don't have to put up with either of them anymore. Hey, I have to go. I'll call you later tonight or tomorrow morning."

"You better girlfriend," she warned. "Don't do anything I wouldn't do at the winery tonight. I love you!"

"I love you, too!" I said back. "Don't worry, other than the sleazy realtor, everyone here has been wonderful!"

I hung up knowing Maggie was truly concerned for me. It was too bad I didn't bring her with me. I could have used the help! She'd freak out at any sight of a bug, however. Maybe it was best she stayed home. I really needed this time to myself.

I eagerly went back to my cleaning. I was now filling one trash bag after another, feeling a sense of accomplishment.

Blade came in to tell me I should set any trash out by the barn, and one of the boys would carry it all away in his pick-up truck tomorrow.

"I'm headed to Marv's place to get some chow for me and the boys," Blade announced. "Do you want anything?"

"Yes, I'm starved," I responded heartedly. "Bring me the biggest and most loaded hamburger he has, plus a diet coke, please."

"Workin' that hard, are ya?" he teased with his sleazy laugh.

"Here's a fifty dollar bill," I said reaching into my purse. "Buy them lunch and keep the change." He looked at me strangely, like I had given him a thousand dollars.

"Well, now that's the best tip I've ever had, ma'am," he

said grinning. He quickly took off before I changed my mind.

When he returned, I decided to take a break and eat outside in the fresh air. The cool fall breeze felt good from the closed in dust of the house. I sat down on the back step to the deck, wishing I had some comfortable lawn chairs. The filling and delicious hamburger made me want to take a nap right here on the deck. Perhaps I could just sit down on the grass and lean against my big beautiful tree sitting so stately in the back yard and take a snooze. I wasn't used to this kind of physical labor, but it gave me a good feeling. I skimmed over the view of the back yard and began to picture how beautiful it could be with all the right flowers and shrubs. There were a few colorful fall mums, peeking out here and there, as if they didn't want to be completely forgotten. Neglect seemed to be the story of this place. The barn needed red paint, which would charm it up immensely. Hopefully, the new owners would see some of these possibilities.

I reluctantly got up, knowing I had to accomplish a lot today. Tomorrow, I would ask Ellie if I could borrow her vacuum cleaner, which would help a great deal. When I got inside, I peeked out the front window to check on any progress. The yard's appearance was improving and they seemed to be working hard. How could this local community ignore this hidden gem as they drove past it each day? Were the Doc and his wife happy to see what was going on?

CHAPTER 10

In no time it was 5:00, and I heard Ellie's voice outside talking to the workers, like she knew them. She came in the back door with a surprising look on her face.

"Things are looking pretty good out there," Ellie complimented. "What's happening in here?"

"Mostly bagging trash and wiping things down," I reported with a sigh. "I must look a mess!"

"Well, you look like you've been working hard all day, but I can see progress," Ellie said looking around the place.

"Tomorrow, I'd like to bring your vacuum cleaner over here, if you wouldn't mind," I said pulling the hair out of my face.

"Sure, whatever you need," Ellie assured me. "Are you ready to clean up and head to the winery?"

"Almost," I said closing up another trash bag. "I'd like to finish up a few things first, and then I'll be over, if that's okay."

"We have a light menu there, so I thought it might do for our dinner tonight, if that's okay," she suggested. "If these bags go out back with the others, I can do that on my way out."

"Have at it," I said handing her the one in my hand. "I'll be over shortly."

Before I left for Ellie's, I went to thank and say good-bye to the two boys. They told me Blade would be coming back for them shortly. I gave them each some cash, which they seemed to be grateful for. They said they'd be happy to help anytime.

It was nearly 6:00 before I got to Ellie's and jumped in the shower. I came in the kitchen to join her feeling refreshed in clean clothes. I was exhausted, but felt extremely proud of what I had accomplished.

"The word sure is out about you being in town," Ellie revealed with a laugh. "Everyone drives by this place, so you can't keep any secrets around here."

"This is a prime location, so someone will surely want to buy it," I noted. "It's such a shame there isn't a place where tourists or family guests can stay when they come to this county."

"There actually is a B&B in Eggersville, some miles from here, but there isn't much else happening around it, so I'm not sure how busy she is or when she's ever open. I think you really have to call ahead, which obviously you didn't take time to do. It's in the old Egger's country store, and one of the family members has restored it. It's very nice and I hear they serve a great breakfast with the German coffeecake."

"That sounds great, but not very handy for my purposes," I said picturing it in my mind. "I wish I could stay long enough to see all these places you keep telling me about."

"You're welcome to come back and stay anytime, for as

long as you like," Ellie offered.

"I was cleaning the upstairs bathroom and wondered if there were any ghosts in the house?" I asked, catching her off guard. "I had been meaning to ask you if there is any truth to the rumors?"

"I would hear things now and then," she said casually. "What has that Blade been telling you?"

"No details, but I did have an interesting sensation while I was up there in the master bedroom," I started to describe. "Despite the whole house being rather cold, I had a very warm, loving sensation while I was up there. It was probably the way the sun was coming in, but it did make me wonder. Do you know if anyone died in that house, since it was a Doctor's office?"

"You'd have to ask some of old timers around here about that," she said shaking her head. "At least you weren't freaked out about what happened! Are you ready to go?"

"Absolutely!" I said, following her out of the door.

The drive was interesting. We passed through Dresden and then Ellie began telling me about Rock Landing, where there was a significant rock structure, very popular with the tourists. We turned onto a gravel road, taking us up the hill to her winery. It seemed to be nestled in the woods, surrounded by a wrap-around deck that offered a pleasant view in any direction. There were just a few cars, which Ellie said belonged to frequent customers getting off from work. When we walked in, all eyes were on the two of us.

"Kate, this is Trout," pointing to the man behind the bar. "Trout, this is my friend Kate, who owns the property next to my house." The tall, thin, young man greeted me with a big smile.

"Welcome to Red Creek," he said nodding.

"I think it's too cool to sit on the deck, so we'll eat in here at the bar if that's okay," Ellie suggested.

"This is great!" I said with my eyes scoping the place. "You have such eclectic décor in here! I love what you've done with the lit, colored wine bottles! There is so much to look at, and it's quite romantic, as a winery should be!"

Ellie laughed. "Coming from your decorating experience, I consider it a compliment," she said graciously. "I like using a lot of the local memorabilia. Folks love to see it and then they share their stories."

"So would you like to start with a tasting of some our more popular wines?" Trout asked eagerly.

"I would, but first, you have to tell me how you got your name Trout!" I teased.

"It goes way back to when I was just a kid. I always liked to go trout fishing, more than anything else," he explained. "The kids started calling me Trout, and it stuck with me ever since."

"I really like the name!" I said making him feel at ease. "How did you end up working here with Ellie?"

"I stole him from another winery!" Ellie interrupted. "I was impressed with his knowledge of wine, the first time I met him. When I found this place, I knew it had real potential, but I didn't know anything about wine. I thought of Trout and made him an offer he couldn't refuse. I also knew I had to have someone to charm all the ladies that frequent here. Another woman behind the bar doesn't do the trick."

I laughed. "Smart move, Ellie!" I complimented.

While Trout began his dog and pony show of wine tasting, Ellie ordered us a big platter of assorted appetizers. I wanted to devour them all at once and chase them down with more wine.

Trout said the place had live music on Sunday afternoons and special occasions. It wasn't long after we got our food that more folks were coming in the door. Ellie made a point to greet each of them, as a smart business owner should.

"How can folks have a couple of glasses of wine or more and drive those country roads home," I asked Trout.

"Most groups will have a designated driver, plus we keep an eye out for anyone getting too loose!" he explained with a big grin.

Ellie could see I was fading away quickly after my two glasses of wine. She knew I'd had a physically draining day, so we called it an early evening, despite the fun I was having, in a very different relaxing environment.

When we got back to the house, she asked if I would like a cup of coffee. It sounded wonderful. We both got comfortable in her small living room. She wanted to know more about Maggie, my best friend, and then I told her about the Beach Quilters.

"Everyone quilts around here but me, I think," Ellie recalled. "The church lady quilters quilt on Thursdays, I think. It's mostly elderly woman now, as all the young women around don't seem to have the time for it. We have a Friendship Circle of a dozen ladies who meet in the evening because most of them work during the day. I enjoy meeting up with them."

"You said a Friendship Circle?" I inquired. "Tell me more!"

"We're friends who vary in age and occupations," she described. "We meet in homes, so we don't want the group any bigger. We try to do a charity contribution once a year, but it's mostly a social group. Living a distance from most cultural things, we make our own fun. When it's my turn to have them in the spring and summer, I have them at the winery."

"Nice!" I said with another yawn. "Speaking of quilting, where did the white whole cloth quilt on my bed come from?" I asked with curiosity.

"That was made by my Grandmother," she said proudly. "I received it when I married and I try to keep it in good shape. It's what gave me the idea to do the whole guest room in white."

"I love it and of course I folded it back so nothing can happen to it," I said to ease her mind.

"So Kate, what are your plans when you get home?" Ellie asked boldly.

"Nothing definite, other than continue to look for a place to live in case my house sells quickly," I reported. "After I sell both houses, I'll be free and clear of anything that belonged to Clay Meyr!"

"Why do you say such a thing?" Ellie asked looking shocked.

"Because I want to cut as many ties as I can from him and his family," I stated bluntly. Ellie looked shocked. "I'm quite unhappy about many things. Clay's drinking cost him his life and made Jack fatherless at such a young age. I also learned recently he was having an affair for goodness knows long. I was such a fool!" The look on Ellie's face filled with horror.

"Oh dear, Kate, I'm so sorry to hear all this!" she said with a gasp. "You poor thing! How does anyone forgive someone who is gone?"

"I'm not looking for sympathy," I said quietly. "I just want out and away! I gave up my own desires and plans so I could be there for him. When I first met Mrs. Meyr, my mother-in-law, she pretty much told me that it was my duty to make him succeed. No doubt, I benefited from the rewards, which kept me going, but he had such a controlling way of using me. He was such a health nut that it drove me crazy. He thought everyone should live like he did. Look, Ellie, I have no one to blame but myself."

"Then, I suppose you have to forgive yourself," Ellie said wisely. "Are you starting to feel some sense of freedom, at all?"

"Yes, I am," I said smiling. "Every step I take, I can taste it."

"You obviously don't have to work, so what will you do with all your time?" she asked with interest.

"I may travel," I said with amusement. "All options are on the table. I better get to bed so I have some energy tomorrow."

"Sure," Ellie said still in shock from our conversation. "I'll have the vacuum out for you, so you don't forget. Will coffee cake still work for breakfast?"

"That's wonderful!" I said giving her a hug. "You've been so helpful. I hope I can thank you one day."

I crawled into bed, feeling the wine and a few aches and pains from my hard working day. There were so many questions I still had about Doc's house. Perhaps I would learn more tomorrow!

CHAPTER 11

Despite a light headache from the wine I consumed, I awoke with energy and excitement. I looked out my bedroom window and could see Doc's house waiting for me. There were more colorful mums blooming along that side of the house which I hadn't noticed before. I wondered who planted them.

"I put on the same soiled outfit I wore the day before and found my way to the delicious smell of brewed coffee.

"Good morning!" I said joining Ellie at the kitchen table.

"I was just sitting here thinking, and I decided I would make us a pot of chili for dinner tonight. You'll be tired, and I can take some time off this afternoon. I make a mean German cheesecake, too which is pretty easy. So does it sound good?"

"That sounds heavenly, for a nice cool night," I said in agreement. "I can't remember when I've had chili to eat."

"Really?" Ellie questioned in surprise.

"You're sure it's not too much work?" I asked politely. "I'll be happy to take you to dinner somewhere."

"Good luck with that!" she teased. "There's not much around here but bar food. I just need to check in at the winery for a little while today. I'll be home for sure by 5:00."

"Sounds great!" I said feeling energized from the delicious coffee cake.

A knock on the back door startled us both. Ellie went to answer, and she announced it was Anna, a friend of hers.

"Good morning!" she said coming in the door. The lady was surprised to see me sitting there.

"Kate, this is Anna," she introduced. "Anna, this is Kate." I nodded.

"Oh, I hope I'm not interrupting anything," Anna said with concern.

"Not at all," noted Ellie. "Please sit down and join us with a cup of coffee."

"Thanks, but I just can't," she refused. "I just wanted to drop off these new brochures of the Village for you to take to the winery."

"Good timing, because we're all out of the old ones," Ellie claimed as she took a few bundles. "I'm anxious to see them. Anna is the Director of the Saxon Village down the road. She and her husband live in the old house on the grounds. Oh, and there are two little munchkins who live with them, too." They laughed.

"Oh, I hope I have time to see it before I go back to Michigan," I said to Anna. "I've heard so much about it."

"I hope you can, too!" she wished. "It's been a lot of work, but so far we just love it! Be sure to take one of these brochures for yourself."

"Kate owns Doc Paulson's house next door," Ellie revealed. "She's been trying to get in shape to put on the market."

"I just love that old house!" Anna said with excitement. "It has been so sad to drive by and see it vacant for so long."

"I couldn't agree with you more," I nodded. "I'm convinced it will show better with some clean up."

"I always envisioned it as a fancy tea room or restaurant, but it would never support itself in this town," Anna assessed. "I hope you find the right person who really cares for its history."

"That's my intention," I claimed.

"I need to run now," said Anna opening the door. "It was nice to have met you, Kate." I gave her a wave.

Out the door she went. Ellie said the young couple was trying very hard to make Borna a success as they bring tourists to the Saxon Village.

"Anna belongs to our Friendship Circle," Ellie noted. "She's also the one that organizes the monthly baking in the outdoor oven in the village. They bake the first Saturday of every month. You can do it yourself, or Anna helps you."

"Oh, it sounds so cool," I said with envy. "That experience sounds like a good enough reason to drive back from South Haven. That is right up my alley!"

"No one bakes bread better than Anna," Ellie declared. "Just like the coffee cake, practice makes perfect, and she's done it so often. There are times when she makes extra loaves to sell and people go clamoring for it. It pays to do it right, whatever you do."

Ellie said that perfectly. I wanted to do things right the next time, whatever I did. I grabbed the vacuum and said good-bye. On my way next door, I was already looking forward to having chili and her wonderful cheesecake.

I set the vacuum on the deck and decided to explore the property a little more. I reminded myself to ask Blade for a better property line description. I walked towards the barn and pulled open the worn, crooked door. The inside was piled high with junk, like broken lawn furniture, dried up paint cans, an old ladder, and some tools I didn't recognize. It would take a whole day to clear this all out, and today was not the day.

I closed the door and went around the back of the barn that looked down the hill side. I saw a leaning fence, which was likely the property line. As I stepped further, I nearly tripped over what appeared to be a large stone. As I looked closer, it appeared to be a very small tomb stone. I brushed away the dirt and leaves to see if I could read what it said. It was too worn to make out anything, surmising it must be very, very old. It had a simple name of some kind with probably a year underneath it. What was it doing here of all places? Did it connect to Doc's life here or before then? I cleared more area around it, so I could come back later and find it more easily. This wasn't anything I was going to ask Blade about because whatever he would tell me, I wouldn't believe anyway. Before going back to Michigan, I would take a picture of it with my phone.

When I got inside of the house, I remembered to call Maggie.

"Well, if it isn't my country girlfriend," Maggie teased when she answered. "I keep thinking about you. When are you coming home?"

"Maybe tomorrow or the next day," I said with frustration in my voice. "There is still so much to do here. You won't believe what I found this morning behind the barn!"

"What, a cow, or maybe a horse?" she guessed with humor.

"No, a small tombstone!" I said with excitement. "I can't make out what it says as it's so old and worn. Isn't that something?"

"Well, it beats any excitement I've had around here, lately," she teased back. "You're having too much fun. Hey, how did the winery visit go?"

"It was pretty fun and it's such a charming place!" I reported. "We had a great time, and the bartender's name was Trout. Isn't that something?"

"Oh boy, this doesn't sound good," she said laughing. "I'm not going to ask any more questions."

"Ellie is cooking for me tonight," I said as I was walked further into the house with my cell. "I really am going to owe her big time when this visit is over. I don't know how I'm going to repay her. So what's new there?"

"The quilters asked about you, of course," she said casually. "Alice said a lady from Nebraska won our blueberry raffle quilt at the festival. Jenny took a fall and is on crutches. That's about it."

"Sorry to hear about Jenny!" I responded. "I still haven't called Carla to see how things are going at the house. I'm hoping she'll take Rocky home for good. I need to get rid of him."

"Why?" Maggie asked in surprise. "That's a terrible thing to say!"

"Because he's never been my dog and never will be," I stated boldly. "I really need to go. I've got a lot of vacuuming to do today. Take care and I love you girl!"

"Me, too!" she added. "Don't work too hard!"

I got busy with the vacuum cleaner, which felt like I was reacquainting myself with an old friend. I was figuring out the attachments, when Blade snuck up behind me, scaring me to death.

"I yelled at you, but you didn't hear me," he said defensively. "Man, are you uptight!"

I wanted to slap the creep, but instead, took a deep breath and shut off the vacuum.

"What's going on?" I asked with little patience.

"You tell me!" he said in a loud voice. "Are you gonna sign some papers today so we can get going on this sale or not? This place never looked better. What's the hold up?" There was nothing about this guy that I liked. I looked for the right words to get my point across to him.

"I'm still trying to clean up around here, by the way, and no, there won't be any signing today," I bluntly stated. His face turned bitter. "Until I feel comfortable about folks seeing this place, I won't be putting any for sale sign up in the yard.

Blade shook his head in disgust and walked towards the back door. "Look, if you aren't comfortable with my time table, I'll list it by owner and put the sign up myself!" I said in a raised voice. From the look on his face, I thought he was going to spit at me.

"Have it your way, ma'am," he said mean spiritedly. "Good luck getting anyone to look at this place without my help. You have no idea what the market is around here. You come from your high and mighty place somewhere and expect everyone here to fall into your hands. They're not gonna pay the big bucks you seem to be dreamin' about. You think sweeping up a little dirt is gonna do the trick?"

"Okay Blade, I've heard enough from you," I said walking directly in front of him. "I have no contract with you. Just because you agreed to meet me here, gives you no right to talk to me this way, or make any of the decisions."

He turned around to go out the back door, slamming it hard on the way. Good riddance, I thought to myself.

I took a deep breath and walked towards the entry way, where I could sit down on stairway. As frustrated as I was, I felt a sense of relief knowing Blade was out of my life. The first thing I told myself was to call Harold's Hardware and get a locksmith to change the locks. Selling it by owner would not be as easy, as he stated. Who would show the house to perspective buyers with me in Michigan? The bigger worry would be what Blade would do to the property with me gone!

CHAPTER 12

While I got back to my vacuuming upstairs, my mind wondered about everything imaginable. When I stopped to take a drink of water, I decided to peek in the attic while it was daylight. I carefully approached the narrow staircase which curved upward. To my delight, it was empty. The coolness of the season was setting in, taking the stuffiness of the summer heat away. The sub flooring showed the enormous space that could have been many bedrooms, if needed. It was too bad the Paulson's never had any children to fill up this big house.

I came down to the second floor, feeling the warmth of sunshine wash over me once again. It was like an embrace I had never felt before. I had to smile, for it was love coming from somewhere, but where? I decided I was hungry and thought of going to Marv's for a sandwich. I decided to walk.

I knew it would be a full house, judging from the parking lot.

When I walked in the door, you could have heard a pin drop. I kept my head up high and walked to the counter where I saw an empty bar stool between two men.

"Hi there, how can I help you?" the young lady with a pony tail said to me from behind the counter.

"Yes you can," I nodded. "I'd like to order a BLT and a diet coke to go."

"Got it," she quickly said as she wrote it on her pad.

"This seat isn't taken, is it?" I asked the bald man to the right, eating his hamburger.

"Not today," he said wiping his mouth. "Fred usually sits there, but don't think he's gonna show up. He's been sick. The flu's going around these parts ya know?"

"Is that right?" I responded.

"I bet you're a Meyr, aren't you?" he said grinning.

"Why yes, Kate Meyr," I said putting out my hand for a hand shake. "Who are you, if I may ask?"

"Eddie Mueller. Pleased to meet you," he said not shaking my hand. He reached for his bottle of beer instead. "I've seen you in the yard at Doc's place."

"That's right, "I began. "I'm putting the place up for sale, so there's some cleaning up to do. The man on the other side of me was now listening intently. "What is it that you do, Mr. Mueller?"

"Heating and cooling," he stated not looking at me.

"Here in town?" I asked with interest.

"Anywhere I can find work," he added.

"Does Harold at the hardware store ever recommend you?" I asked as an idea formed in my mind.

"He better," he jokingly said with a big laugh. "Harold and I go way back."

"Well then, Mr. Mueller, I need someone to check and clean my furnace and the two fireplaces at my house," I explained. "I was going to call Harold for a reference."

"Why sure, but can't today," he said with a much friendlier voice. "How about I come first thing tomorrow morning to take a look?"

"That would be great," I happily said. "I need to be getting back to Michigan the next day, but I would feel better if I knew those things were taken care of."

"Here's my card, ma'am," he said handing me a card from his shirt pocket. "If I have to change anything, where can I reach you?"

"I'm staying at Ellie Meer's house next door, so I'll write my cell number down on a napkin," I said reaching across to the napkin holder.

"None of my business, of course, but why don't you just move in there?" he asked as he leaned back from his stool.
I laughed softly. "I live in South Haven, Michigan," I began to explain. "My husband was killed in a car accident not too long ago, and now I need to sell some of our property, which is why I'm here."

"Money, huh?" he asked nodding like he knew everything about me.

"No, it's not about the money," I sternly said in defense. "Frankly Mr. Mueller, I didn't even know much about this place till after he was killed."

"I'm sorry to hear that Miss Meyr, and please call me Eddie like everyone else around here," he said with a big grin. "I'm happy to have the work after a dry summer, so I'll be sure to see you in the morning."

"Here's your order ma'am," the bar girl said handing me

a paper bag. I handed her a twenty dollar bill and told her to keep the change. She was thrilled.

I walked out of Marv's place knowing I had successfully completed my first visit. I walked to the back of the house, and despite the cool breeze, decided to sit on the steps of the deck to eat my sandwich. I came to the conclusion that as long as I was friendly and didn't become intimidated by anyone, I could be accepted around here.

CHAPTER 13

By late afternoon, I was running out of energy. I saw Ellie's car was home most of the afternoon, so I decided to call it a day.

I was just about getting ready to leave when I thought of Carla and how naughty I was about checking in with her. I pressed on her number.

"I was just getting ready to leave your place, Kate," Carla said somewhat breathlessly.

"Sorry I haven't called sooner, but I've really been busy here," I said feeling badly. "How are things there? Is Rocky doing okay?"

"I'm taking him home with me today, as a matter of fact," she noted. "It's a lot easier. I think he misses you!"

"Well, I can't quite say the same," I admitted. "I wish you would keep him Carla, or I'll just have to find a complete stranger to take him."

"Oh, Miss Kate, I don't know," she debated. "I'll think about it. Before I forget, James has called here a couple of times wondering if you were back from Borna."

"Did he say what he wanted?" I asked with wonder.

"No ma'am," she answered. "He said to call him right away when you got back. There have been more folks driving by the house to check it out. You may want to see what's going on with your realtor."

"Yes, I will, and hopefully we'll have a buyer soon," I responded.

"What's taking you so long to come home?" Carla asked impatiently.

"That's a good question Carla. This is a small town here, and I just can't list this place without it looking more presentable. It needs some cleaning up before I can list it," I explained. "Everyone's been so sweet and helpful. I'm staying with a nice single lady that lives next door."

"So in other words, you're enjoying your stay," Carla guessed. "There's nothing wrong with that, after what you've been through."

"It has been pleasant, despite some work," I described. "The house is in such need of love and attention. It's been vacant for a long time."

"It sounds like you're talking about yourself, Miss Kate," she bravely stated. I really didn't want to go where she was taking me.

"I've got to go now," I said changing the subject. "I'll be home in the next couple of days."

I locked up the house and went back to Ellie's, wondering what James may have wanted. It was more than likely about another business issue he was dealing with. Why didn't he just call me on my cell?

I walked into Ellie's kitchen to the smell of heavenly, hot chili. In the middle of her kitchen table sat the cheesecake she talked about. The table setting of blue and white Dresden dishes enhanced her blue and white décor. This was too much like playing house.

"Welcome home!" Ellie said coming out of her bedroom. "I bet your beat! How about a glass of wine?"

"That sounds wonderful after I clean up a bit," I happily responded.

"I put some clean sweatshirts on your bed, in case you're running out of clean clothes," she offered. "We can put some jeans in the washer if you'd like."

"That's a splendid idea," I praised, going to my room.

When I joined Ellie in the living room for a glass of wine, I knew I had to break the news to her about letting Blade go. She listened intently as I shared every detail.

"He's a piece of work, alright," she said shaking her head in disgust. "I don't blame you!"

"Harold is going to send someone over in the morning to change the locks," I added. "Do you think I have to worry about him doing something vindictive this evening?"

"He better not!" Ellie said raising her voice. "Did you leave both your porch lights on?"

"Yes," I said nodding. "He's so angry, it does concern me."

"I have a realtor, around fifty miles from here, we can call," Ellie offered. "He may sign you on as a favor to me. Blade's right about one thing. Realtors avoid signing anyone in these small towns, simply because they don't want to make the drive to show any perspective buyers!"

"I'll buy a small for sale sign I saw at Harold's Hardware, if I have to," I said feeling frustrated. "By the way, do you know Eddie Mueller?"

"Oh sure," she said as we walked to the kitchen to eat.

"He's coming in the morning to clean the furnace and the

two fireplaces," I said helping myself to the sliced bread. "I met him when I got a sandwich at Marv's place this afternoon. He seemed nice and said Harold recommends him."

Ellie laughed. "Why you're just getting to meet everyone around here," she teased as she served my bowl of chili. "You can meet even more folks if you go to the Friendship Circle with me tomorrow night. They all know about you and would like to meet you. It's at Anna's place this time, and she always goes overboard with food, so it can be our dinner."

"You know I have no decent clothes for socializing," I reminded her. "I shouldn't be prolonging my visit."

"A clean shirt will do fine, plus they know your circumstances," she explained. "We all dress casually."

"It does sound fun, and you've got me curious about this group," I said between bites of chili. "This is so good Ellie. Did you make this heavenly bread?"

"No, I got it out of the freezer," she noted. "This is actually some of Anna's homemade bread which I purchased some time back. Maybe she'll have an extra loaf to sell you, to take home."

"Wonderful," I added. "I need this cheesecake recipe from you, too. Clay never wanted anything like this around the house, so I never attempted to make it. It's a heavy texture, yet light."

"That's the German way!" she exclaimed.

We continued the cozy conversation around the table as she shared small town stories. It was indeed different than South Haven. After several yawns, I helped clear the table and decided to turn in.

CHAPTER 14

Knowing I had a full day of work ahead of me, I left Ellie's house at an early hour. Walking towards the house, I wished all the windows could be clean, but knew it wouldn't happen. I knew I had some scrubbing ahead of me today in more important places, which would be a challenge.

Eddie knocked at the back door at 9:00. He seemed to know his way about the house and made his way to the basement. Looking out my back window from the kitchen, I saw one of the young men who had been previously working in the yard. He was loading up his pick-up truck to haul away my trash. I rushed outdoors to greet him with my gratitude.

"Good morning, ma'am," he politely said. "Do you have any more trash before I take this away?"

"I think everything's out," I assured him. "I'm sorry, but I didn't get your name, and I really want to thank you for returning despite me dismissing Blade."

"My name is Charlie Wells, but folks here call me Cotton because of my white hair," he explained. "I'm glad to do what I was asked to do. Blade likes to act like a big shot around here, but I ignore him to get work when I can." He seemed to blush.

"Here's a hundred dollar bill, and I'm sure I can find a few other things to do around here if you're available!" I offered. "Oh, that's too much," Cotton responded as he backed away. "It won't take me long to haul this away, and then I'll be happy to check in with you on anything else you might need."

He took off in a rapid fashion. Money sure talked around here with so many out of work. It was one thing I had over Mr. Sleazy, at least.

I continued my chores and was determined not to take a lunch break after a hearty breakfast at Ellie's house this morning. Eddie came up from the basement steps to give me an update. He had done extensive cleaning and put in clean filters but had not attempted the fireplaces. He took time to warn me of a rather hefty bill, but I told him not to worry. When I inquired about how much central air cooling would cost for the house, he lit up like he had just won the lottery. I calmed him down by telling him if the house didn't sell right away, I may at that point have to invest in central air-conditioning. He went back to his work, and I couldn't help but wonder once again why this place had been so neglected.

Cotton quickly returned, and I had just the job for him.

"There's an old ladder in the barn I'd like you to bring in," I instructed. "Hopefully, it's in working order because I'd like you to wipe down all the light fixtures for me."

"Why sure," he eagerly said going out the door.

By 4:00, Eddie was gone and warned me not to use one

of the fireplaces because it needed more extensive cleaning. The one in the upstairs bedroom was good to go. When I wrote him his check, he was very grateful.

"Say Eddie, do you know a good plumber around Borna who you can recommend?" I asked thinking of the house's poor water pressure.

"Why old Gabe Grebing is the best around these parts, but he's trying to retire," he answered. "He's been training his son though, so I'd give him a call. I have his number."

"Is his wife Helen Grebing, the best coffee-cake maker in town?" I asked with interest.

He gave a loud chuckle. "By golly, it sure is!" he said slapping his hands together. "It didn't take long for you to find that out I bet!"

"It's delicious!" I exclaimed. "I'm hoping she'll give me the recipe!"

"Don't count on it!" he joked rather sincerely. "I don't know anyone who's been able to get their hands on it!"

I heard Cotton coming down the stairs with the ladder. "Hey Eddie," Cotton yelled out as Eddie was about to go out the door. He turned in surprise.

"How's that new baby of yours?" Eddie asked Cotton.

"You have a new baby?" I asked in shock.

"I sure do," Cotton responded blushing. "She's just over a month old now. It's our first."

"Good heavens, Cotton, I thought you still might be a teenager!" I responded. They both chuckled.

"I'm 21 ma'am," he said proudly.

"Did your wife work before the baby?" I couldn't help but wonder.

"She was helping out Sarah White with some house

cleaning jobs," he explained. "When I don't have work, we can only hope Sarah can use her." I was making a mental note, that now I had found a future house cleaner, if I needed one.

"Let me know if you decide on the air-conditioning, Ms. Meyr," Eddie said as he told us good-bye. "Tell Susie I said hello!"

Cotton nodded with a smile. "Thanks, Eddie," Cotton replied back. "Do you want this ladder back out in the barn? I cleaned it off, in case you would need it again in the house."

"That's a good idea," I said, still thinking about Cotton and his young family. "It's none of my business Cotton, but how do you make ends meet with hardly any work around here?"

"There are a lot of us around these parts in the same boat," he answered defensively. "We get by somehow, and Susie's mom helps out when she can."

"Well, if I lived around here, I'd keep you and your wife busy," I bravely said.

"I wish you did, but you've been more than generous, ma'am," he said with his head down. "If there's anything you need me to do, after you're gone, just let me know."

"As a matter of fact, I'll pay you a little extra, if you can keep an eye out on this place once in a while when you drive by," I suggested. "I will leave my cell number with you in case you see something unusual."

"Oh, why sure, but you don't need to pay me for that!" he offered.

When he saw I included an extra tip, I told him to buy his new baby something pretty. He gave me a big smile and would have hugged me for sure, but his shyness kept him in place.

After Cotton left, I walked into the front of the house to

inspect the clean chandeliers. I heard a car drive up, but I didn't look out to see who it was.

All of a sudden, the back door swung open and in stomped a bearded man, a woman, and what looked like to be three teenagers. I was startled to say the least, and speechless as I looked at their dirty appearance. How rude, I thought. Did they think no one would be in the house?

"Hey, hey," I finally yelled out. "Can I help you?" Everyone scattered about the house as the grungy looking man came closer to me.

"Yeah," he nodded. "We're here to buy this place!" I wasn't sure I was hearing him correctly.

"What?" I shouted out in disbelief. I could hear the teenagers now running around the rooms upstairs. "I'm sorry mister, but I am the owner of this house, and it's not for sale!" I couldn't believe the words that just came out of my mouth. He laughed and really began to stare me down from head to toe.

"That's not what I heard," he said like I was joking with him. "We want this house, and if you're the owner, I guess you're the one to cooperate with us. Maybe you misunderstood my intentions here."

"No, I don't think YOU understood what I have clearly told you!" I said defensively, raising my voice even louder than before. "It is not for sale, and I want you and your family out of my house right now before I have to call for some assistance!"

"You better rethink that Miss," he threatened. His face turned to stone. "We'll leave, but we'll be back. We know about this house, and it works just fine for what we need." I kept staring at him, like he wasn't scaring me. "Hey, kids, get in the truck! Mavis, get those kids out of here! Just how much are you askin' anyway?"

"Get out now!" I yelled, ignoring his question and opening the kitchen door. He winked as he took his time walking past me. His kids swiftly ran past me without a word, and they piled into the back of the pickup-up. Mavis, who I guessed to be his wife, obediently left and got in the truck with her head down. I closed the door and locked it immediately. It hadn't dawned on me to lock the door while I was here working!

I was shaking. Did that really happen? I looked out the window and tried to memorize the license plate, without success. Where did these creepy people come from? Where did they get their information about the house? There was no way they could afford a place like this anyway, from the looks of them. Did they think it wasn't occupied, and they could just move in? Did I dare leave the house now, like I had planned?

I got my cell phone and called Ellie to explain what just happened. She said I should lock up, leave lights on in the house, and get on over to her place.

I did as she said. I told myself I could finish up here in the morning before I would leave town. Right now, I just wanted to be safe.

Ellie was waiting for me with the door open like she had been watching me walk from my house.

"I have a glass of wine ready for you," she said with a welcoming smile. "I think you need to notify the Sheriff's office about this." We both sat down at the kitchen table. "I'm so sorry this happened, Kate. This is out of the ordinary. All I can think of is they didn't see your car and decided they would check things out!"

"Who does that?" I asked, still shaken. "It was so scary seeing everyone swarm into the house as if they were going to take it over that very minute. Do you think Blade had something to do with this?"

"Who knows," Ellie said shaking her head in disbelief. "See what the Sheriff's office has to say."

After a few swallows of wine, I felt calm enough to call and tell my story over the phone. All they could really tell me was they would check out a description of the truck and for me to keep an eye out. They told me since the house was not locked, they didn't really break in and do anything unlawful. From the conversation, they didn't seem to be near as alarmed as I was. That was unsettling to me.

"Do you think I should sleep over there tonight?" I asked Ellie, after I hung up.

"Don't be silly," she responded. "The way you yelled at them, they're probably long gone from here. We don't have to go to Friendship Circle tonight if you're not up to it, Kate."

I paused, not knowing what to say. I didn't want to ruin Ellie's evening. I told her I would give her an answer after my shower. Just when I was feeling loved and secure here, this crazy incident had to ruin it.

CHAPTER 15

A hot shower relaxed me, and I knew I couldn't let my experience take away Ellie's evening with her Friendship Circle. When I joined her in the living room, I told her I thought the meeting would be a good distraction for me after all.

"You'll be meeting nice, normal, fun loving people tonight," Ellie assured me.

Ellie offered me one of her warmer jackets, and off we went. We turned off of Main Street and followed the signs to the Saxon Village. When we turned off to a narrow gravel road, I felt a bit concerned but kept my observations quiet. In no time, we pulled up to a white framed farm house, which was surrounded by woods, open fields, and a log cabin village which Anna had described so well.

Other ladies were arriving about the same time so we walked into Anna's house together. Friendly greetings were exchanged as if they knew I would be attending.

"I'll wait till everyone's here, before I do any introductions, Kate," Ellie said as we found our seats together. Anna's living room and dining room were connected with a wide arched opening, so the crowd could easily be expanded. On her large oval dining room table was a wide assortment of goodies displayed beautifully on a lace table cloth. I immediately spotted a variety of homemade breads that looked delicious. I heard Anna tell one of the ladies that her husband had taken the children out for pizza for the evening.

Everyone smiled at me while they waited for Ellie's introductions. As Ellie had described, the women's ages varied, but overall they were a good looking and friendly group.

"I'll start by telling you only their first names, Kate, to make it easier for you to remember," Ellie stated. They all stopped their chatter, to listen more intently.

"It looks like Emma is the only one absent this evening," Ellie began. "She is our most senior member and doesn't mind reminding us of that." They all snickered like there was a hidden story. "She had another commitment I think. Ruth Ann is an amazing art quilter, Kate. Although she has her hands full being a full time caregiver, she is able to accomplish some quilting. You should see her sewing room!" Ruth Ann blushed. "Kate is a pretty good quilter, too by the way!" They all smiled with approval. "Ruth Ann just lives down the street here in the old Lueder's mercantile building. They live upstairs in a very nice apartment. The downstairs is still vacant, right?"

"Yes," Ruth Ann responded. "We still hope some kind of business will want to locate there. It's so spacious, so it'll take a while, I guess."

"Is that the really large building next to Imy's Antique shop?" I asked with interest.

"Yes, the biggest building in town," Ruth Ann bragged. "I have my hands filled with Mother, or I'd be tempted to try my hand at some kind of retail." That comment seemed to surprise most of them who were listening.

"Sitting next to her is Esther, who is a native of Borna," Ellie continued. "She is best described as the expert gardener of our group. If you have any questions about growing things, it's Esther you seek out!"

"She can also give a pretty good hair cut by the way," voiced Ruth Ann. Esther was now shaking her head with embarrassment.

"I forgot," admitted Ellie. "She used to have a beauty shop here in town, but now she just cuts for a few people." I gave her a big smile of approval.

"Mary Catherine is another native of Borna," Ellie continued. I gathered that being a native of the area carried some weight. "She moved back here from Boston not too long ago to be closer to her aging parents. She is a darn good writer, so she can work from any place. She is still in culture shock, but she's adjusting." Many laughed. I thought how courageous she was.

"You can say that again," Mary Catherine said with humor. "There is plenty to write about here!"

"So you do freelance writing?" I asked in admiration.

"Yes, but I have regular periodicals I write for that keep me afloat financially," she explained.

"Ellen is our chief of entertainment," teased Ellie. Ellen shook her head. "She can put on any event and decorate it like no other. You should see her house! Ellen would have a lot in common with Kate because she can make everything beautiful!" They all responded with praise.

"Ellen, you're way ahead of me!" I assured her.

"Peggy just got married less than a year ago, right?" Ellie noted. Peggy nodded in response. "She is anxious to start a family. Her husband is employed by the lumber yard here.

"Betsy moved here after her divorce was final. She is living temporarily with her parents but is looking for a place to fix up."

"Sorry, Kate, not a house the size of your place," Betsy teased. "My husband and I restored a couple of houses, so I know enough about restoration to be dangerous." Everyone chuckled. "I need to find something I can afford, so I can work on it as I go along. There are plenty of places off the main roads, so I'll take my time till I find the right place."

"I don't think you have to go off into the country roads to find rundown buildings," Ellie noted. "I have a couple places in mind I'll share with you later." Betsy nodded.

"I admire your willingness to go through that process, Betsy," I added. "As a decorator, I am better suited on the fun side, not where walls and plumbing need to be!" She smiled as she agreed.

"Charlene has lived here all her life like the other natives," Ellie noted. "She is the daughter of the coffee cake lady I told you about. She and her husband work at the Dresden Bank."

"Oh Charlene, I got to taste your mother's famous coffee cake, and it's wonderful," I praised. She smiled but made no comment. She probably got sick of hearing that. She definitely looked like the most conservative of the group. She seemed the shyest of them all, which surprised me since she worked at the bank. I wondered if she'd ever lived anywhere except Borna. She probably met and married a fella from here.

"Of course you've met Anna," Ellie said as she finished

the circle of folks. "Thanks for having us tonight."

"Welcome to our circle, Kate," Anna said very graciously. "If you ever visit again, please feel free to join us on a regular basis."

"I am so happy to meet you all," I began. "Ellie has spoken very highly of all of you. I have been very fortunate to have her help while I'm here in Borna. I have to tell you this town is a little gem I wasn't aware of." They all smiled and some nodded. "I have to say, for someone who loves to bake, I am quite impressed with all the baked goods I've sampled! I'll be going home a pound or two heavier for sure." They now chuckled.

"So home is South Haven, Michigan?" Ruth Ann asked with interest. "I take it it's a pretty good drive from here!"

"It's a good day's drive for sure," I said nodding. "As most of you know, I have recently become a widow and Doc Paulson's property was purchased on my husband's side of the family. You could say I really knew nothing about its existence. It's a lovely place, and I am determined to find a buyer that will be a good neighbor for all of you!"

"We hope you do, too," chimed in Betsy. "I've noticed just in the last few days, it's looked better on the outside."

"Thanks, but it really needs a total renovation," I shared.

"We've been having a great time," Ellie said changing the subject to a more positive one. "I hate to see her leave."

"When are you leaving?" asked Charlene as she filled her coffee cup.

"I want to leave tomorrow morning, but there are still some last minute things I need to do," I explained. "Hopefully, Ellie will put up with me another night."

Anna interrupted us by telling everyone to help themselves to refreshments.

"I wish I knew more about Doctor Paulson and his wife," I interjected.

"Emma may know more than some of us," responded Ellen. "Her memory is amazing and she tries her best to keep up with the area's history."

"No one ever mentions Mrs. Paulson, and I think it's because she was always out of sight in the house," added Charlene. "I heard she helped quilt at church, but otherwise she really wasn't active in the community. Would you all agree?" Most nodded and agreed.

"That's the way things were back then with women and children," commented Ellie. "They were to be seen and not heard." They all chuckled.

"Have any of you ever seen a photo of her?" I asked as I got more curious. "Surely there has to be a wedding photo somewhere."

"You'll probably find something on their marriage at the history museum," Ellen claimed. "It's turning out to be a wonderful resource for all of us and a place to donate some our family memorabilia."

"I wonder why they didn't have any children." I asked next, even though no one would surely have the answer.

"Maybe they chose not to," Betsy said with humor. "He probably had access to birth control methods his patients didn't even know about!" They all had another chuckle.

"Betsy!" Ellie scolded with humor.

As the evening progressed, the only order of any business was when Ellen reported that the group had received a thank you note from the Oswald family, who suffered a fire a month ago.

What impressed me throughout the evening was how

each and every person connected personally with me. They were touched that under my grieving circumstances, I was trying to deal with the property here in Borna. Almost half of the friendship circle were single, and I'm sure in a town this small, their social life was limited. I wondered how these unique individuals ever connected.

"I felt bad and guilty coming back here after my divorce," Betsy quietly admitted. "It was a culture shock and things were so different than when I left. I thought I would go crazy the first week, but instead, I found peace and a loving community where I could raise my child." Hmmm, interesting. "My son loves having his grandparents nearby. From what I hear, the local schools are very good. I don't do much other than go to work." That sounded rather sad.

"Do you want to call it a night, Kate?" Ellie asked as she finished her coffee. "I know you had a long day, and you were nice to accommodate my plans tonight."

"See how well Ellie takes care of me?" I teased as I got up from my chair. Seeing we were getting ready to leave, several ladies said they were glad they had met me.

"Anna, I hope to see the village better in the daylight, sometime in the future," I said as I walked her way. "I can't wait to check out that outdoor oven."

"Anytime," Anna said with a big smile. "I'm sending some of my bread home with Ellie for your breakfast tomorrow."

"That would be wonderful!" I said putting on my jacket. "Thank you so much. This was an interesting evening."

"Are these ladies always this nice?" I asked Ellie as we got into the car.

"I have to say they are," she replied. "They all have such kind hearts, and yet they are all unique in their personalities.

One of the things I appreciate about them is they're not a gossipy group."

"That is in itself, unique!" I noted with a chuckle.

When we got back to Ellie's kitchen, she poured herself a glass of wine and asked me if I cared to join her.

"I am way too tired to think or drink right now, Ellie," I confessed. "I'm so glad I went this evening. It was the perfect diversion to my horrid afternoon."

"So, what is your game plan tomorrow?" Ellie asked as she kicked her shoes off. "I'm available to help you in the morning before I go to the winery."

"It's just odd and ends," I described. "The first thing I want to do is get a for sale sign from Harold's Hardware. Cotton left me the ladder in the kitchen so I'll be able to get to some places I couldn't reach before. I am leaving you one of these new keys in case you need to get in when I'm gone. I'm thinking I may leave one with Cotton, since I told him to keep an eye out. I can trust him, right?"

"Oh, sure, but I really don't think it's necessary," she said sipping her wine. "Is there a particular event or reason to get on home so quickly?"

I looked at her like she was joking. "I have a realtor to put a firecracker under, a dog without a home, and probably a stack of bills to pay," I said sarcastically.

She nodded. "I hope you can figure things out for yourself, Kate," Ellie said sadly.

"I do, too," I said becoming more frustrated. "Right now, my life has a lot of resentment and anger, which isn't productive, so I'll just say, Good Night Irene!" She laughed and threw me a kiss.

CHAPTER 16

I woke up feeling totally rested. It appeared my sleeping habits were improving. Perhaps it was the country air. I was somehow managing to erase Clay's lover, babe, and his bad choices out of my mind for now. My immediate concern was only to keep 6229 Main Street safe till I found a buyer.

I packed up my things in case I could get away in the afternoon. The weather was indeed getting colder, but the sun was now shining brightly.

When I joined Ellie in the kitchen, she announced she was skipping church to help me with any last chores at the house. Despite my objection, her mind was made up. She said she would go check on the winery in the afternoon.

"It's a good day for some of my chicken and dumplings," she proclaimed. "I make a lot of noodles at one time and freeze them. They should hit the spot for us at lunch time."

"Oh, it sounds delicious," I said with a yawn. "I'm not

sure I've ever had what you're describing, but isn't it a lot like chicken noodle soup?"

"Yes, and no," she said as she prepared the broth. "It's thicker for sure. When I was growing up, we either had fried chicken or chicken and dumplings for Sunday dinner. I guess it will be something I think about making every Sunday. My Mother would roll the dough out in big sheets, and I would help her cut them into squares. Some people drop dumplings into the broth. That isn't done around these parts." Either one sounded great to me!

"I can't wait!" I said picturing the perfect comfort food. "I wish you wouldn't go to such trouble. I keep thinking I could have left for home this morning had it not been for those creepy people that stormed in the house."

"Forget about that!" Ellie advised. "Let me make sure this is going, and then we'll go on over together.

"Okay, if you insist," I said giving in. "I'll just have one more little slice of this cranberry bread." Ellie laughed at my indulgence.

As we walked on over to the house, Ellie commented how much better things were looking. When we got inside, she asked if she could see the upstairs. I was surprised she had never taken liberties to check it out. As we walked up the stairs, she was immediately impressed with the lovely wide staircase and hall when we got to the top. She was also amazed at the size of the bedrooms and all the closets.

"You've got to see the attic," I encouraged. "It's huge. However, be careful on the staircase going up, as it curves." She was ready to explore, so up we went.

"Wow, Kate," she said as she got to the top step and onto the attic floor. "Look, this window looks out onto the street.

This view is incredible, and the ceiling's high enough to walk around up here. They could have had a big family living here with all this space. Perhaps this is where the Mrs. spent her time, if she was never seen much."

"Do you really think so?" I asked wondering.

"Well, Emma said one time that the Doc was a drunkard," she said with a chuckle. "Isn't that hilarious? I can't tell you if it was true or not."

"What?" I gasped. "I never heard that before!"

"It's a small town Kate, so who really knows!" Ellie said lightly. "Now if he was one to get drunk, I could see the Mrs. hiding out wherever she could."

"How in the world could he practice medicine if he drank?" I asked with confusion. Ellie shook her head. "Let's go back downstairs."

I told Ellie since Cotton left me a ladder in the house, I wanted to explore the small cabinets above the hall closets. I told her I was scared of heights and didn't want to go up the ladder without anyone else around.

"I'll go down and get it," Ellie offered. "It's in the kitchen, you said?"

"Yes, but I can go," I said feeling helpless.

"I am used to schlepping at the winery, so I'll go," she offered.

"What is schlepping?" I tried to picture it.

"You'll know in time," Ellie answered laughing as she went down the stairs.

I stared up at the cabinets and wondered when they had been opened last. Hopefully, the old fashioned looking latches would open.

"This ladder must be over one hundred years old, Kate,"

Ellie said coming slowly up the stairs. "You were smart not to get on this without someone else around. Be careful. I'll climb up, and you hold on to the ladder."

I held my breath as she opened the latch on the first closet.

"I don't have a flash light, but I'm afraid there's nothing in here but some spider webs," she informed me as she carefully came back down. "At least there weren't dead critters of any kind."

We moved the ladder to door number two, and she repeated her attempt to find something.

"Sorry, Kate. It's empty as well," Ellie said in disappointed tone.

"I sure was hoping there would be something from the Doc's records stored up there," I said with disappointment. "Maybe we'll get lucky behind door number three like in the TV show."

"Cute Kate," Ellie said as she climbed up to open the last cabinet. She was hesitant before reporting.

"What?" I inquired with impatience.

"There's a package wrapped in brown paper and string," she stated. "I'll try to reach it and hand it to you. I don't think it looks heavy."

"Really?" I asked as she just let the package fall to the ground. "Oh, Ellie!"

"It's pretty covered with dust and spider webs, but the string will probably break easily after all this time," Ellie noted as she waited for me to make the first move. We both stared at it as if it could be a bomb about to explode.

"It's all yours," Ellie joked. "It's your house and it's finders keepers on this, unless it's all cash!" We both gave a nervous chuckle.

"Wait. I want to take a photo on my phone, the way it looks right now," I said going down the stairs.

When I returned, Ellie watched as I took step by step photos of its discovery. The package felt soft, and once the paper was unfolded, it appeared to be a quilt. It was tightly rolled. The thought occurred to me that there could be something bad rolled up inside. We opened it up very slowly for a full view. We both were shocked to see the black embroidered message boldly stitched near the center of the quilt. It read, "FORGIVE US OUR TRESPASSES, AS WE FORGIVE THOSE WHO TRESPASS AGAINST US." I was speechless.

"There are passages and quotes all over this quilt," Ellie observed. She picked up the corner and read, "LEAD US NOT INTO TEMPTATION."

"Whoever did this was certainly religious, I'll say that!" I said looking closer.

"Here in the corner is a name with some dates, Kate," Ellie revealed. "It says, JOSEY, AUG.30 TO SEPT 2, 1916. Whoever Josey was, she didn't live very long. It's strange there's no last name!"

"Oh Ellie, I think maybe the name on the little tombstone in the backyard is Josey. It was a short name like that," I said thinking hard.

"What tombstone?" Ellie shouted in shock. "You never said there was a tombstone on the property."

"I may be mistaken, but it was just one name on a good sized stone that reminded me of a child's tombstone," I recalled. "It was nearly all buried, and it's pretty worn from the weather. My plan was to go back later and look at it, but I never had a chance."

"This corner says, "ELOISE, JUNE 6 TO JUNE 9, 1917,"

Ellie read aloud. "This little gal didn't live but three days, it appears. Do you think this was made by Mrs. Paulson? They didn't have any children, but maybe it was because they didn't live."

"How sad," I said as I sat on the floor. "I do think back then, women lost more children from miscarriages although I don't think we should assume that just yet. Here it says, 'DELIVER ME FROM EVIL.'"

"Isn't it supposed to say 'DELIVER us FROM EVIL'?" Ellie noticed. "This is weird!"

"This really is sad," I said pointing to another corner. "It just says, 'I'M SORRY'."

"I think our quilt maker was in a pretty bad way, if you ask me," Ellie said sympathetically. "What was she sorry for? It could have been left by one of the renters, don't forget."

I nodded. "The top is all different sized blocks, like she didn't have a pattern or plan for it," I observed as I examined it more closely. "It's never been washed. She may have made each block and then decided to make a quilt. All the embroidery floss is black making it depressing. Maybe she wanted the wording to look more like scripture in a book."

"It is a depressing quilt, let's face it," Ellie noted. "I don't think this was made to be a pretty quilt. Did you notice all these small tiny brown speckles on most of the fabric? Does it have any batting?"

"I've seen enough antique quilts to know these brown speckles are from lack of air in the storage process," I revealed. "Maggie calls it blemishing. Yes, it has a thin batting, which is the old cotton. If held up to the light, you would probably see flecks in the cotton. Some like to say they are cotton seeds, but that's incorrect."

"Well, if you're not the quilt authority, Miss Meyr!" Ellie praised.

We continued sitting on the floor a bit longer, as we turned the quilt various directions. There didn't seem to be anything organized about the quilt, as if it was made as she went along in life. The main message of forgiveness was off center, which spoke to thoughtlessness and carelessness of the work.

"DIE IF YOU WILL," Ellie said aloud as if were frightening her. "What's that supposed to mean?"

"We've got to put this away," I suggested. "It's creeping me out, and I don't have any more time to waste on this. Do you by chance have an old sheet I can wrap this in? We have got to get rid of this awful paper. This is the worst possible way to store this. It hasn't had any air in ages, plus this paper is an acid product."

"You're taking this home with you, aren't you?" Ellie asked curiously. "Sure, I have some old sheets."

"No, I can't take this quilt out of the house, Ellie," I said firmly. "It really doesn't belong to me and it's hidden here for a reason. It has to belong to somebody, don't you think? I'll wrap it in the sheet and put it back where I found it. Hopefully, the owner won't mind that I removed the paper."

"You're nuts, Kate!" Ellie said shaking her head in disbelief. "What if someone forgot it was here? It's your house now, don't you see? "She saw me shake my head to the negative. "Okay, I'll go get a sheet while you run to Harold's to get a sign."

"Deal," I said folding up the quilt. "Leave the ladder here."

As I drove to Harold's, I thought of the saying, "Be careful what you wish for, for you may get it." The quilt made me sad.

Finding this quilt wasn't the exciting treasure I was hoping to find in the house. The way it was packaged, it almost looked like it was supposed to be mailed or saved for someone. The good part was I corrected a bad storage situation, so it could survive.

Harold was surprised to see me, and even more so when I asked where he kept his for sale signs.

"Is that ole Blade to tight to furnish you a sign," Harold teased. I laughed not really wanting to explain.

"I'm afraid Blade is on a different time line than I am." I said as briefly as I could.

"These aren't very big, but the good part is, your house has such great visibility." he explained. "We sell a lot of these to folks who can't afford to sell through a realtor. It works because buyers feel they can get the place for a cheaper price when the owner doesn't have to pay a commission."

"I'll take a couple of those," I said walking to his counter. "I really like your little store. It seems to have everything you would ever need. Thanks for helping me out."

"Heading home are ya?" he asked as he put the signs in a bag.

"I am," I said nodding. "I have folks keeping an eye on the place. I'll be back again, if or when it sells.

He smiled with approval. "Good luck, but ya know winter's about to set in around here, and that means less traffic going by here," he added. "I wouldn't get your hopes up too much, Ms. Meyr."

"It's Kate, remember?" I reminded him. "I happen to know there are a lot of people employed at the lumber yard who can afford to own a house like this. It's perfect for a large family." Harold smiled again to humor me.

Harold smiled again to humor me. "Well, good luck to you, Kate," he said giving me a wink. "You have a safe trip home, ya hear?"

"Thanks," I said winking back.

When I returned to the house, Ellie was in the kitchen, sizing up the room. The quilt was wrapped nicely in her white sheet on the counter.

"You know, if this were my kitchen, I'd knock out this pantry and open up this room," she said with her hands on her hip.

"I thought the same thing, Ellie," I added. "I think some exposed brick in here would be attractive, too!"

"I didn't know if I should say anything, but while you were gone, Blade pulled up here in your drive and turned around," she said in a concerned tone. "He probably thought you went home to Michigan since your car wasn't here or next door."

"That man is creepy if you ask me!" I said in disgust. "I wonder how long my sign will stay in the yard. If it disappears, will you go to Harold's and replace it for me? I will pay you."

"Of course, I will silly," she said nodding. "I don't want you to worry about anything. I think we should have some lunch. I'm starved. I hope you're ready for a real country treat. I think I can smell it all the way over here!"

"I'm ready girl!" I said following her out the door.

CHAPTER 17

Going back to Ellie's house was like going home to the heavenly comforts in life. While she prepared our table for lunch, Maggie called on my cell phone.

"I'm missing you, girlfriend!" her familiar voice said. When I heard her voice, I too was missing her.

"I miss you, too!" I had to admit. "I'm leaving first thing in the morning so I figure on Tuesday we can meet up for lunch. Would that work for you?"

"Sounds great!" she said eagerly. "Everyone's been asking about you."

"I need to check in with Carla today and confirm with her I'm coming home," I said to remind myself. "I haven't heard a peep from my realtor, so I guess I'll look for another one when I get back."

"We had our first snowflakes yesterday," she noted. "It didn't amount to much, but it appears our fall is going to be cut short."

"It's been colder here, too," I shared. "Ellie has been nice enough to let me borrow some of her warmer clothing. The foliage is still pretty colorful here, Maggie. I would love for you to visit here with me when I come back. It really is beautiful country."

"Sure, I'd like that, too!" she said without hesitation.

"We are about to have some lunch, so I need to go," I said looking at my hot bowl of chicken and dumplings. "Ellie has truly spoiled me with good food and wine. I'll bring you some of her Red Creek wine specialties."

"That sounds great," Maggie replied. "Be safe coming home, okay?"

"Will do and love you!" I said before she sent her love.

I sat down and carefully tasted the chunky chicken and noodles in the heavy broth. It was perfectly seasoned, and I felt it could cure just about everything, including a hearty appetite. I immediately sang praises to one of the best cooks I had ever known.

"So do you think Maggie will agree to come with you to Borna some time?" Ellie curiously asked.

"She might," I said between bites. "She and I have been through a lot together. You can have all these so called friends in your life, but very few are really true friends, if you know what I mean. I'm looking forward to seeing her, but every time I think about going back to my house, I tense up inside. I almost feel almost nauseous."

"Well, under your circumstances, I wouldn't wait for your house to sell," Ellie advised. "You find a place that's to your taste and move there as soon as you can. There's no point dragging it out. This is a big turning point in your life right now. For once, you, not Clay, gets to decide where and how you want to live! It's real easy to slip into another submissive situation when your friends and relatives are telling you what they think is best for you. You are a smart and capable woman Kate. I see how you're making decisions on your house next door and how beautifully you interact with the community. When you told me that you didn't bake much because Clay said it wasn't healthy, I wanted to scream. Don't you know how bizarre that sounds to an independent and normal woman like me? You are a big girl, Ms. Meyr!"

"I know, trust me, I know," I confirmed. "It was just easier to go along with his wishes. I picked my battles, and there were few of them." I got up and started to pace the floor. Ellie had ruffled a nerve, which embarrassed me.

"Oh darn it," Ellie said with a sigh. "I didn't mean to upset you. Sit down and finish your lunch. It's your last night here, so I think you should come to the winery when you're finished and we'll celebrate." I smiled and sat down.

"I think that might be nice, except you must help me stick to only two glasses of wine," I teased. "I am determined to get an early start.

"Whatever you say, big girl!" Maggie teased back.

CHAPTER 18

Trout was glad to see me walk in about 7:00 that evening. I scanned the place for Ellie, but didn't see her.

"Hey, there!" Trout greeted me as I approached the bar. "Ellie said to tell you she had to make a quick kitchen run, but that she'd be right back. She said to order anything you want and it's on the house."

"No problem," I said as I took a stool by two young girls. I nodded to them. They seemed to be having a good time. "Trout, before I leave tonight, I need to take about six bottles of your Red Creek labeled wine home with me. Give me three red and three white. Will you choose them for me?" "Be glad to!" he said as he served someone nearby.

"So girls, what kind of wine would you suggest I have tonight?" I asked boldly.

"Oh, I'm all about red wines," the blonde girl eagerly said.

"I usually have a beer, but tonight I'm drinking one of

their cabs," the brunette said as she pulled her hair out of her face. "Are you from here?" I thought she was being rather bold, as she looked sternly at my face.

"No, I'm visiting," I simply stated. "I'm a friend of Ellie's, but I'll be going back home to Michigan tomorrow."

"Oh, of course, you're that lady who owns the Doc Paulson house on Main Street, right?" The blonde said with a friendly smile.

I smiled back at her. "Yes, I'm Kate Meyr," I said extending my hand.

"I'm Karen, and this is Sarah," she responded. "We live about twenty minutes from here, and try to meet up once a week. Sarah's got a thing for this cute bartender here, or we wouldn't come as often."

I laughed. "He is pretty cute," I added.

"Sorry I had to leave, Kate," said Ellie's voice behind me. "I see you've met the girls. They make this place look pretty good, don't you think? Would you girls like to join us at a table for a bite to eat?"

"Oh, sure," voiced Karen. "We just gave Trout our pizza order."

"That sounds good!" I said looking at Ellie. Do you want to split one? Maybe the chicken/pineapple you've talked about!"

"Sure, let me go turn the order in," Ellie said leaving us.

"So do many singles come here?" I asked, assuming they were single. They grinned.

"Some do," Karen quickly answered. "Unless you want to hang out in one of the smoky bars around here, this is about the only place to come. We like the no smoking here. Of course, having the outside deck helps for those who smoke.

If you go in one of those bars, your clothes smell to high heaven the next day. The guys can be pretty rough there at times, too."

"I bet you're right!" I said in agreement. I was thinking of Blade as a good example.

"So you're putting Doc's house up for sale, huh?" asked Sarah. I nodded. "It would make a really nice restaurant. There's not a table cloth place for miles around here."

"Hey, does it have a ghost like they say?" asked Karen. "Trout told us once that a renter there used to come in here and talk about a ghost. He told Trout he was going to be moving as soon as he could."

"Oh really," I pondered. "I haven't had any ghosts appear, however I am trying to find out more about the house and its original owners."

"Well, there has to be some juicy stories about a doctor's office for heaven's sake," joked Karen. "Don't you think babies may have been born there, and some folks may have even died there? It's not like we have a hospital anywhere close by."

"You bring up a very good point," I said giving credit to her. I did need to think about that further.

Ellie arrived at our table with our pizzas and another round of drinks. My wine glass was still nearly full, so I passed.

"So, Kate, I take it your single?" Sarah asked with a flirtatious tone.

"I am," I happily said. Yes, I am, I'm confirmed to myself.

"So are you hanging out with anyone?" Sarah continued to probe. No one but Ellie I thought about saying.

"Aren't you being nosy," chimed in Ellie.

"Well, both you gals are very attractive and shouldn't have a problem finding anyone," Karen added. "Ellie gets hit on a lot here, but she's always so cool about it."

"I'm sure she does, but I bet she's all business," I defended. "She seems pretty darn happy if you ask me."

"Thanks, Miss Kate," Ellie said laughing.

"At this point in life, I want to surround myself with fun friends," I noted to them. "Yes, it can include some fellas." I blushed as they laughed.

It was good for Ellie and me to be with young girls who were full of fun and new conversation. The pizza was some of the best I ever had. Ellie said it's all about the dough. Leave it to her to have her own special touch. Ellie had truly created a place which was open for a variety of folks who loved wine, enjoyed a lovely atmosphere, and had friendly service. If I lived here, I could envision coming to this bar alone now and then, just to enjoy a glass of wine and fun company.

To my surprise, it was Ellie who suggested we head home. I said my goodbyes to both the girls and Trout. I felt I had known them all for a long time.

CHAPTER 19

When I woke up the next morning, it seemed so dark outside. I checked my watch, then jumped out of bed and into the shower. Shivering, I put on my jeans and sweatshirt I had worn the first day I arrived in Borna.

To my surprise, Ellie was up and had the coffee ready. She was still wearing her night time sweats and big puffy house slippers. She was really her own person, which I so admired.

"Any effects from the wine last night?" Ellie asked as she poured my coffee.

"Just good ones," I joked. "I slept like a baby."

"I sure hate seeing you go, Kate," Ellie said as she sat down at her kitchen table. "I put some bread and coffee cake in a zip lock bag for you to take home."

I smiled. "I'm all set with Red Creek wine and German baked goodies," I bragged. "What more could a girl ask for." She laughed. "I don't know how I can begin to thank you, Ellie. I couldn't have accomplished so much on this visit without you."

"You have a point there," she teased. "Look, I'm not good with goodbyes, so let's just say we'll call or email, okay?"

"I'm good with that," almost breaking into tears, I turned away.

"You should take that extra jacket of mine you've been wearing," she advised. "I think you may need it if you get out of the car." I accepted with a nod.

We chatted at the table with our coffee, for a short while longer, knowing our goodbyes would have to happen. Ellie walked me to the car. I told her I would be putting the for sale sign in my front yard before I left. We embraced with a big hug, and Ellie immediately went into the house. I knew this was hard for her as well as me. I took a deep breath and started my car to head next door for the last time.

When I pulled into my drive way, something told me that the most secure way to leave 6229 Main Street was to leave my for sale signs on the front seat next to me. The thought of nosy strangers milling around my empty home was unsettling. I turned the car around and headed out of Borna.

As I drove towards the interstate, I felt like I was saying goodbye to a beautiful place and lasting friendships. Part of me felt liberated and the other part sad. This trip had been so good for me.

When I finally got on the interstate where my mind could go on auto-pilot, I began replaying the great memories of the last few days. At least they overshadowed creepy Blade and the scary family who invaded my house. When I stopped for gas, I put on Ellie's jacket, which smelled like her cozy house. Before I got back onto the highway, I called Carla to tell her I would be home later in the evening. When I reached her, she said my answering machine was full of messages. She said she had assured James I would call him as soon as I returned. The report on Rocky was fine, and she would continue to keep him till I decided what to do with him.

I just couldn't quite figure out the urgency of James' calls. I thought I was done with him and Clay's family once the estate was settled. As I continued towards home, I had to switch my mind to a South Haven mode. My first priority would be to find a place to live. I had thought so often, I wanted a simple, plain, condo with no upkeep, but after my experience in Borna, I realized how much I liked playing house. Perhaps I should be looking at some cute, little, historic homes, where I could have a small garden, a great kitchen for baking, and a white picket fence. It would be perfect for my antiques and quilts. How fun it would be!

It was late at night when I pulled into my prestigious subdivision. Maggie always teased me about living in the neighborhood of the rich and famous. The house was dark except the light in the hall which we always kept lit. The outdoor motion lights greeted me when I pulled into the garage.

I opened the door, turned off the alarm, and didn't hear Rocky's patter of feet, which usually greeted me. Perhaps he wasn't such a nuisance after all. He was missed. I walked straight into my large bedroom, wanting to crash right on top of the bed. Besides James' calls, I listened to my messages, which were meaningless to me. Having the realtor say many people were calling about the house was a joke, as I knew there were many, nosy folks, just curious about the asking price.

Without turning on the lights, I undressed and put on my favorite, white cotton pajamas. All I could think about was Ellie discovering no FOR SALE sign in my yard. I'd have to call her in the morning and explain before she ran to Harold's for more. For some reason, it gave me a chuckle and off to sleep I went.

CHAPTER 20

I awoke to bright sunlight coming in my window. I turned over and mentally planned my day. A smile came over my face when I remembered I would be having some of Ellie's coffeecake with my morning coffee. I was also anxious to meet Maggie for lunch at Clementia's, which was a nice sports bar downtown. We would have a lot of catching up to do.

As I showered and dressed, I looked about my closet and bedroom realizing I still had much to get rid of. Most of these clothes I would never be wearing again and I would rather have a unique antique dresser and wardrobe for the few things I would be keeping.

The phone rang, and I saw it was James. I reluctantly answered. He wasn't wasting anytime.

"It's about time you got back home," James said in a teasing voice like we were best friends.

"Hey, what can I do for you?" I casually asked. "I got home late last night and saw you called."

"Sure did, and I was wondering if I could stop by to see you this morning?" he asked in a more desperate voice.

"I have an 11:30 appointment, but before then should be fine," I reluctantly agreed.

"Great," he immediately said. "I'll be by in about an hour." Why his purpose couldn't be discussed over the phone was beyond me!

I was savoring my coffeecake at the kitchen table, wishing I could have met Mrs. Grebing herself, instead of her daughter, at the Friendship Circle. I bet she was a special lady. My cell went off, and to my delight, it was Ellie!

"You made it home safely, I see," Ellie began.

"Yes, and overwhelmed, but I'm here!" I confessed. "How did you know to call me while I was enjoying your coffeecake?"

She laughed. "I think you are a real foodie," Ellie teased.

"You know, I think you're right!" I said laughing with her.

"Was it my imagination, or did you forget to put the FOR SALE sign in your yard?" Oh dear, she must have been looking out the window.

"Aren't you a nosy neighbor?" I accused in fun. "I just couldn't do it yet, Ellie. Once the sign goes up, it's up for grabs to anyone who can afford it. It's not the house it's really supposed to be. Does that make sense? I really would like to upgrade it a bit more, so it gets an owner who can afford to take care of it. It may mean the asking price will go up, but I think the Borna community deserves something better for this house with all its history."

"I see," she said somewhat confused.

"It's been sitting there all this time, so until it's in better shape, just tell folks it's not for sale. If a qualified person inquires about it, have them call me."

"Oh boy, I can't imagine how Blade is going to interpret this!" Ellie warned.

"We'll keep him guessing, that's what!" I suggested laughing. "I could care less what he thinks! I've got a busy day, starting with a mysterious visit this morning with Clay's brother, James. Wish me luck there. Is everything okay otherwise?"

"Yup. Heading to the winery shortly," she said matter of factly. "I thought I better call you first and check on the sign situation. I'm glad I don't have to stop by Harold's!" We both laughed. "I'm glad the place is gonna bring you back for another visit. Have a good day and keep me posted!"

It was so good hearing her voice. We shared the same sense of humor that Maggie and I did. I almost wanted to say, "Love you," like I did with Maggie. When I hung up, I saw James pull up in his fancy, black Mercedes. I said a little prayer, hoping this visit would go well. I couldn't help but wonder if my husband Clay was witnessing this.

After a somewhat strained greeting, James came inside and immediately took off his coat.

"It looks like we're going to have an early winter," he said uninterestedly. "So, I understand you just had a visit to Borna?"

"I did," I said with hesitation.

"I wondered if you knew why my Dad purchased that piece of property?" he inquired getting to the point.

"Sure, but perhaps I need to hear more!" I politely said.

"Our Dad had a relationship with someone at the lumber

yard there, and it not only became a business relationship, but a friendship which made my Dad feel compelled to purchase this property from him. I think his friend convinced him it was a great place to go hunting and fishing, but frankly, as you may know, our Dad, nor any of us, did any of that."

"I see," I said, just trying to listen.

"I'll be honest with you, Kate," he began with some hesitancy, "I was shocked when Clay left that property to you, since it was in the Meyr's side of the family. We still have a business relationship with the East Perry Lumber yard there." He now got up to pace the floor. "Since you are totally out of the business now, I wondered if I could strike a deal with you to purchase that property. I would probably be doing you a favor, since I heard you'll be putting it up for sale." I was at a loss for words.

"Were you ever there?" I softly asked.

"Yes," he nodded. "A long time ago, my Dad and I flew into St. Louis and drove to that part of the world. I thought we'd never get there. The town certainly has nothing to offer, but the lumber yard does quite well, for sure. I understand you have it listed with a local realtor there."

"No, as a matter of fact, I've changed my mind," I said with a slight grin on my face.

"You did?" he quickly questioned.

"The realtor was pretty obnoxious and unprofessional to be honest," I described.

"Well, I'm sorry to hear that," he said calmly. "I hear he's the only one in town. Perhaps it's just as well because I'd like to make the purchase directly from you. I think you, of all people, can understand it's only right, it stays in the family."

I looked at him strangely. "I thought I was part of the

family," I questioned as I felt offended. I now got out of my chair.

"Oh, of course, I didn't mean it that way," he quickly responded. I knew now where he was going, and I was trying to find the right words.

"I'm not surprised you're being so direct here, but I find it most interesting that Clay wanted me to have the property and not you," I bluntly said. "He could have easily arranged it, and I wouldn't have thought a thing about it. The reality is he left it to me."

"I understand and now you want to get rid of it!" he said raising his voice. "What does that tell you? He obviously wanted you to have the money from it, so I'm willing to provide you with the appraisal value. I don't know what you would be asking, but I'll be happy to pay for an appraisal for you. If you feel you need something beyond that, within reason, I can do that." I took a deep breath.

"That won't be necessary because the property is not for sale, right now," I stated looking directly into his eyes. He stared me down, and I could tell he really wanted to yell or strike me. "I've started renovating the house to make it more appealing to the buyer. It's not very marketable right now. It's been terribly neglected, thanks to the Meyr family by the way. The town of Borna deserves a better structure in the heart of their community. If it sells in poor condition, chances are the owners won't have the means to improve or maintain it."

"And just who do you think is going to be able to afford such a fancy house in that God-forsaken town?" he said in anger.

"Maybe no one," I came back to say. "It's a real gem in my

estimation and so is the little God-forsaken town you just mentioned. I think Clay would be pleased I took the interest to improve it."

"That's a bunch of bull," James said in disgust. "Spare me your sentiment here. I think you just want to be spiteful to our family. Clay said you were different, and now I'm seeing what he meant." I wanted to slap his face.

"Different? Yes, perhaps Clay's mistress would have been more to your family's liking," I suddenly blurted out. "I'm sure you know who she is, so you decide. I really appreciate you thinking of my best interest James. Clay would appreciate it." His face turned red. He was at a loss as how to respond. He grabbed his coat, without saying another word, and left the house. I couldn't watch him drive away. I was shaking, but I felt as if a big rock had just been lifted off of me. I was free.

CHAPTER 21

While changing clothes to meet Maggie, I was thinking my Father-in-law would have actually been proud of how I handled James. Leaving this property to Clay, and not James, was intentional, I'm sure. James had plenty of money, so why would he care if I owned the house in Borna? It could only be greed.

I couldn't wait to share the details of James' visit with Maggie. There was no one else who would understand. She was waiting for me in the sports bar's entrance, where I rushed in and hugged her. We asked for a booth, and quickly decided we'd celebrate our reunion with a wine cocktail.

"I have some Red Creek wine for you in the car," I revealed. "I think you'll like what Trout, the bartender, chose for you."

She laughed. "You're trip was quite an adventure, wasn't it?" she asked patting my hand from across the table.

"Yes, indeed it was," I said smiling. "Besides such beautiful country, the people are so nice!"

After we ordered our BLT sandwiches, I told her about my morning visit with James. She was totally shocked and angered by his comments. She said after his behavior, James should be the last person I sell it to.

"There's something I haven't told you about Clay," I said after I took a sip of my cocktail. She looked at me strangely. "Clay was seeing someone. I only know her by "babe", and I don't know where she lives or how long he was seeing her, but I have voice mails and text messages to that effect."

"What?" she asked way too loudly. "Clay? How could he?" Her eyes were tearing up. "You were the perfect wife in every way! What the heck was he thinking?"

"I think I may have been part of the problem," I sadly admitted. "The girl he admired and fell in love with disappeared under his control. I knew I was giving up some independence, but I wanted him to be successful and happy."

"Too bad you couldn't have found this out while he was still alive," Maggie said angrily. "Together, we would have fixed his goose and hers, too!"

"You know, I was so angry about him drinking, and then I find out this!" I shared. "This affair doesn't affect me like you would think. He paid a price for his wayward life, and now I need to move on. I can't do anything about any of it!"

Maggie shook her head in disbelief. "Oh honey, you are way too kind, but I see your point!" she conceded.

We continued our conversation hitting on a variety of topics. She always asked about Jack. I told her he was pouring himself into work with a new project, and how much he was like his Father in so many ways. She knew he and I tried to connect with a phone call on Sundays, and by texting back and forth. I grieved more for Jack not having a Father than me not having my husband. After a three hour lunch, we finally said our goodbyes.

On the way home, I drove through the oldest part of South Haven, which had smaller, older, homes. They seldom came up for sale, and I was not finding any for sale signs. South Haven had a terrific association for preserving their history and architecture. The red harbor light house was their key signature, and there were fund raising efforts going on, to do another renovation. Thousands of tourists took pictures of the red beauty each year, and it was also the most perfect area on the beach to catch a gorgeous sunset. Property in the beach area was sky high and usually not for sale.

I dreaded going home. Not even Rocky would be there to greet me. However, I liked being alone when I could do things I wanted to do. Maybe I would heat up my fancy oven and bake something!

CHAPTER 22

I got home around 5:00, and my cell was ringing. When I looked to see who was calling, to my surprise, it was Ellie.

"Hey, Miss Borna, what's up?" I cheerfully asked.

"I'm fine, but I'm calling to actually give you a message from your favorite person!" she teased.

"And who would that be?" I asked without giving it a thought.

"I had a little visit from Blade at the winery today, and he wanted me to give you a message," she began to explain. "I think he thought you probably wouldn't take his call or return his message."

"What's going on?" I asked impatiently.

"He said he had a buyer for the house," she stated with a pause. "He was also fishing for an explanation as to why there wasn't a FOR SALE sign in the yard. He wanted to know if you had sold it."

"What did you tell him?" I anxiously asked.

"There's more," she said, before she would give me an answer. "He said the buyer made an offer above what you were going to ask when you first discussed the sale with Blade."

"Oh really," I responded. "Why would he care about the sale now, since I don't have it listed with him?"

"Oh, I'm sure he's baiting you with this fish to see if you'll sign with him to get access to his buyer," she predicted. She snickered. "I told him you wanted to do more with the place before you sold it, but he dismissed the idea right away, saying you'd be crazy to do so with a buyer in your hand."

"I'm not about to contact him, Ellie," I stated. "If someone is serious about the place, they're going to have to contact me directly. I don't have to go through him. Frankly, I don't believe him. I have a buyer interested here in South Haven who told me to name a price, and he'd buy it."

"Are you kidding me?" she asked in disbelief.

"Clay's brother, James practically threatened me to sell it to him this morning," I revealed. "He tried to make me feel bad, saying the property should have stayed in the Meyr family to begin with. He's willing to pay me off, in other words."

"This is crazy, isn't it?" she surmised. "Did someone discover gold on the place or what?" We both had a chuckle.

"Before I forget to tell you, I ran into Emma at the bank, and she said she might be able to help with more information about the Paulsons," Ellie voiced with excitement. "She also said how sorry she was, she didn't get to meet you at Anna's house."

"Wonderful!" I exclaimed. "Did you tell her about the quilt we found?"

"Oh, no girl," she stated firmly. "You better keep that under your hat right now since it's still kept in the empty house. I still think you should have taken the quilt home with you."

"You're probably right, but I don't feel it really belongs to me," I shared. "I'll pay Emma a visit as soon as I can come back. Have you seen Cotton coming around to check on the place?"

"Not really, but I'm not here most of the time," she admitted. "I keep an eye out, whenever I can."

"I know you do, and I really appreciate it," I said sincerely. "I will try to return as soon as I can, but I still haven't a clue as to where I will move to. It's really starting to stress me out."

"I know," she said with sympathy. "Don't worry about things here. Try to focus on one thing at a time."

After we ended our conversation, I wished I could have run next door to her inviting kitchen for a glass of wine and good conversation. Why all this sudden interest in Doc's house? I think James just wants the house for spite, knowing Clay and his father passed him by. He'd probably let it sit and rot, just to say he got what he wanted. I also wondered how Blade was going to react when he realized I was going to ignore him.

CHAPTER 23

"What do you mean I can have this?" Carla asked in disbelief the next morning. "You don't even know where you'll be living and what you'll need!"

"I just want to keep what is meaningful to me," I said calmly. "If you don't want any of the things I mentioned, you won't hurt my feelings. I would just ask if you don't care to have them, please call Goodwill to pick them up."

"Oh, Miss Kate," she said shaking her head. "I sure hope you don't regret some of this one day!"

"I'm already regretting some things, Carla," I said sadly. "I may as well be blunt with you. Did you know Clay was having an affair?" She gave a frightful look.

"Are you serious?" she shouted. "Clay was not my favorite person, and he drove me crazy at times, but I sure thought this man was crazy about his wife. Are you sure you know what you're talking about?" I nodded. "Did you know before his accident?"

"No, I didn't," I said feeling weak as I sat down. "I have all the proof I need, and now it doesn't matter, anyway." I was so tired. I just wanted to run away.

"You knocked yourself out for that man," she said in my defense. "I could call him some choice names right now!

"I'm not looking for sympathy, Carla," I said to calm her down. "From the way he was drinking, he obviously was unhappy. He already has paid the price of his poor decisions, so I have to leave it at that. Can you understand now, why I'd like to get rid of some of these things?"

She nodded. "Does our sweet Jack know any of this?" she asked next.

"No, and he doesn't have to," I stated. "He loved his father, even though he knew he had faults. He doesn't need to have any more pain. I don't think he'll be home for a while, which I understand. Right now, news from me or home isn't helpful to his grief, so I need to respect that."

"Okay then. I'll have another look at some of the furniture," Carla said after she gave me a little hug of support.

I spent the rest of the afternoon looking on the computer for any new listings of houses for sale. I knew my bad attitude was getting in the way of considering any of them. I was looking for anything that could be wrong with them. I loved the shoreline, but the hefty investment made me think twice about any commitment right now.

After I heard Carla leave, I poured myself a glass of wine. I was too tired to think of eating anything. I was ready for another pity party, I supposed. I really didn't cry much after Clay's death. Anger kept getting in the way of any sadness. I went to the sunporch to watch the sun go down. It was my favorite part of the day. I laid my head back on the lounge chair and wondered what Ellie was doing tonight. Did she have a full house at her winery? I wonder what Emma would be able to tell me about the Paulsons? If the quilt belonged to Mrs. Paulson, she was a mighty unhappy person. It was a sad, dark quilt which was asking for forgiveness. Forgiveness for what, I wondered? If someone stole the quilt while I was gone, I'd never forgive myself. Should I tell Ellie to go rescue it and take it to her house, for now?

I pulled a nearby knitted coverlet over me. I pulled it over my head, thinking maybe some answers and comfort would come to me.

CHAPTER 24

I woke up in the dark to the constant ringing from my cell phone. I was still cuddled up on the lounge chair when I reached for the phone. I saw it was Ellie, but it went to voice mail before I could get my bearings. Her voice mail said to call her, as there was some vandalism at my house. My stomach sank to feeling nauseous. How can things get worse? It was 2:00 am when I quickly returned her call.

"I'm sorry I had to call you at such an ungodly hour, Kate," Ellie said, apologetically. "I hadn't been home too long from the winery when I heard a car or vehicle speed out from your drive way. It appeared suspicious so I went over to check it out!"

"So was it anything?" I frantically asked.

"Yeah, the first thing I noticed was your narrow cute window in the kitchen was broken and had a big hole in it. The basement window below it was also broken. As I walked around the outside, I saw another basement window, on the back of the house, was busted, too."

"Good heavens," I said in disbelief. "They didn't hurt the stain glass windows, did they?"

"No, from what I can tell, that's it," she reported. "It doesn't appear they were there to steal anything. They just wanted to vandalize it. It's probably some young kids out for a joy ride, which happens around here on the weekends."

"Did you call anyone?" I asked as I pictured the horrid scene.

"I did, but they pretty much blew me off, saying they'd be out first thing in the morning to take a look," she reported with disappointment. They gave me a number to call to have someone board up the windows, but that's about it. I'll go over in the daylight and clean up any mess. If you want me to call Harold and have some of his guys replace the windows, I will."

"Oh Ellie, that is asking way too much!' I said in dismay. "Yes, have Harold fix them and send me a bill. Just leave the inside mess for me to deal with. Thank you so, so much!"

"I'm glad to do it!" Ellie said trying to comfort me. "I'm sorry this happened. I wish I had gotten a better look as they drove away. It could have been a lot worse!"

"You're right," I said thoughtfully. "Thanks again."

Now being wide awake, I went to the kitchen and put on some coffee. I took this incident personally. Everyone in town had to know I was trying hard to make the place better. This had Blade's name all over it. Why would kids want to break those windows? Who knows what he'll do next. Having Cotton and Ellie check on the place was not going to do the job. It was my place and my responsibility. My house wasn't selling, and I didn't have a place to move to, so what was I doing sitting here?

I decided that in the morning I would take some kind of action, but I wasn't quite sure what it was going to be. I would visit the realty office in person to see if there were any serious prospects. If not, I could make another quick visit to Borna. When I returned the first thing would be to install a security system of some kind. I had the money, and it would help me and poor Ellie, who felt so obligated to check on my house every day. I went to my bedroom to try to get a few more winks of sleep, but trouble in Borna was determined to keep me awake.

As tired as I was, I finally dressed to start my day. I was anxious to go to Harbor Realty as soon as they opened to speak to them about my house.

They seemed surprised to see me, and I was lucky enough to catch Mary Carpenter, when she came in the door, behind me. Mary was the prestigious realtor in South Haven. Maggie said she had the connections to sell a house like ours, so without a thought, I listed it with her. So far, I wasn't impressed.

"There is absolutely no need to panic, Mrs. Meyr," she said as she poured herself a cup of coffee. "Would you like a cup?"

"No thanks and I'm not panicking," I said bluntly. "I realize a house in this price range may take a while to sell, but I wanted to hear directly from you if there were any serious prospects. I want to go out of town, but would happily postpone my plans, if you told me someone might be interested."

"Right now, I'd say you'll own this house for a while," she said playing with her hair.

"Have you been aggressive in trying to sell it?" I quickly asked in response. She looked at me as if I insulted her big time. "My contract with you is up the end of the month, so I'm going to be listing it elsewhere, if there isn't some kind of interest."

"My goodness, Mrs. Meyr," she said in surprise. "We are doing everything we can! Do you have a place to move to? Is that why you so anxious?" I knew what she was getting at.

"I just may," I said leaving her to wonder. "Well, I need to run now, so thank you for your time." She looked like she had seen a ghost.

I came out of the office and walked a block down to the harbor, where my car was parked. It was a beautiful sight to see all the sailboats lined up, waiting for a visit from their owners. I sat down on a nearby park bench to gather my thoughts. Was I really thinking about what I was thinking about?

Yes. I did have a home to go to when I thought about her question. It wasn't here in South Haven, but a house which needed my attention. Perhaps I was looking for love in all the wrong places, as the song goes. I could set up temporary residence in Borna while I updated the house. I could always come back here when the house sold. If I called a mover today, I could make my move on the weekend. Carla could keep an eye on things while I was gone.

After feeling a surge of adrenaline, I thought of my best friend Maggie. I'd have to convince her it wasn't permanent and how the idea would be good for me. If I had some luck, she might consider a visit to Borna soon. This sounded like a sensible plan to me. Ellie would be thrilled about my return, but I'd have to make sure she knew I would be staying at 6229 Main Street.

I was convinced James and his family would try to muddy my name since I didn't commit to playing ball with him. Jack was seldom home and was creating his own life in New York City. It didn't make sense for me to sit here in South Haven waiting for something to happen.

CHAPTER 25

I waited a couple of days before calling Maggie and Jack because I wanted to make sure I was going to go through with my decision. My last call would be to Ellie, to announce I was on my way.

I spent the next two days deciding what to take, what I wanted to sell, and to give away. I made sure I took a couple of unfinished quilt projects with me. However I couldn't imagine when there would be time to work on them. The one project was a Christmas gift for Carla, which was nearly finished.

My bed, a game table with matching chairs, clothing, linens, quilts, a couple of lawn chairs for my deck, and personal toiletries would be all I would need for now. All the things I had been accustomed to were no longer important to me. I was tempted to over pack on kitchen items, but that would be optimistic since they would be tearing up the kitchen.

I met Maggie downtown for dinner at Tello's, my favorite Italian restaurant. Maggie's husband traveled a lot, so she was usually available when I called. She anxiously approached me when she saw me at the table. I knew she was expecting news of my living arrangements, and I started my conversation by explaining my visit at Mary Carpenter's office.

"So, Maggie, after feeling frustrated about not finding a place suitable for me, I realized it was because I already had a home, that I happen to love, waiting for me." I said at the end of my story. "This unfinished business in Borna is calling my name, right now."

Her face turned sad. "So how long will you be gone?" she asked like a little child.

"Well, I can't say for sure, but I don't want to get snowed in down there," I explained. "Ellie said snow doesn't usually come till well after Christmas. I want to be back here for Christmas because Jack will likely come home. If my house sells before then, I'll be home sooner."

"You're excited about all this, aren't you?" she asked, knowing the answer. "You've been a different person since you went to Borna."

I smiled. "I probably am!" I admitted. "As a decorator, I can't wait to get my hands on that barren house. I know I have only visited there, but I already feel connected, if you know what I mean. It's such a charming and unassuming village, surrounded by so much more!"

"James is going to be very angry with you!" she warned.

"It doesn't matter what his family thinks anymore," I reminded her. "I really loved Clay's parents, but they're gone now."

Maggie paused awhile before speaking. "If I come to visit, will you make me work?" she joked. I had to laugh at the thought.

"More than likely," I nodded. "You'll also have to share my king size bed because that's all I'll have. That's going to be more difficult than sweeping up saw dust!" We laughed.

"I'll be lost without you," she said seriously. "I don't have another close friend."

"Anyone of those beach quilters will be happy to hang out with you, anytime," I encouraged. "We can talk every day on the cell, too! I love South Haven. It will always be home to me, but having this project right now is just what I need to get my mind off of all this darkness surrounding Clay's death."

"You're probably right, Kate," she finally said in agreement. "You deserve some happiness. However, you're going to work your butt off doing it. Do you realize what you're getting into?"

We poured more wine and started to enjoy the evening like we always did. When we said goodbye on the sidewalk, we hugged and once again said, "I love you."

Since Maggie took my news so well, I was ready to call Jack and tell Carla in the morning about my plans.

After I got into my pajamas, I called Ellie on her cell knowing she would be at the winery at this late hour.

"Hi Trout," I began. "This is Kate Meyr. Is Ellie there?"

"Well Kate, hello!" he greeted. "She just happens to be standing right here, so hold on."

"Hey there!" she said with surprise in her voice. "I sure didn't expect to hear from you tonight. I was actually going to call you in the morning to tell you that all the broken windows have been replaced."

"Oh, good!" I responded. "I couldn't wait to tell you I'll be arriving this weekend! I am sending a small moving van with me, the same day, so I can stay in the house while I'm working on it. I can't keep taking advantage of you next door. I have no prospects of the house selling here, so thought I'd be of better use in Borna!"

"Well, that is big news, but you know you are welcome to stay with me any time," she added. "I'm glad you're giving me some warning so I can turn the heat up in your house. It's a good thing you had the furnace looked at before you left. We've been having some pretty cold days lately."

"We have, too," I added. "I want to meet with Harold right away about a list of contractors in the area. I may stay till Christmas, but then I need to get back. I think Jack will be home."

"That's awesome, Kate," she replied. "We'll have a grand Thanksgiving together!" That sounded so good to me right now.

"Has everything been okay recently at the house?" I had to ask. There was a pause.

"Pretty much so," she answered. "There's nothing to worry about. We'll discuss it when you get here. Just be careful on your drive, ya hear? I'll have dinner ready for you, when you get here."

"Thanks for everything, Ellie," I said with excitement.

What did she mean saying "pretty much so?" I felt as if my child was being unattended and the babysitter was holding back on something so I wouldn't worry or get my feelings hurt.

CHAPTER 26

When Carla arrived early the next morning, she knew something was happening. I joined her in the kitchen to tell her about my plans. I could tell she was holding back tears as she tried to make herself busy.

"You're always going to have some responsibility here," I assured her. "Your paycheck will continue, plus you're taking care of Rocky for me. I hope it becomes permanent. I seriously want you to take some things you said you were fond of. I have the furniture marked, that's going in the van."

Finally, she spoke. "I just hate what Clay has done to you and Jack," she said in frustration.

"I do, too, Carla, but it may turn out to be one of the best things that's ever happened to me, when it's all said and done," I assessed. "I feel badly mostly for Jack. Whatever happens, we will always be friends and share Christmas together for sure!"

"What about Jack?" she said wiping a tear away. "What

does he think of all this?"

"When I called him this morning to update him on things, he seemed pretty impressed by what his Mother was about to take on," I explained with a smile. "He promised he'd be home for Christmas, and he asked me to email him pictures of Borna. I think it's a relief to him that I'm not alone here, crying in my bedroom. He knows we'll be there for each other as time goes on. This goes for you too, Carla."

I gave her a hug, and then we went to work dismantling the game table. As I packed and moved things, Carla cleaned up right behind me.

My cell phone rang, and it was Maggie saying she'd like to stop by in the evening to give me a little going away present. I told her I would welcome her company, but she couldn't stay late with my early plans the next day.

After Carla left in low spirits, I showered and put a pizza in the oven for Maggie and me. I would have liked to have jumped into bed, I was so tired, but I knew Maggie was having a tough time with me leaving.

Maggie arrived just as I pulled the pizza out of the oven. We poured some wine and went into the den, where I turned on the gas fireplace. She handed me a wrapped present which looked and felt like a book. I opened it up and the title on the book read, "My New Life." I saw the blank pages and knew it was a journal for the new life I was starting. I smiled.

"This is wonderful Maggie," I said happily as I held it up. "I've been terrible about journaling lately. I have too many negative thoughts to put into words." She nodded as she understood.

"I know," she said quietly. "When you expressed those feelings awhile back, I thought how sad it was. This is time to start anew, so now you can! Someone once said, "Just because your life is changing, doesn't mean you have to."

"Thanks, I get that," I reassured her. "I'm still me, and I'll make my first entry tonight! I hope I won't be too tired to write when I turn into a Borna work horse." We laughed.

"Just keep your eyes open and forget the past as much as you can because there could still be a possibility of a new romance out there for you," she teased.

"You have got to be kidding me!" I said loudly. "After life with Clay, I'm done with men! Besides, I don't think there are too many eligible bachelors in Borna!"

"There might be a widower farmer who's looking for a cook!" she joked. "If he hears about your baked goods, he'll be calling on ya!" We shared another laugh.

"Stop it, you're crazy girl!" I said joking back.

Our conversation got crazier as we continued to eat and drink. Maggie tried to turn the conversation towards who "babe" was in Clay's life, but I didn't want to go there!

"You know Sandra Meyr wouldn't speak to me at Rotary Club this week," she noted. "She's probably furious about how you told off her husband!"

"Oh, boy!" I responded. "I'm afraid you're going to pay the price, for being my friend."

"They were never my friends," Maggie claimed. "They were just nice to me, because of you. Good riddance, I say."

"Maggie, you are such a dear friend!" I said as endearingly as I could. "You will be in my suitcase all the way to Borna. I do hope you'll think about visiting, soon." She leaned back with a smile on her face.

We said our goodbyes, and I went to bed dreaming of the rolling hills waiting for me.

CHAPTER 27

It was a clear, chilly, fall morning when I loaded my car. I knew more bitter cold days were ahead, and I hated the thought. This year however, I would have a real, wood burning fireplace going all the time and a hot oven for baking. I'd leave my sewing room messy, and I'd entertain as many diverse people as I could find. Clay would be rolling over in his grave!

The drive was going more quickly than my first trip, and I eagerly awaited going into a warm house at 6229 Main Street. While I waited for the movers to arrive, I could build a fire with the wood stacked out by the barn. After everything was unloaded and my bed assembled, I would be heading to Ellie's for a nice hot meal. Life was going to be good!

I was near the turn off to Highway A, when my cell phone went off. I saw that it was James so I pulled to the side of the road. I figured after our encounter, this had to be important.

"Hi, James, this is Kate," I said in a friendly manner.

"Kate, I know you're probably not very happy with me right now after my remarks the other day," he began. "I'm sorry." He then paused like I was supposed to say something. "I wanted to ask you once again if you would consider selling me the Borna property that Dad purchased? I feel I owe it to him to keep it in the family. The additional income should be helpful to you, and as I told you before, I would pay your asking price. We both have been through a lot of stress lately, and I just think we need to do the right thing, here." I couldn't believe what I was hearing all over again. I took a deep breath, to stay as calm as possible.

"I understand how you must feel, James, and I'm truly not trying to be difficult," I said calmly. "The property IS staying in the family. Clay left it to his wife. If he wanted you to have it, he would have chosen to do so. Borna is a charming community and the house has wonderful possibilities and history." I could hear his heavy breathing in the phone. "The timing of your call is interesting because I'm in the car right now heading to Borna. I'll be there till Christmas to get some work done on the house."

"You can't be serious, Kate!" he said raising his voice. "Why in God's name would you want to do that?"

I continued to stay calm as I answered. "I have my reasons, James, and right now, this is a good diversion for me after the difficult past months," I explained in a normal tone.

"Oh please!" he boldly said. "This is not a way to get back at Clay. I know you're angry and there's no excuse for the way he drank and carried on. He probably didn't realize in his state of mind the property would go to you."

"My intent is not to prove anything, James," I said in earnest. "Why do you begrudge me so? I haven't done anything to your side of the family. I loved your parents."

"If you loved them so much, then you should give back what isn't yours!" he demanded. "If you insist on playing hardball, I can do just that. You'll be hearing from my lawyer." He then clicked off the phone.

He was going to get a lawyer to get 6229 Main? That beats all! What was I missing here? He sure didn't need the money, however the greedy get greedier I guess. My blood pressure was rising as I got back on the road.

As I slowed down on the curvy roads ahead, so did my blood pressure. Somehow, I knew James couldn't really hurt me. The last thing I wanted to do after Clay's death was to communicate again with my lawyer, Susan Wake. Perhaps he just was just trying to scare me.

It was dusk when I drove into Borna. I drew a sigh of relief knowing I had friends in this village. Ellie's car was there, so she was probably cooking the dinner she offered. I pulled into 6229 Main Street and wanted to wave hello. Everything looked the same, except a lot more leaves were covering the property. That would be a job for Cotton, I immediately thought. Before I got out of car, I called to check the whereabouts of the moving van. They thought it should arrive in about an hour. I was relieved, and it gave me time to unload my car.

When I walked in the kitchen, the temperature was nice and warm. As I walked around the first floor, I couldn't help but wonder why this house had become controversial. I was pleased it appeared to still be pretty clean from my last visit.

When I walked into the kitchen, I forgot how outdated and forsaken it was. This was going to be my first priority. Any woman looking at this house to buy, would judge the kitchen.

At least with electricity, I could make something quick in the microwave I brought, and also make coffee in the morning.

It was dark when the moving van arrived. Now the excitement could begin. I went out to meet the movers and give them instructions. I was interrupted by Ellie's loud happy voice, giving me a cheerful, welcome home.

"Oh, Ellie, it's good to be back!" I said with excitement as we hugged.

"What can I do to help?" she immediately offered.

"I'm going to tell the movers what room to put things, and you can bring a few more things out of my car, if you like," I suggested.

We all kicked into action. When they placed the small game table and chairs in the huge dining room, it was rather humorous. The comfy loveseat from my bedroom looked lost in the large living room. The 6X9 Oriental rug I brought for the entry hall was perfect. I had them place the smaller Oriental right in front of the fireplace in the living room. It would suit my needs on this visit, just fine.

Watching them assemble my king size bed in the master bedroom was surreal. I had plenty of closets to hang clothing and hide boxes for now. After the movers were finished, Ellie helped me make up the bed. "This white quilt is beautiful!" Ellie said as we arranged it on the top of the bed.

"Thanks," I said with pride. "I designed it myself, and I had them quilt it for me at my local quilt shop. I figure it will go with anything here. I also brought a couple of other antique quilts."

"This looks like a wedding quilt like the one I have." Ellie said as she smoothed her hand across the stitches.

"It was supposed to be just that, but the cousin I made it

for cancelled the wedding," I explained. "I was pretty happy about it!" She laughed.

"Are you hungry?" Ellie asked as we came downstairs.

"I'm famished, but I'm more interested in relaxing with a glass of wine after such a long day," I shared smiling. "I'll see the movers off. It looks as if they're about ready to leave."

I thanked the two nice fellas and advised them to get something to eat at Marv's down the road before they got on the highway. They were happy with the recommendation and said they would be on their way.

I wasted no time closing up the house to get to Ellie's. I left the back porch light on to be safe. I had forgotten how dark the country nights were here compared to South Haven.

As I entered Ellie's house, the smell and charm brought back wonderful memories.

"I want you to try this new red wine we just labeled last week," Ellie said as she opened it with a cork screw. "It's called "Red Velvet," like the cake."

"Count me in!" I said eagerly holding my glass. "What smells so good?"

"An old fashioned pot roast with carrots and potatoes," she said as she poured our wine. "I've got a nice tossed salad in the fridge as well. How do you like the wine?"

"I'm lovin' it!" I happily said. "This is all too much!"

We talked non-stop through Ellie's delicious meal. I couldn't believe how much I consumed. Where was this ferocious appetite coming from? It wasn't till we finished that I told her about the phone call from James on the way here.

"What kind of case would he have if he gets a lawyer?" Ellie asked in anger.

"I don't know, but I will not sell it to him, ever!" I assured her.

"Well, Blade is spreading rumors around here," Ellie revealed. "He's saying you reneged on a contract with him."

"What?" I gasped. "I had no contract! I decided I'm not going to use any realtor. I want to decide who owns this place. I really hate anyone around here thinking I'm dishonest or mean."

"Don't worry; they know Blade is full of hot air," she claimed. "When I have to opportunity, I'm making sure to tell them it's not true. I think everyone around here likes you! I haven't said anything, but I've seen his truck pull in and out of your place more than once. He knows I saw him one time for sure. I hope you don't find anything disturbed or missing."

"I do, too," I added. "How could I have such a bad guy in both places?"

Ellie had to chuckle. "You have something they both want, girlfriend!" Ellie joked. "Are you okay sleeping there tonight, or do you feel a bit strange on your first night back?"

"I hadn't thought about it, but there's no reason I should be," I defended. "I'm not running from that creep nor will I be intimidated!" Ellie nodded giving me a thumbs up.

"Once everyone knows your back, they'll help keep an eye out for you," Ellie assured me. "Keep your cell by your bed, and if you hear anything, call me. After 10:00, there's hardly any traffic that goes by here."

"Have you seen Cotton lately?" I curiously asked. "He told me he'd keep an eye out."

"I haven't seen him at all since you left," she revealed.

"That's rather odd, as he seemed to be eager to do so!" I stated.

After I helped Ellie clear the table, I announced I was exhausted and was heading to bed. I reminded her I was going to Harold's first thing in the morning.

"Do you have a coffee pot?" Ellie asked.

"Yes, I'm in great shape as long as I have electricity," I answered. "I also brought my microwave, so I'm good!"

"Well, here's some coffee cake for in the morning," she said as she handed me a zip-lock bag. "I knew it would be a nice welcome home treat for you!"

"You're too much, Ellie," I said giving her a hug. "I'm having them gut the kitchen first so I may be mooching from here more and more when it comes to food.

She giggled. "I'm here!" she cheered. "Now go home and get some sleep in that awesome king size bed of yours! Do you want me to walk you over? It's pretty dark, like you said."

"I think I know my way, Ellie, but let's make a deal where we watch out for each other by watching till the first inside light comes on, okay?" I suggested.

"Good idea!" she said as she opened the door.

CHAPTER 28

I turned on the lights in two rooms so Ellie would know I was home. I got out my coffee pot and set the timer to go off for my morning coffee. I looked about at all the boxes standing everywhere as I made my way up the stairs for the night.

I ran the water for my first bath in my antique, claw foot tub. The wait for the water to rise was well worth it as I laid my head back to relax. I wanted to fall asleep right there. I told myself I would revisit the mystery quilt in the closet first thing in the morning before going to Harold's.

As I headed for my familiar bed, I turned out all the lights except in the hallway since I was still a stranger to the house at night. As I crawled into the comforts of my own bedding, I realized I had a little slice of South Haven right here in Borna.

Hours later, I awoke very suddenly when a vehicle sped

past my house. I felt as if the morning had already come. There was a warmth surrounding me like the morning sun. I went to the bathroom, looked at my clock, and discovered it was only 3:00 in the morning. How could it all be so warm and bright in here? I thought the experience was quite odd, but still feeling exhausted and sleepy, I went back to bed with feelings of love and comfort around me.

I awoke, feeling totally rested, to the smell of the coffee floating its way up the stairs. I put on my robe ready to tackle my ambitious plans for the day.

After I finished my cherry crumb coffee cake, I took the ladder from the kitchen and made my way up the stairs to visit the quilt. I was anxious to find out if it had been disturbed.

I opened the latch, and there it was just like I'd left it. I carefully came down the ladder and took the quilt to the empty bedroom across the hall from where I slept. I took the sheet it was wrapped in and opened it up on the floor so I could spread out the quilt. It was so wonderful to see it totally opened for the first time. It took my breath away in a sad sort of way. It wasn't a pretty quilt, but it was like no other I had ever seen. I wanted to stay and study it further, but my day was planned for other duties. I took another sheet from my box of linens and covered it up so the daylight coming into the room wouldn't fade it.

I decided to get ready for my long day. As I came down the stairs, my cell phone rang. It was Maggie.

"I made it here, and I'm up and at 'em!" I said before she could say hello.

"Did the van arrive in timely fashion?" Maggie asked immediately.

"Everything's here!" I said with excitement. "I'm off to see Harold at the Hardware store!"

"Are you sure you and Harold don't have something going?" she teased. I laughed. "It sounds like an exciting day for you!"

"I'm glad you didn't call last night because I was really wiped out from the trip," I explained. "After a meal at Ellie's, I went straight to bed!"

"I kept thinking about you," she said on a more serious note. "I'm off to see our beach quilting friends. They will have lots of questions. I'll just tell them you're happily off to the hardware store! They'll get a kick out of that." We chuckled again.

"Please tell them hello and tell them I'll be try to be at our annual Christmas luncheon," I instructed.

"Will do and tell Harold hello!" she said with a laugh. "I love you, gal!"

"Love you, too!" I said hanging up. I smiled picturing her drinking coffee in South Haven.

I grabbed my purse, notepad, and heavy jacket as I went out the door to visit Harold. Seeing Borna in the daylight, once again, made me smile.

CHAPTER 29

"Good morning Harold!" I cheerfully said approaching his counter.

"Well, Miss Meyr, a little bird told me you'd be paying me a visit," he said with that same jolly smile on his face. "Ellie stopped by yesterday to get a few things on her way to the winery and said you were coming back to do some more work on the house."

"She has been such an amazing friend and neighbor," I marveled.

Harold seemed to know what I was wanting, so at his suggestion, we went back to his small cubicle of an office. Stacks of catalogs and unfiled papers, looking centuries old, were stacked about on his desk. I got out my note pad to write down names and phone numbers of contractors for various things. As he looked on his list, he made comments about them.

"You sure are going to a lot of work to just turn around and sell the place," he stopped to say.

"Perhaps, but I have to improve the kitchen for sure, or no one will want to buy it," I explained. "I want to knock out a wall and put in new cabinets and appliances. I'll need someone that does custom woodwork, I'm afraid."

"Well, we used to have access to such a fella in these parts, but he's become too famous. I heard he doesn't do residential work anymore. He's quite talented in wood carving as well. His name is Clark McFadden. He's even done custom work for the Governor, movie stars and the like."

"Wow! Then I guess I'm out of his league." I said with disappointment.

"He doesn't live far from here. He has a secluded, rustic log cabin near Indian Creek," he described. "You know how them artists can be! " He laughed like there was an inside joke. "They say he gets darn good money for his work now. I've got his number, so I'll put it down anyway. He may have a good carpenter he can recommend for ya."

"Oh, that'll be great, Harold," I said thankfully. "Sounds like I couldn't afford him, anyway."

I picked up a few other things to purchase and gave him a hug. As I was going out the door, Anna was just coming in. She was happy to see me back and reminded me that on the first Saturday of the month was when they baked bread and coffee cake in the outside oven. She said they had a group of school children on a tour a couple of days ago, and they made pizza in the oven. I was impressed to say the least. I told her I would mark it on my calendar.

When I got back to the house, I poured myself another cup of coffee. Despite the brisk fall morning, I took my two, yellow director's chairs I'd brought with me and set them on the deck. I sat down and stared towards the barn remembering the small tombstone I had discovered there. Although I was curious to see it again, I knew I would have to put off for another day.

I heard a noise and turned to see it was Cotton pulling up in his pick-up truck.

"Hey, welcome back, Miss Kate!" he said as got out of his truck.

"You're just the person I want to see!" I greeted cheerfully. "How about joining me for a cup of coffee?"

"That's the best offer I've had all day!" he said grinning as he looked at my two bright chairs.

"Have a seat. I'll be right back," I offered as I went inside.

"It sure is a mighty nice day!" Cotton said when I returned with his coffee. I nodded.

"So, Cotton, was everything cool while I was gone?" I bravely asked as I sat next to him.

"You mean besides the broken windows?" he asked scratching his head. I nodded once again. "I'm sorry Miss Kate, but Blade said if I ever stepped foot on your property again, he'd never give me another piece of work. He's pretty miffed at you. That's the nicest way I can say it."

"Well, you just tell Mr. Blade you work for me now!" I bravely stated without thinking. Cotton looked surprised. "What can he do to you then?" He shook his head in wonder.

"You don't know Blade like I do," he warned. "You're a fine lady, Miss Kate, and you're doing the right thing by fixin' up this house here. However, Blade seems to have a lot of dirt on many folks in this town, and he uses it to get what he wants. I have to remember I have another mouth to feed with the baby and all."

"I will pay you a decent weekly wage," I offered with mixed feelings. "If I can trust you, there will always be work here for you."

"But what happens when you leave and sell the place?" he cautiously asked.

"We'll work out something, don't worry," I said sympathetically. "There is a lot of work to be done around here. Are you afraid he'll harm you, if you work for me?" He looked down at the ground. "I can't ask you to do something, if you feel it would hurt you. I'd like to meet your wife Susie, too. There will possibly be some work for her in the future."

He thought it over. "I will talk it over with the wife," he finally said. "I sure appreciate your offer."

"Sounds fair enough," I said as he got up to leave.

"Thanks for the coffee," he said smiling. "That was mighty nice of you. Where'd you get those sunshine chairs?"

I laughed. "They do bring a little sunshine, don't they," I said blushing. "I brought them from Lake Michigan, you might say. They now have a different view, but just as beautiful!" He laughed as he got back in his truck to leave.

CHAPTER 30

The next week seemed like a blur and yet a high at the same time. I made more decisions in one week than I made all of last year in South Haven. I got lucky meeting nice and sincere business folks who needed work and were willing to help me.

The contractor I chose was extremely helpful in suggesting things I hadn't thought of. He was eager to put his men to work right away with winter at our door step. He also mentioned I would need some custom cabinet work done, which he, himself, wasn't qualified for. He also mentioned Clark McFadden and how talented he was.

Cotton was busy raking leaves and doing yard clean-up. There was a lot to be done before the first snow. He stacked firewood near the house in the wrought iron holder, I had purchased at Harold's. He also gave me a wonderful idea as we chatted on the sunshine chairs one morning. I told him how I seemed to perch on my sunporch at my home in South

Haven more than any other room in the house. He suggested we add onto the deck with a nice sunporch which would extend the length of the back of the house. I could picture it immediately and was very grateful for the suggestion. With a lot of glass, there would be a wonderful view to the back farmland. Making the decision early made it easier for the contractor as well, since it affected the back door.

I finally got to meet Cotton's wife Susie when he came by to pick up his paycheck. I went to the pickup truck and introduced myself. She was holding their little girl who was wrapped in a worn, cotton baby blanket. I thought about the many baby quilts our Beach Quilters had made for charity and wished I had some to give her. I made a mental note to have Maggie send me a couple of them.

On one of my many trips back and forth to Harold's for supplies, I noticed I had been passing "Imy's Antique Shop." It never looked open, and I assumed it was a business that had been there some time back. It was in the building where Ellie said the first post office in Borna, operated. The sign was handmade and very small which is why I hadn't noticed it at first. The windows were cluttered with merchandise, so there was nothing to entice me off the road. I saw a car parked in front, so decided to stop. When I walked in, a very pretty lady was working on a piece of furniture. I asked if she was Imy. She nodded and blushed, as she apologized for her appearance. I introduced myself, but she said she already knew me.

Her shelves were mostly filled with dusty Depression glass, which she obviously was fond of and hadn't sold in some time. There was a little bit of everything to catch my eye, plus her prices were more than reasonable. She was extremely pleased when I walked out with a rocking chair to sit by my loveseat, a worn oriental area rug for my upstairs hallway, a Victorian quilt rack, and some pretty, cut glass wine glasses. Imy, in her excitement, helped me get everything in the trunk of my Mercedes. I had to leave the lid up, but I was just a half mile down the road. I told her I would check back once a week to see what she had new. She couldn't thank me enough. I couldn't wait to tell Ellie and Maggie about my bargains.

When I got back to the house, Cotton helped me unload the car. He thoughtfully wiped down the quilt rack and rocker before carrying it into the house. I laid the rug over the deck banister to air out.

When I took the quilt rack upstairs, I first thought about using it for the mysterious, forgiving quilt, but I really didn't want to fold it up. I liked seeing it laid out and being able to study the messages, as I walked by. Now the rack seemed perfect for the two antique quilts that I brought with me. One was a red and white Irish Chain and the other was a blue and white Drunkard's Path pattern. I loved two color quilts more than any other. I put one on each side and placed it in my master bedroom.

After I came downstairs, I built a fire in the fireplace to take the evening chill out. I sat in the rocker and had to laugh at how it squeaked at each rock. If this chair could talk, I said to myself, perhaps it would tell me where it had been before. Maybe it had rocked many babies to sleep, or perhaps an elderly lady used it until she died. I wanted to think it was from Borna as Imy believed it was. It would now serve a new purpose here at 6229 Main Street.

CHAPTER 31

Later as I was sweeping up some sawdust, Ellie called my cell phone.

"Have you heard the forecast?" she asked with concern.

"Not really, but I know it's getting colder!" I responded.

"Well, tomorrow we're due to have our first snow storm, so I thought if you might want to get out from that workshop you're in and come to the winery tonight," Ellie suggested. "Our cook is making his famous gumbo, which always tastes pretty good on a cold night. We're expecting a pretty big crowd with the weather getting bad and all."

"I think it's a great idea!" I immediately said. I was ready for a little fun!

"I'll have to work the counter with Trout, but you can sit at the bar and keep us company," she suggested.

"Sounds good, as I could use a break from this mess," I said excitedly.

"Okay, I'll see you then," she said hanging up.

Knowing I had some pleasant plans for the evening gave me some energy to finish up early and clean myself up. I had lost several of my fingernails, doing my chores, and assumed I wouldn't be getting a manicure around here anytime soon.

The workmen also talked of the storm as they prepared to leave. I was used to this kind of weather in South Haven, but I could tell this storm was more dramatic, and now the talk of the town, here in Borna.

I put on my heaviest, wool sweater and clean jeans, knowing the crowd would be casual. I kept on the back porch light, but wanted to have a dusk to dawn light installed soon.

When I walked in the door of the winery, there was one seat left at the bar. Ellie spotted me and told me they had saved the seat for me. Trout said hello, and as I looked about the room, I saw some familiar faces that included Anna with her husband, and Harold was at a table of eight having a good, ole time.

For once, I didn't feel like I was the big elephant in the room. Most of the folks ignored me and were busy chatting and responding to the festive, background music.

My gumbo arrived, and the man sitting next to me asked if I had ordered it before.

"Get ready for a chaser," he warned with a grin. "Kelly makes it pretty hot for most folks." His jolly round face chuckled when I took my first spoonful.

"I only took a small bite, and he was right. It was a good thing I had a bottle of water handy with my glass of wine. Ellie laughed when she saw my reaction.

"Add a little of this sugar to tame it down a bit," she said as she handed me a sugar bowl. I did just that.

On my way to use the restroom, Harold stopped to introduce me to his wife, Milly. She was plump and jolly just like Harold. He proceeded to go around the table introduction everyone. They all greeted me politely. When I came out of the restroom, Anna stopped and approached me with a very handsome man I had never seen before.

"Kate, I want you to meet Clark McFadden," she nicely stated. I nodded with a smile. "Clark, this is Kate Meyr. She owns the old Doc Paulson house and is fixin' it up."

"Are you THE Clark McFadden, the wood artist and carpenter?" I asked blushing.

"I suppose I am," he said modestly.

"Harold gave me your name to call," I said as I admired his stature. "He speaks quite highly of you!"

"Call me for what?" he innocently asked.

"I'm afraid I got a little carried away knocking out some walls in my kitchen, and it's going to require some custom cabinetry," I explained. "Would you be interested in taking a look and giving me a bid when you have some time? I heard you are pretty much in demand!"

"I'm afraid I'm pretty committed for some time, plus I don't do that kind of work anymore," he casually said.

I was disappointed with his direct answer, but I was taken back by how his appearance and manner didn't match the typical picture of a carpenter. He reminded me of someone, but I couldn't place who it was.

"Oh, I'm sorry to hear that," I finally said. "Can you recommend anyone?"

"I'll give that some thought," he answered with little interest. "I always thought that house had real potential. I can't believe it's been vacant for so long."

"I find it hard to believe, as well," I said in agreement. "I'm not from here, and I suppose I've given fresh eyes to the place."

"Excuse me, Clark," the waitress said. "Your take out order is ready at the counter."

"Well, nice meeting you, Miss Meyr, but I need to run," he quickly responded.

"You as well," I murmured as he walked away. What a handsome man! I wondered what his wife looked like.

"Sorry that didn't work out," Anna said. "He did a great job on one of log cabins at the village, some time back. I know he's in the big time now, but thought it wouldn't hurt for you to meet him. He's not married, and I've never seen him with anyone. He's in and out of town a lot. I think he gets take outs here frequently when he's on his way home." Well, she answered my question.

"Thanks, Anna," I said with disappointment in my voice. "I appreciate that."

I went back to the bar, and Ellie was staring at me as if she was waiting for a serious report on what just took place.

"I see you just met Clark McFadden, our local celebrity," Ellie teased. "Can you believe what a looker he is?" I laughed and shook my head. Ellie was such an observer of people, which was perfect in her business.

"He may be a looker, but his personality is lackluster, I'm afraid," I replied. "He may have a big head from all the hype he's getting, but he does remind me of someone."
"Sure, it's Sean Connery, the best James Bond we ever had!" Ellie boasted.

"I think you're right on, Miss Ellie!" I said sipping my wine. "Too bad he's not doing cabinetry any longer.

"He's quite the loner, did Harold tell you?" Ellie asked with interest. "When he does come in here, he's alone and orders a single malt scotch or our best Cabernet. He drinks it slowly while he's waiting for an order of food to go. Now and then, some ladies try to get his attention, but he politely respond, and then turns to mind his own business." For some reason, it made me chuckle.

"Did I detect a bit of an accent from him?" I asked curiously. Ellie nodded.

"He's from Scotland," she added. "So is Sean Connery, so maybe he's related!" We laughed. "He's very nice and good for my business, but don't count on him for much conversation. I think he likes this area because most folks leave him alone. I heard he has a really neat log cabin right on Indian Creek."

"Well, he wasn't much help to me, but no big deal. I'll find someone," I noted.

The crowd continued to thicken, and Trout and Ellie were too busy to talk to me. I hated making small talk with just anyone. I felt like a bar fly sitting there, so decided to leave. I waved to Ellie and then walked over to say goodbye to Harold's table.

With light flakes already falling, I knew I made a good decision to head home. When I pulled into my driveway, I truly missed having a garage. I was a spoiled Michigan girl, I supposed.

When I got out of my car, I noticed something rather large lying in front of my deck steps. In shock, I realized it was a young deer. I didn't panic till I saw a gunshot wound on his neck. I stepped aside thinking how odd it was to find it here! I carefully stepped over the step to avoid it. When I got to my door, I saw a dead possum lying there. From the blood I was seeing, I knew he had also been shot. Now I knew this was no accident but a deliberate act to scare me. It gave me an eerie feeling making me want to throw up before going inside the house.

I bravely took a deep breath and unlocked my door. So much for the deck light keeping bad guys away from here, I thought! I was too sickened to call anyone, and with the bad weather, I didn't want anyone coming to the house. Cotton might be the only one to have a theory on this, but if I called him this late, I would wake the baby and he'd try his best to come over. I decided to deal with this in the morning.

I locked the door and kept the deck light on. As I walked up the stairs to bed, I knew someone was trying to scare this little city gal so she would go back home. I kept my cell phone near me and lay awake trying to analyze the horrid sight. What would Maggie think if I told her this? I knew she'd tell me to get myself back home before I got hurt. Besides better lighting, I now would have to consider a security system as soon as possible. I could only think of two people who would not want me to be safe here.

CHAPTER 32

The next morning, I jumped out of my bed to see if my gruesome gifts were still at my doorstep. I took one quick glance at the snow covered souls, making me lose my morning appetite.

I knew Fred, one of the drywallers, would be arriving soon so I went upstairs to dress. I felt badly for anyone who had to see this horrible mess and hoped the word would not get out to the rest of Borna.

A heavy knock on the door told me Fred had arrived. I rushed down the stairs and saw it was Cotton instead.

"What the heck is this all about?" he shouted. "What a bloody sight you have here! Did you know this was out here?" I nodded as he stepped inside.

"I came home to this mess last night, but I didn't want to call anyone at such a late hour," I timidly explained.

"Go get your camera or phone to get a picture of this

before I haul them away," Cotton instructed as if he were in charge.

When Fred arrived, Cotton explained what was going on and asked him to help put the animals in the back of his truck. Fred shook his head in disgust. There was still blood all over the deck, but I ignored it for the time being. I decided to bring in my snow covered sunshine chairs for now and was grateful no blood had splattered on them. I brushed off the snow and folded them to bring inside. It looked like we'd be getting more snow, as the wind howled in the dark, cloudy sky. It reminded me once again how much I despised winter.

Trying not to appear shaken, I left Fred in the kitchen with a cup of coffee in his hand. I went upstairs to call Ellie. She was horrified when I told her what greeted me last night. She thought I should report it to the Sheriff's office, but I told her I didn't want to be known as the whining widow at 6229 Main Street. I said if I found a horse's head in my bed, like in the Godfather movie, I would call. She got a kick out of that. Ellie said the winery would be closed because of the weather so she invited me to join her for some vegetable soup she was making. I said I would gladly be there, as I needed to escape for a while and assess my intrusion. I tidied up a bit and was getting ready to leave, when Carla called on my cell.

"Hey, Carla, I was thinking of you all with this snow storm we're having," I greeted. "I think you all started it up north!" She chuckled.

"I saw it on the news," she noted. "We are so cold here the last snow we had continues to hang around. They say we'll get another couple of inches tonight." I knew Borna wouldn't be hit as bad, so I took it as good news.

"So, is everything okay there?" I finally asked.

"Well, I have some good news and some bad news," she hesitantly said. "The good news is you may have a serious nibble on the house," she reported. "This couple has been here twice to look at it."

"Well, maybe Miss Mary is finally getting on the ball to market the place," I said with satisfaction. "So what's the bad news?"

"A man stopped by yesterday and asked for you," she began. "I told him you were out of town. He said he was here to serve you papers to appear in court and wanted your address."

"Appear in court for what?" I asked defensively.

"He wouldn't say of course, but I hope I did the right thing to give him your address in Borna," she said shyly.

"Of course, but no one can divorce me, take my children away or sue me for an accident!" I said jokingly.

"Don't be silly, Kate. This looked serious!" Carla said with a sigh. I took a deep breath before I continued.

"Well, now they know where to find me," I said sheepishly. "How's Rocky doing?"

"I think he's missing the luxurious home he had with you, but he's adjusting," Carla reported with a laugh. "How's the house coming along?"

"Very well, but I keep making changes," I reported. "Have you seen Maggie by chance?"

"Not lately, but I know she is missing you!" she added. "Where will you be going for Thanksgiving Day?"

"Ellie said she's in charge," I said smiling. "If her invitation list keeps growing, she'll have it at her winery."

"I need to go, Kate, and I'm sorry I had to call you about this," Carla said apologetically.

"It's okay, thanks," I said in closing. "You and Rocky take care!"

When I trudged through the snow over to Ellie's warm and inviting kitchen, I was wearing my worried face because of Carla's recent news. Ellie was watching as she opened her kitchen door.

"I think there's about eight inches of snow out there!" I announced as I slipped off my boots.

"It's not supposed to stop till later tonight," Ellie reported. "If it wouldn't be for that darn wind, it would be gorgeous out there. The sunlight makes it all glisten. Here's some coffee unless you've already had your fill."

"I think I need something stronger," I suggested. "My day just got worse." Now she took on the same worried look as me.

I told her about my phone conversation with Carla. After I go to the part about being subpoenaed, she sat down to absorb it all.

"So that darn brother-in-law of yours decided to get a lawyer after all and give you a little trouble." She said with a smirk on her face. I nodded.

"I just don't understand what he thinks he can do, and for goodness sake's, why?" I asked in frustration.

"He's obviously angry with you Kate, and he has the money to harass you for not cooperating with him," Ellie assessed. "I'm sure he has hopes of weakening you. Now Blade on the other hand wants to fight you with blood. He thinks you're fragile and dumb, like most of the women he probably knows." I had to laugh. "I don't know which of the two is worse, but they aren't worth the ground they walk on."

Thanks, Ellie," I said with affection. "You've got it all figured out, alright. I wonder how soon I'll get served."

"They'll have to have the county sheriff or bailiff come out and do it," Ellie stated as if she had inside knowledge.

We leisurely ate our delicious soup and tried not to talk anymore about my gruesome situation. Ellie reported she may have as many as twenty people coming for Thanksgiving. She was planning to have it at the winery since it would be closed for the holiday. I offered to make a couple of salads because I didn't know what appliances I would have at that time. She asked me if there was anyone I would like to invite, and I thought of Cotton and Susie. I knew her mother lived nearby, but I thought it might be a nice treat for the two of them. Ellie thought it was a good idea. Then I shared with her about asking Maggie to send a couple of baby quilts for their baby.

"I may invite some of the single gals in our circle if they don't have places to go." Ellie suggested. "My aunt and niece are usually with me for the holidays so they've been invited."

"Oh, I'll look forward to meeting them," I said.

I finally left the comforts of Ellie's home and tromped through the snow on my way home. When I took off my winter garb, I went upstairs and turned on the light in the quilt room where Josephine's quilt laid on the floor.

I sat down on the floor and tried to concentrate once again on some of the sayings embroidered on the quilt. "DELIVER US FROM EVIL," I read aloud. What evil?" DIE, IF YOU WILL," I read next. Who would put such a horrid statement on a quilt? There was so much hurt and sadness on this quilt. What could Josephine have done to make her feel so guilty she needed to ask for forgiveness?

Forgiveness was a very big word that demanded an explanation. Could I possibly forgive Clay for all he had done to me?

It would be easier if I knew Clay was sorry for what he had done to me. Would I ever know that? Should it matter? What if Clay had future plans with "babe"? What if he had plans to ask me for a divorce?

I knew God would want me to let go and forget. What would he have me do with James and Blade? Why was I being challenged like this? I hadn't done anything to Clay, James, or Blade.

As I got up from the floor, I read, "THEY KNOW NOT WHAT THEY DO", which was stitched very small in one corner. That was a phrase to ponder for Jesus said that on the cross.

CHAPTER 33

The next morning, I lay awake for a good while. There was so much to digest. I planned to start my day with making my first appearance at Concordia Lutheran Church. I'm sure some wondered why I had not attended before now. My church in South Haven was huge, so this tiny church would indeed be a new experience I was looking forward to.

I came downstairs to a very quiet house since no workers were scheduled. Because it was chilly, I wanted to make a fire, but it would not be a wise decision since I was leaving for church.

I hurried to make the 9:00 service. As I walked in, I saw many familiar faces, but the one I zeroed in on was Emma. Ellie told me she might have information on the Paulsons.

My comfort zone in churches or theatres always took me to a seat at the end of the aisle. I always wanted an easy exit as I was somewhat claustrophobic. Luckily, I was able to sit right next to Emma, and she gave me a big grin. I thought she was so cute for her age. Her hair was always perfectly done, as if she stepped out of the local, beauty parlor. Her clothing, however outdated, was becoming to her and always accessorized like the orange hat she was wearing today. I could tell she was her own person, in her own time, which I loved.

The pastor had a simple message about giving our time to needy causes and sharing our talents with the church. Perhaps it would include me, in time. I was impressed with the newly decorated church and its addition of the fellowship hall. I knew Ellen went to this church, so she likely had a say in its décor.

After the service, I introduced myself to Pastor Hermann, who seemed to be about middle age with a gentle nature about him. Emma followed me out to the vestibule, where we could sit in the comfy wing back chairs to talk. They were serving coffee in the fellowship room, off to the side of us, but we both decided to pass.

The first thing I wanted to share with Emma was the unusual quilt, Ellie and I found in my house. She nodded and said she was pretty sure Mrs. Paulson would have made it.

"You know, my mom said she was very dedicated to getting to church each Sunday, but she seldom came to help quilt," Emma said as her hands seemed to shake. "It was probably because she was needed most of the time at Doc's office. My Mom felt sorry for her because the rumors flew about the Doc drinking so much. It had to be hurtful to her. Mom thought she blamed herself for not being able to have children."

"How sad," I responded. "If she was the one who made the quilt, she was feeling much more than sadness. I can't wait for you to see it."

"I will try to come this week, but right now, I have to run to get to my son's house," she explained as she rose out of her chair. "I can't wait to see what else is being done over at your place, my dear. I am so happy you are fixin' up the ole place. I just hope you get some nice folks to buy it after all your trouble." I smiled and nodded. I seemed to be doing a lot of smiling lately.

"It's been pretty much fun for me, Emma," I cheerfully stated. "I love decorating, and when the appliances arrive, I'll be able to so some baking which I also enjoy. Everyone in Borna will know when my oven gets going. I hope the smell will go far and wide!" She laughed.

"I can't wait for it either!" she said as she wrapped a scarf around her neck. "I'll see you this week. Say, you might want to think about bringing the quilt to the Friendship Circle next time."

"Sounds like a good idea," I said walking alongside her to the door.

On my way home from church, I stopped to get a take out, chicken dinner from Marv's Place. Ellie said his fried chicken was marvelous, and it sounded like just the thing for a Sunday meal. He had a good after church crowd from what I was seeing. When I walked in, it smelled like a Grandmother's kitchen instead of a grocery/bar kind of place.

After I gave the girl behind the counter my order, a voice behind me said, "I'll have the same Audrey, but double up on the mashed potatoes."

I turned to see it was Clark McFadden. He nodded at me with a business like acknowledgement.

"Oh, good to see you," I said awkwardly. "I hear Marv's

fried chicken is wonderful!" He nodded again with barely a smile.

"How's the renovation coming along?" he asked very matter of factly.

"Tomorrow my appliances arrive, but I still have no cabinets!" I said with a bit of sarcasm.

"Sounds like you may have gotten the horse before the cart, then!" he criticized with half of a smile. Was he being rude, or was he trying to be clever? I wasn't sure what to say.

"Maybe," was all I could come up with in response.

"Here ya go, Kate," Audrey said as she handed me my take out bag.

"Enjoy!" Clark said without cracking a smile as I brushed past him. I nodded once again with my frequent Borna smile.

When I got home, I was both miffed and baffled at this strange man. No wonder he wasn't married. He had the personality of dried toast. It was a good thing, others told me about his manner, or I would have taken his attitude personally.

I built a fire and curled in my loveseat as I ate my lunch. Just as described, it was delicious, but it was enough for two meals. I saved half of it for another time. Now I was ready for a long winter's nap. I felt entitled since it was Sunday. As I got comfortable, my phone went off. It was Jack calling for our Sunday phone conversation.

"Hey, Mom," he greeted as always.

"So glad you called, sweetie," I said happily. "I just finished lunch and was going to call you. What's happening these days?"

"Well, as a matter of fact, I've been hanging out with this girl, Jenny," he revealed with a pleasant tone for a change. "I was with her again last night, and she reminds me of you, Mom." I laughed wanting to apologize.

"Where did you meet her?" I asked wanting to know more.

"A friend of mine at work introduced us," he noted. "She's a good Lutheran, as you would say. I thought of your reaction right away! She teaches kindergarten and has a terrific sense of humor!" We both laughed.

"She does sound about perfect, Jack, so don't screw it up!" I teased.

Our very pleasant conversation continued. Jack wanted to know about selling our home in South Haven and how I was coming with the house in Borna.

When I hung up, I felt Jack was happy for the first time since his father's death. It sounded like having attention from this girl was just what he needed. Oh how I wished I could hug him right then.

Feeling energized from Jack's call, I skipped the nap and pulled out Carla's quilt from the large basket I kept by the fireplace. If I were really intending to get this done by Christmas, I needed to give it some attention. I opened it up, to assess how much more quilting had to be done. I hadn't done anything regarding quilts since Clay's accident. As I started to make those first stitches, it was awkward, as I started to make those first stitches, but then it all fell into place once again. I loved the therapy hand quilting provided. My mind wondered off as I stitched away. It was brainless work, which created beauty and productivity. While being quilted, quilts had a way of coming to life. What could be better than quilting by an open fire on a winter's Sunday afternoon?

CHAPTER 34

Monday morning brought sunshine, which started melting the snow. My appliances were due to arrive, and hopefully they would be in working order by the end of the day. It was a huge investment for this house, but I felt it was worth it.

Cotton was painting the insides of my closets today. I was trying hard to keep him busy. I knew I was lucky to have him.

While I was upstairs sorting laundry to wash at Ellie's later, Cotton hollered up the stairs for me and told me to come down right away. I thought perhaps the appliance truck had arrived. When I got to the bottom of the stairs, Cotton gave me a strange look and pointed to the front door, where a uniformed officer stood waiting.

By his appearance, I knew his purpose in coming to see me. I slowly opened the door with my Borna smile.

"Miss Kathryn Meyr?" he formally asked.

"That's me," I responded politely.

"This is for you!" he said handing me an envelope.

"Thanks, "I said closing the door. It was quick and done!

I watched the bewilderment on Cotton's face, as he still patiently held the paint brush in his hand.

"I knew this was coming," I began to explain. "My husband's brother is contesting Clay's will. He thinks this property here in Borna should have been left to him instead of me."

"Well, if I ain't heard it all!" Cotton replied in disgust.

"I'm not worried," I said walking to the kitchen. "He's just a bitter and greedy man." Cotton followed me to hear more.

"Why would he want to put you through more grief?" Cotton asked. "No one's been coming to this place for years, and now he wants it?"

"All good questions, Cotton," I replied. "If Clay and his Dad would have wanted him to have this place, they would have put him in the will."

"Hey, look what's here!" Cotton shouted as he looked out the back window.

"My oven?" I anxiously asked. He nodded with a big smile.

"I'll put my paint away and find out if I can be helpful," Cotton quickly said.

"Thanks," I happily responded. "Fred and I will make sure they're put in the right places." Fred stopped nailing the baseboards and looked out the window.

The commotion began with too many chiefs and not enough Indians. It didn't take me long to get the message. I was best kept out of the way.

I went upstairs and decided to call Maggie. She would want to know the subpoena, did indeed, arrive.

I caught her while shopping, which wasn't unusual. I told her the subpoena had arrived, and I was to be in court the week after Christmas.

"That so and so!" she said angrily. "What a great Christmas present for you! Why isn't he paying attention to his business instead of harassing you?"

"What do you mean by that?" I asked confused.

"Meyr Lumber just laid off some more people which included my brother, by the way!" she revealed. "The morale around there is terrible. Since they're non-union, the employees don't have much recourse. I hear things have really suffered since Clay died."

"Good heavens, I had no idea!" I said in shock.

"There were always rumors, but Sunday's paper had an article on it," she reported. "I'll save it for you. Some of those employees have been there over twenty-five years."

"Oh, that's horrible to hear," I said feeling ill. "If the company is struggling financially, why on earth does James want to buy this place in Borna?"

"My brother thinks James has been using company resources for his own personal use," she added. "According to the article, the whole board, including him, received their annual bonuses. I guess it's at the expense of the employees."

"I just can't believe how quickly this could happen!" I said harshly. "Clay and his Dad valued those employees and treated them well, which is why they never unionized."

"Thank goodness you're out of the family, Kate," Maggie stated firmly.

"I wish I really was Maggie, but they don't seem to be

done with me just yet," I answered. "Hey, on a more pleasant note, my appliances are being installed as we speak! That's a good day for me! I figure by this evening, I'll smell some of my blueberry muffins!"

"You're crazy, my friend, but I love ya!" Maggie said as we ended our conversation.

By 9:00 pm, everyone had gone home, and I was all alone with my instruction books and warrantees. I found myself staring at my new appliances like they were objects from outer space. Somehow, these brand new specimens invaded my historic home in Borna. They were so clean and sterile compared to the other worn patina in the house. Hopefully, I would find the nerve to use them. Once the cabinetry would connect them, they would look like they belonged.

Surprisingly, I was mentally too exhausted to drag out the supplies and utensils to make muffins. I decided instead, to turn in early and make them first thing in the morning.

I soaked in the tub as I kept thinking about James and the troubles of Meyr Lumber. I wondered if they were in trouble when Clay was alive. He never discussed his work with me or wanted my opinion on anything. I guessed I was just the trophy wife and Jack's mother. My emotions and concerns were always dismissed by him telling me not to worry my pretty little head about anything. I think women know when they're truly, emotionally connected to their husband. I never felt confident enough to admit there was something missing in our marriage. I wondered if "babe" was ever included in his most intimate thoughts.

With everything going through my mind, I found it impossible to sleep. I finally gave up and went downstairs to fix myself some Chamomile tea to help me sleep. The house was very quiet until I got to the bottom of the stairs. Suddenly, a vehicle sped by the house gunning its engine. It was frightening, so I turned on the front porch light to look out the front door window. In the dim light, I saw trash scattered all about my snowy, front yard. Tin cans, containers and papers were blowing every direction. This was no accident! Could it be teenagers, playing a prank, or was it my dear Blade wanting to harass me into leaving Borna?

I didn't know quite what to do or who to tell. By morning, the debris would be all over the neighborhood. It was dark and very late, so I convinced myself to get up before dawn and pick up what I could.

When I got back upstairs, I just had to call Ellie. She was a night owl so thought she might be awake. When she answered however, I could tell I had awakened her.

"I'm sorry to call you so late, Ellie, "I cried.

"Kate, what's wrong?" she asked in panic.

I told her about the loud car and the trash. She couldn't believe it! I told her she might see a milk carton or two on her lawn in the morning. We decided to meet up in the early morning, to assess the damage.

"I hope you're keeping track of all this nonsense, Kate," Ellie scolded. "Chances are it won't happen again, but somebody's luck is going to run out soon!"

"It does sound like Blade's doings, again, doesn't it?" I admitted.

"No question," Ellie stated. "He likes to play dirty because he is dirty."

CHAPTER 35

After very little sleep, I turned over to see the alarm clock was at 4:45. It was still very dark, but I made myself get up and dress for the trash pick-up at 6229 Main Street. I put on the coffee and found a large trash bag to gather up the debris.

I walked out into the cold darkness, hoping there would be little traffic to witness my activity. By now, I could see the trash had traveled. The good news was it showed up clearly on the white snow. Ellie must have been watching for me because she appeared about five minutes later with trash bag in hand. She picked trash up along the road side and anything blowing outside my yard. When she got to my place, we giggled when she told me she picked up some disposable diapers. After we gathered what we could, we thought it best to go inside and get warmed up, with some coffee.

"If you're not in a big hurry, I'll whip up some of my blueberry muffins!" I offered.

"After all your bragging, I'm not gonna pass that up!" she joked. "How about I get a fire going here for ya?"

"Oh, Ellie, you are just too much," I praised. "What kind of a friend helps you pick up trash in the dark and makes you a fire?"

"What kind of friend would make you breakfast on such an early cold, morning?" she asked in return.

We carried on in fun as we watched the sun come up. Each of us had a good view of the sunrise from the back of our houses. We continued chatting, sitting in front of the fire, waiting for the muffins to bake. I confessed to Ellie, making the muffins again was like getting back on a bicycle. It made the whole house smell like home again.

Fred showed up about 7:00 to work on the baseboards so Ellie left to go home. He was more than happy to have one of the muffins. Watching him take the first big bite was worth the task. He smiled immediately. He shared he was thankful to have an inside job on this cold day and the muffins were a bonus.

My objective for the day was to drive some distance away to a national chain grocery store. I could feel the adrenaline kick in at the thought of doing something which most folks did every day. Now I could cook, but if my groceries had to stay in boxes and bags for the time being, so be it. I also had a brand new empty freezer which could now store everything I loved.

I found the store Ellie told me about and entered like a little kid in a candy store. I grabbed the cart and started throwing everything in but the kitchen sick, as the saying goes. Filling a soon to be pantry from scratch was very exciting. I enjoyed every minute of choosing enough food to feed a family of five for a long time. A young man helped carry all my bags to the car when I finally left. With all this food, I wanted to start thinking about doing some entertaining. So many folks had been nice to me, and it was now time to pay back.

When I returned home, Fred was gone, so one by one, I carried the bags to my kitchen and lined them up all in a row. I took the refrigerator and freezer items and arranged them neatly in my new appliances. I visualized just where my pantry would go, but for now, it was still an empty space. When I put my coat away, there was a knock at the back door.

To my surprise, it was Clark McFadden. I opened the door not quite knowing what to say.

"Hey, there!" I nervously began with a big smile. "Would you like to come in?"

"I was nearby and thought I'd take a look at your kitchen to see if I could at least be helpful, with a little free advice," he explained without a smile. I couldn't believe it.

"Oh, why sure," I mumbled. "I would appreciate it very much. I still haven't hired anyone, so perhaps someone will come to mind when you see what has to be done. Please take off your coat. Would you like some coffee?"

"No thanks," he immediately responded. "I don't have long, but I have to admit, I've been very curious about what this house looked like inside. I wouldn't mind a short tour if you have the time."

"Why of course," I said detecting a small smile from him. "For someone who has such a fondness of wood, you'll appreciate the woodwork for sure. Let's start upstairs." He followed me up, which made me a little uncomfortable as we remained silent.

With little small talk, his eyes gazed on every nook and cranny. Now and then he would caress the woodwork as we walked along. I was surprised when he agreed to see the attic. His comments were few, but his admiration of the wood said many things. When I opened the door to the quilt room, he gave me a strange look for an explanation. He nodded as I told him about the special find in the upper cabinet. I told him I was still analyzing the inscriptions. He had no response.

When we came back down the stairs, he became more talkative.

"I can't believe this woodwork survived like this, over time," he marveled. "I heard there were renters in here for a short while, which could have been terribly risky. Someone could have taken a paint brush to some of this."

He was fascinated when I showed him the layout of the Doctor's small waiting room and where he saw his patients.

"Living in the same house with the doctor's office had to be challenging," I noted. "They had no children, so the noise wouldn't have been an issue." He nodded and smiled.

When we got back to the kitchen, he saw my grocery bags all neatly lined up. He gave me a questionable look, like I must have an explanation.

"I just got back from grocery shopping," I confessed. "Now I can cook and bake again, so the floor will have to hold my groceries for now. If you would've arrived five minutes earlier, you could have helped me carry them in." He didn't respond.

He pulled out a notepad from his shirt and started scribbling in silence. Without solicitation, I started telling him what I envisioned, between the kitchen and the dining room.

Surprisingly, he seemed to agree with most of what I suggested. He did make some comments, I frankly didn't understand. I picked up on a slight sense of excitement as he made his notes. Was he now sorry he didn't say yes to the job?

"So, do you know anyone I could call to accomplish this?" I asked interrupting his concentration. He put his hands on his hips and looked directly into my eyes, as if he was going to tell me to leave him alone.

"Are you in any hurry on any of this?" he asked as he looked over the room.

"Does it look like I am?" I said with a laugh. "I'm willing to live out of grocery bags till I find the right person to do this the right way. I do have to go home to Michigan for a short Christmas visit, but then I'll be back. I'd like to put it on the market as soon as the kitchen is finished." He seemed to be listening intently as he calculated.

"Okay, I'll do the job, if I can work at my own pace," he said somewhat reluctantly. "I have other projects I'm committed to. Do you have a limited budget?" I looked at him with a grin.

"No budget and you can absolutely work at your own convenience," I said nodding. "I'll open an account wherever you tell me to."

"That won't be necessary," he added. "I have those already established. I think I can make this all look unique to the time period and functional as well." I couldn't believe what I was hearing!

"Oh, thanks, Clark," I said wanting to hug him. "When can you start?" He looked at me shaking his head in disbelief. "I think it's a very fair question to ask." He nodded with a smile.

"I'll start ordering some things tomorrow after I draw up a few sketches," he commented as he walked about the room.

"Surprise me with whatever you decide to do," I added with excitement. "I am honored to have your work in my house. Should I pay you something up front, or as we go along?"

"I'll take one of these muffins here, for starters," he teased as he reached into the basket of muffins on the table. "They smell really good, so a down payment in muffins works for me!"

"That works for me, too!" I chuckled.

"I may be by this week to get started," he said as he walked out the door taking the last bite of the muffin in his hand.

That was that! I had scored big time and didn't know how I did it. The smell of the muffins must have been the turning point! This guy was totally strange. How could he be so creative and attractive, and have such a dry personality?

I couldn't wait to share the news with Ellie. As soon as I saw him drive away, I called Ellie at the winery and told her of my surprise visit from Clark McFadden. She cleared her throat before giving me a response.

"And you only had to give him a muffin as a down payment?" she joked.

"They are mighty powerful!" I joked back. "How many do you think it'll take to complete the job?" We laughed. "What do you think it was that changed his mind?"

"I think he not only finds your house intriguing, but you as well," she teased.

"Oh, please Ellie," I immediately answered back. "I haven't given him any personal attention, and I certainly didn't beg after he turned me down. I've seen his type. Some men are full of themselves, and I don't bite or play games with them."

"Exactly my point, Miss Meyr," she fired back. "That's why he finds you intriguing!"

"I think it was the smell of my great muffins!" I chuckled.

"Don't flatter yourself too much, girl!" Ellie warned.

"I think Mr. McFadden and I share some things in common at this stage in life," I surmised. "I don't know his past, but you can just about guess he likes his life just the way it is right now."

"Sorry, Kate, I have to go," Ellie interrupted. "Trout is yelling for me. Please stay out of trouble, okay?"

"I'll do what I can!" I promised.

I felt energized with Clark's commitment and went to the kitchen to toast my own success with some of Ellie's Red Velvet wine. It had been so long since I'd had happy, little moments like this! Life was looking up!

CHAPTER 36

The next week, Clark showed up to begin working. He mostly measured and did a little frame work. I got the message right away that he didn't want to be interrupted with small talk so I made myself disappear when he stopped by.

It was also the week the baby quilts arrived for Cotton's little girl. Maggie included some handmade stuffed toys from Emily, one of our Beach Quilters, and a knitted sweater her mother had made. Cotton and Susie were delighted and asked for their address to send a thank you note. I extended a Thanksgiving invitation to the two of them, but they were going to Susie's mother's house.

I also attended my second meeting of the Friendship Circle. This time it was at Ellen's house. Her husband was one of the owners of the East Perry Lumber Company in Borna. Her house was as lovely as she was! She definitely had quite a talent for interior decorating and seemed to have the money to do it with. She was also the social butterfly of the community, it seemed, and had the Friendship Circle in the palm of her hand. She was very gracious to me, and I liked her very much. As wives of lumber yard owners, we actually had something in common. However, it was obvious, she was able to be herself, unlike the Kate Meyr I knew.

Attending the Friendship Circle meeting also meant I could continue to pick Emma's brain for information on Dr. Paulson and his wife.

On my way home from the afternoon meeting, I made my weekly stop at Imy's Antique Shop. She was happy to see me again and informed me during the winter she would just be open on the weekends. Imy had an eye to turn something insignificant into something attractive and useful. I saw three stripped bar stools in a row, as if they were waiting to be varnished or painted. They were for sale as is, so I decided to purchase them for the island I planned for the kitchen. I asked if she would paint them red like the little bench she had sitting on the counter. I also spotted some Victorian Redwork shams that were in perfect condition and very inexpensive. This type of sham would be a good accessory for my two color quilts. One said, "GOOD MORNING" and the other said, "GOOD NIGHT". I wished they were in German like some I had seen before. She was happy with my purchases and said she would deliver the stools when they were finished. I knew she was also curious to see the house.

Every time I ventured out to run errands, I wanted to explore the surrounding villages I kept hearing so much about. Each little community had its own little history going back to Germany. I could see why merging any of them together would be difficult. Some of the villages were predominantly

Lutheran and some Catholic. The locals knew who was who, and even though they were somewhat territorial, they all had respect for one another. No one had ever criticized one over the other. The ladies at the Friendship Circle were very sweet to one another, and I never picked up on any unkind gossip. Was it because I was new to the area? What they were saying behind my back would likely be very interesting.

Ellie said there would be a Christmas Church tour before Christmas. She said it would be a perfect opportunity for me to visit all the churches as well as sample wonderful baked goods from the area. It was an annual candlelight event that sounded wonderful. If my timing allowed, I was determined to go. There sure seemed to always be a lot going on in this part of the county. I heard repeatedly about the East Perry Fair and picnic. When I arrived in Borna, I had just missed the Saxon Fall Festival at the Saxon Village. It sounded wonderful, and judging by the photos I saw, it looked very authentic and fun! Was I forgetting I, too, came from a fun and beautiful part of the world?

CHAPTER 37

The next morning dawned cold and dreary so I decided to make a fire before having some breakfast. I heard a car pull in the drive, and lo and behold, it was Clark McFadden. He never came this early to work. I was still in my robe, but I had no choice but to answer the door.

"Good, I was afraid you might still be asleep," he said coming in the door without an apology for arriving at such an early hour.

"Excuse my appearance, but I was just making a fire and haven't gotten upstairs to dress for the day," I mumbled. "Would you like some coffee?"

"No, thanks," he said as he avoided looking at me. "I won't be here long. I'm on my way into the city to complete a job."

It wouldn't have made a difference to excuse myself so I went quickly up the stairs to get dressed. I looked in the mirror, and my hair was a mess. Who would be cutting my hair in Borna, I wondered? Would it be Esther, who used to own a beauty shop? I had perfectly straight hair and was always jealous of Maggie's cute, natural curls. Maybe this was the time to change my hairstyle! It was almost long enough to do a cute, pony tail like I once had as a young girl, except I wasn't a young girl anymore. I'd have to get Ellie's advice on this matter.

I did look presentable in my brand new, white, terry cloth robe, which I purchased before my trip. With workman coming in and out of this house, I was going to have to be more careful about my appearance. It bothered me more around Clark because he was always so neatly dressed, and I didn't want him to think I was a slob from up north somewhere.

After a change of clothing, I came down and entered the kitchen to get myself a second cup of coffee. I was determined to find out more about this guy, whether he wanted conversation or not.

"I hear you live in a nice, little log cabin down by Indian Creek," I began. "That sounds really unique and private."

"Yes, I do better work that way," he answered as if he was giving me a hint to be quiet.

"Do you have any neighbors?" I asked. "Ellie has tried to tell me where Indian Creek runs along Borna."

"It's pretty peaceful," he said walking in and out of the kitchen. "No close neighbors."

"I can't believe tomorrow is Thanksgiving," I stated. "Do you have plans, or do you have family around here?" Now he looked annoyed.

"No, and that's okay," he said in a softer tone.

"You know, Ellie is having a nice little group at the winery tomorrow," I informed him. "I think you would be very welcome, and the food will be wonderful."

"Ellie has a kind heart, but I have some work to get done," he answered. I wanted to ask what he did for fun, but I thought I had reached my quota for questions.

I took my coffee to sit by the fire hoping he might join me in conversation, but that didn't happen.

"I'll be out of here now, Kate," he announced five minutes later. "I took some measurements which will allow me to do some construction at my studio. I'll be back in a couple of days or so." I nodded. "Have a nice Thanksgiving!" He didn't even give me a chance to say the same before he was out the door.

He no more than got out of the driveway when Cotton pulled up in his truck. I was always happy to see him. Cotton was always talkative and happy to be employed. He knew I appreciated his efforts.

"Come on in," I greeted in the cold air. "It's frightful out there!" He looked frozen, and he wasn't dressed warm enough, in my opinion.

"Clark is already gone for the day?" he asked his voice shivering.

"Yeah, he's going to do some of the construction at his studio," I responded. "I can't figure that guy out. Would you like some coffee?"

"Sure, but I just wanted to stop by and ask you something," he asked with a serious look on his face.

"Shoot!" I said pouring his coffee.

"I wondered if you'd like a real live Christmas tree for this house of yours?" he asked with a bright smiling face. "You said you'd be gone only a week or so in Michigan, so I thought maybe you'd like to enjoy a bit of Christmas here in

Borna." I was caught off guard at the thought. "I found the perfect tree, right on your property, Miss Kate. It's nice and tall and perfectly shaped. It's just off the road a piece. I could get it put up for you the day after Thanksgiving so you have time to enjoy it."

"Oh, wow, how really nice of you Cotton," I said happily. "I already envision a lot of decorations already going up around here, but I don't have anything to put on a tree. I certainly have boxes of ornaments back in South Haven, if Carla hasn't given them away!"

"Harold's store is selling boxes of lights, which is really all you need," he noted. "I can make you a stand to set it in. However he sells those, too!"

"Well, then I guess we will give it a go, if you don't mind the work," I said in agreement. "I haven't had a real tree since I was a little kid. I love, love the smell, which I have not forgotten!"

"Most folks in these parts have a real tree," he added. "I'm always on the lookout for some of the churches, which need good sized trees. I sure wish you'd be here for Christmas instead of going back for a stressful, court date."

"Well, my biggest joy in going back will be seeing my son, Jack, who hasn't been home since his father was killed," I revealed with a smile. "My lawyer said I really don't need to show up personally in court, if I don't want to. I have a woman lawyer who is quite good. She says it's a slam dunk for me. No one can take the property away from me since it was in my husband's will. I hope she's right!"

"It's pretty sad, if you ask me," Cotton said, shaking his head. "I may be speaking out of turn, Miss Kate, but I think you're making this place your home, and you don't even realize it. I told Susie there would be no way you'd let anyone else buy this place with what you're investing. I think Blade knows it, too, and the thought of it is what's making him angry." I couldn't believe what I had just heard. Cotton was a brighter guy than I was giving him credit for. I wasn't sure how to respond.

"I think you may be right, Cotton," I finally agreed. "It would have to be just the right person for me to sell this house."

"Your son lives in New York, your in-laws are suing you, and your house is almost sold; so why would you want to stay back there anyway?" Cotton inquired. I paused as it made me think.

"I do love Borna and the people here, but what will I do, once this place is all finished?" I said trying to make sense of it all.

"You'll know the answer when the time comes," Cotton said with assurance. "This place won't be done anytime soon, and you'll have plenty to keep yourself busy."

"Well Cotton, you may have just given me permission to do what I probably had in the back of mind all along!" I said laughing. He grinned from ear to ear.

"You'll stay then?" he asked with excitement.

"I'll think about it, but right now, bring on the tree!" I shouted with enthusiasm. "I may be in South Haven, Christmas Day, but my Christmas spirit belongs to Borna!" We both wanted to jump for joy!

CHAPTER 38

Thanksgiving Day was very cold, cloudy and windy. I got up early to make two apple pies, instead of salads which was my original plan. The delicious smells warmed up the house. They would join other wonderful desserts at the winery in the late afternoon.

I decided to pass on church giving me a pang of guilt, but I planned to visit nature, which always brought me in touch with my faith. I was curious where Cotton had spotted the Christmas tree. I had paid little attention to the rest of my acreage behind my house. I decided this morning would be a good time to assess what was mine and enjoy the scenery along the way!

As I walked along, shivering, I was convinced East Perry winters were just as cold as South Haven. However, there was more dampness in the air than what I remembered in South Haven. The best part of the Missouri winter was the snow never lingered on for days as it did back home.

There it was! This had to be the one. Across the ditch, alongside of the road, stood a stately, tall pine tree that was perfectly shaped. As I walked closer to it, I noticed there were smaller trees around it, growing at different heights. It looked like a family. I smelled it as I got close and pictured it in my large, living room. Clay never allowed me to have a live tree in our home. I gave my silent approval and headed back home. I walked briskly as I thanked the Almighty for my new life here in Borna. I asked him to help me make the right decision on where to live. Shivering even more, I turned around to head back to my house as I thanked him for the beautiful Christmas tree. When I reached the house, I felt invigorated by my walk and ready for Ellie's big dinner.

I think I may have been the last to arrive at the winery, judging by all the people. Ellie had transformed the place into a warm and formal dining room. She lined up many tables together, in one long, line and covered them with white table cloths. Fall arrangements with candles traveled up and down the center showing off Ellie's personal sets of lovely chinaware.

Many folks were gathered around the bar area where there were various wines and beverages to choose from. I was surprised to see Clark McFadden talking to some of them, especially since he turned down my suggestion to come. I purposely went to the opposite end of the bar to avoid him. I heard some of them telling him goodbye, so when I turned around, he appeared to be leaving with a takeout order, as I had seen him do before. Now he was coming towards me.

"Enjoy your dinner," he said with a half-smile. "I know it'll be delicious. I was going to roast myself a pheasant, but my time just didn't allow it. I think I smelled Kelly's cooking all the way to my place." I nodded with a smile.

"My, you are a busy man," I said flippantly. "Happy Thanksgiving!"

"You as well," he said going out the door.

Well, if that didn't beat all! At least he didn't totally ignore me. Roasting a pheasant sounded just like someone living in a log cabin would do!

Before we were seated, I made my way around the room making sure I had met some of Ellie's relatives who were invited.

When we were all seated, Ellie herself welcomed everyone and said a prayer of thanksgiving.

Trout began the series of toasts, which seemed to circulate around the table. I was beginning to wonder if we were there to eat or drink.

I took a swallow of my wine and decided to join the gaiety of the moment. Something told me this was the time I should announce my intentions to stay in Borna. Once I did that, I couldn't back out! I tapped my knife on the side of my water glass to get everyone's attention. They quieted down immediately in surprise. The looks on their faces were priceless. I raised my glass to begin.

"I have an announcement to make!" I said looking directly at Ellie. She looked at me in wonder.

"Go for it, Kate!" she yelled from the opposite end of the table. She couldn't possibly know what I was about to say.

"I want to share the news that I plan on making Borna, my new, permanent home!" I spilled out rather quickly. There was some hesitation like they didn't believe me. "I have some things to settle at my home in Michigan, but I will return permanently to continue the restoration of the house I have fallen in love with. Your friendship and hospitality has made me feel welcome, and I thank you! Happy Thanksgiving to you all!"

Everyone cheered and applauded. Ellie got out of her chair and came over to hug me.

"Oh my goodness, Kate, I'm so happy!" she said trying not to cry. "When did you make this decision?"

"I'll tell you later," I whispered in her ear. "I'm starved."

"Let the celebration of food begin!" Ellie ordered to her servers.

The meal featured turkey and ham with wonderful German side dishes. There was a round table with every dessert you could imagine displayed for us to serve ourselves. I couldn't believe all the food, which seemed to be a huge part of Borna's social life. Everyone there made a point to personally wish me well in my new home. There were also sincere offers to be helpful, which I appreciated very much.

When I returned home in the early evening, I was in a celebratory mood so I called Jack to wish him a Happy Thanksgiving. When he answered his cell, he was at his girlfriend's parent's house for dinner. I didn't want to keep him long on the phone, but I was happy to see he was in a family environment for the holiday. We said our goodbyes easily knowing we would see each other soon for Christmas. I didn't want to tell him about the lawsuit over the phone, nor did I want to announce my decision to move from South Haven.

CHAPTER 39

Just as Cotton had promised, the next morning at 10:00, he showed up with my Christmas tree. He had another guy with him, who helped him cut it down and lift it onto his truck. Cotton had constructed a homemade stand and placed it on the deck before inserting the large tree. As they brought it into the house, I instructed them to place it right in front of my large living room window where everyone driving by my house would be able to see it from the road. The pine tree smell filled the house immediately, and we all admired the perfect specimen. They both insisted they had to be on their way, so I gave them each a fifty dollar bill as a little Christmas bonus. I would have had to pay a fortune for this large tree in South Haven. The fact it came from my very own property made it extra special. I couldn't wait to get off to Harold's Hardware to purchase strands of white lights. A call from Maggie delayed my trip.

"Hey girlfriend, when do ya think you'll be arriving?" Maggie immediately asked.

"I'm not sure," I answered in all honesty. "I'll have to watch the weather forecast when Christmas day gets closer. Why?"

"I'd like to have a little party for you, since you've been gone for so long," she explained. "I know you won't be decorating for Christmas here because Carla said she thought your house was about to sell."

"Well, that's good news, if you just talked to her, because I still don't have a contract," I reported. "I wish you would forget the party, Maggie. It is a sweet thought, but in my limited time there, I need to pack and spend time with Jack. Of course, you and I need some time, too. Thank goodness, I don't have to fit in time with the Meyr family."

"I don't blame you there, but why do you have to hurry back so soon?" she asked with concern.

"I'm under construction here, for starters, but also because Borna is now going to be my new permanent home," I stately as softly as I could. "I wanted to tell you in person, but it just can't wait. Jack doesn't know yet. I'll tell him when I see him." Maggie paused as the news hit her.

"I'm not surprised," she finally responded sadly. "I told Carla, I had a feeling you would not return here to live. You are sounding way too happy! I have to admit, I'm sad about not having you here on a day to day basis. Nothing will be the same. I hate what's happened to you, Kate, but you deserve to find some future happiness."

"Oh Maggie, thanks. You and I are friends forever. You should know that!" I said wanting to cry. "I am so tired of feeling angry and sad. Darn, I didn't want to cry!" I stopped to sniffle. "This house and Borna have given me hope and energy to be my old self again!" Tears kept coming. This was going to be harder than I thought it would be.

"It's okay, it's okay," Maggie repeated sympathetically. "I'm kind of jealous, really. I know how much you love South Haven, so I know you'll visit. Plus, I'll be sure to do the same! It will be different though!"

"Thanks for understanding, Maggie," I said in closing. "Happy Thanksgiving, and I love ya!"

I had to get a hold of myself after we hung up. Maggie had been through so much with me. I knew my news had hurt her. I wanted to share the excitement about my great Thanksgiving Day and my beautiful Christmas tree, but that would have been rubbing salt in the wound.

Trying to think of only the tree, off to Harold's I went. I bought almost every package of lights he had in stock. He had a good chuckle when I told him that Cotton found a tree for me on my property.

"Say, I heard there was a pretty, important announcement made at Ellie's Thanksgiving dinner!" he teased. I nodded and smiled.

"I hope I'm doing the right thing, Harold," I said as I paid my bill.

"We knew some time ago, you were falling in love with Doc's house hook, line, and sinker!" Harold admitted with a chuckle in his voice. "Say, if you don't mind me sayin', you ought to take a second look at Clark McFadden!" He gave me a wink.

"What?" I gasped. "What do you mean by that?"

"I think he's pretty taken with you, and that's sayin' something!" he teased.

"You are so full of it, Harold!" I said about to go out the door.

"Let me tell you, Clark McFadden doesn't have to go back to building cabinets anymore with his career!" he claimed. "He can name his price on wood carvings and the like. He took your job for another reason, I think." He winked again at me and waved as I went out the door.

When I got in my car, I realized I was now a member of the community. I had become part of the town gossip. Harold loved to tease everyone, so I took it as a form of flattery. I blew off his summation of Mr. McFadden. He just wanted to tease me about something.

When I got home, I called Ellie and invited her over for a tree-trimming cocktail before she went to the winery. She gladly accepted and seemed quite jealous of my new arrival.

Before she walked in the door, I already started pulling out the lights from the boxes. She praised the tree as she walked around it. We got the ladder, and I climbed up, while she held it steady and fed me the lights. It was a sight to behold. It didn't need a single ornament with all its natural beauty. We were having a gay time with our little party, recalling Christmas memories, when Trout called to say he needed her at the winery.

After she left, I sat there with all the lights off, but the festive tree. It was a spiritual moment as I had so much to be thankful for. Life was good, and I was going to have a Merry Christmas!

CHAPTER 40

While I lay in bed the next morning, I thought of my future plans. Suddenly, I felt the same, warm light take over the room as I had before. I knew it was all supernatural, but I didn't care. It was a warm loving message to me. I couldn't explain it, but I loved and embraced it. When I looked out the window from my bed, the day was cloudy and darkish, but inside my bedroom, it was a bright, sunny, warm day.

I started thinking about Clark and hoped he would be coming over today. I didn't want him to catch me in my robe again so I got up and showered before going downstairs. I seemed to be challenged by his coolness towards me.

I was eating a slice of toast when I heard a vehicle drive up. It was Clark, but he was taking his time getting to my door. When I answered the door, I cheerfully greeted him, despite the somber look on his face.

"I hope you're not going anywhere today," he said coming

in the door.

"No; I'm here for a while anyway," I curiously answered. "Why?"

"I noticed all your tires have been slashed!" he divulged as nicely as he could.

"You're crazy!" I yelled. "No way!" I opened the back door to the cold wind and ran towards my car to see for myself. Clark slowly followed.

I couldn't believe my eyes! Every tire was maliciously sliced with rage and anger. They were totally flat. I could only think of one villain who would be so cruel.

"Let's go in out of the cold," Clark suggested.

I slammed the door shut in frustration. I wanted to scream to the top of my lungs. "I can't believe this guy!" I shouted.

"You know who did this?" Clark asked innocently.

"Oh yes, oh yes!" I said pacing the kitchen floor. "He's broken my windows, lain dead animals on my door step, and dumped trash all over my front yard! I should have known he wasn't finished with me."

"Who in the world would do that?" he said looking shocked.

"Blade Schuessler!" I loudly accused. "He's been trying to get me to sell this place and get out of Borna. He claims he has a buyer and wants me to sell. He's been telling people I have reneged on a contract with him to sell the house. I NEVER had a contract with him." Clark looked shocked trying to absorb it all. I was shaking.

"You've reported all of this to the County Sheriff's office, I hope," stated Clark.

"No," I said shaking my head. "Not everything. I thought he was just throwing a little tantrum, and he'd eventually go away.

I didn't want to stoop down to his level and let him think he was scaring me."

"You sure don't want this to continue, Kate," Clark wisely advised. "You've got to report this. He probably thinks you're afraid to do so. I've seen this guy around town and wondered what he did for a living. He looks the part, I might add!"

"I'm getting a security system since I plan to live here now, but I'm not sure it will even help," I confessed.

"You plan to stay here?" Clark asked like he may have heard me incorrectly. I took a deep breath to explain.

"Yes, I decided a couple of days ago," I stated still pacing the floor.

"Do you think this Blade guy knows this?" he quickly asked.

"It's a small town, so I'm sure he does," I conceded. "I made the announcement at Ellie's Thanksgiving dinner."

"Then he'll be angry, which may be why he left you a present, this morning." he noted. "I know a guy who works for Casey's Tires who can come out and fix you up with the same kind of tires. They do a good job, and I can call them if you want me to." I took a deep breath and nodded.

I was seeing a softer side of Clark, but the last thing I wanted was for him to feel sorry for me.

"Thanks, Clark, and I will definitely call the Sherriff's office and make a report," I said softly. "I realize now, I should have called them sooner."

Clark immediately got out his cell and went by the door in the kitchen to make his call. I went to the living room and let a few tears burn down my face. I didn't know anger could create tears. I didn't want Clark to see this side of me so I looked out the glass of the front door. For some reason, I never wanted to show emotion around any man. I was used to not getting much sympathy from Clay. It was just easier to ignore everything and tell myself it didn't matter.

Clark quietly came up behind me to say they would be here within three hours. When I turned towards him, he saw the blurriness of tears in my eyes.

"I'm sorry. This isn't like me," I said wiping a tear away.

"Nonsense," he said shaking his head in disgust. "You have taken on an unnecessary amount of harassment here. You've done nothing to deserve this. Everything you've done to this house is first class, which is quite a gift to this community! I join many folks here who are mighty glad you decided to stay!"

I didn't respond.

Finally, someone from the sheriff's office arrived, and my emotions were now intact. Clark remained at the house working, so I registered my complaint in the living room where he was not likely to hear. There wasn't much sympathy from the officer, when I told him about the other incidents which were not reported. He was helpful in giving me a reputable, security system company who had done some work in the area. Before he left, he took pictures of my flat tires and the back of the house.

When he left, Clark asked if I would like to get out of the house for a bite of lunch. I think he knew I could use some cheering up, but when I agreed to do so, I didn't want him thinking it was anything but an act of kindness.

He talked about a great BBQ place he liked about five miles out of Borna. I liked the idea very much.

"We'll be back in plenty of time to be here for the tire repair," he said as he prepared to leave with his tools.

I felt strange getting into his SUV, which seemed to be

very clean considering his line of work in the country. I tried to make as little small talk as possible, knowing his personality. When we turned off a side road, I mentioned I wasn't familiar with it and how I looked forward to exploring more of the countryside.

When we arrived, Clark was the perfect gentleman opening the car door for me. The tiny, run down structure was called The BBQ Shack. The inside only held about six tables and chairs. Clark said they did a big carry out business, which he frequently took advantage of. Clark confessed the food was not as healthy as he liked. He ordered a rack of ribs, but no sides. I ordered a pulled pork sandwich with an order of fries.

I shared with Clark my plans for when I got back to Michigan. I told him I had arranged for a mover to come, but it would be a challenge because I wanted to spend as much time as I could with my son, Jack. When I added the news of going to court because of a law-suit instigated by my brother-in-law, he looked speechless. I could tell he wasn't sure if he should ask questions or mind his own business.

"That's pretty, heavy stuff your dealing with right now, Kate," Clark said after he took a healthy bite of the ribs. "Now, it's none of my business, but why in the world, would your brother-in-law be suing the widow of his deceased brother?"

I answered as briefly as I could about the dynamics of owning the Borna property. I told him my lawyer said I had nothing to worry about. I also agreed with the whole mysteriousness of it all.

"I'm hearing Meyr Lumber is letting go a lot of employees as if there is a financial crisis," I shared. "That makes me wonder why he would spend more money buying this property here in Borna,"

"Sounds like he now has more personal money at his disposal if he's cutting back at the company," Clark theorized with BBQ sauce on his face. I had to snicker.

"I'm sorry, but I can't take you seriously until you wipe some of this sauce off your cheek," I teased. I took one of my fingers to point out the area. He broke down and give me a smile as he wiped the sauce with his napkin. He was embarrassed, but I managed to get a grin out of him.

"Okay, probably not a good idea to eat ribs in public," he added still smiling. "I get these to go and get as messy as I want, in the privacy of my own home, you see." I nodded with a smile.

"I see!" I replied with a grin. Was I flirting? "We better get back, in case the tire guy comes. I also need to get my carpenter back to work." He grinned getting up to pay the bill.

"Already paid up, Clark," the girl at the counter told him. "Your friend took care of it!" He turned around and crinkled his gorgeous eyes in wonder.

"What are friends and bosses for?" I teased. "It's a tax write off, right?" He chuckled and said a modest, thank you.

On the way home, he told me he had to go out of town to Springfield to deliver a wood carving to a client. He wasn't sure how long he would be gone. Our conversation was much more relaxed than when we left the house. I shared a few more plans with him about the sun-porch and garage addition.

"I can help with the sunroom finishing if my time allows," he offered surprising himself. "I probably shouldn't have said that!"

"Too late," I joked. "I'll count on it."

CHAPTER 41

During the next week, I felt I was finally making some progress on my future home. It took just one day to get the security system in place, which helped my piece of mind regarding Blade. Now, I just had to get used to really using it, like I did with my house in South Haven.

Cotton and I had assessed my property and decided exactly the best spot, for my garage, since the sunporch design had expanded. Because I was using some of the same carpenters, it likely wouldn't happen till spring, when the weather would break. Eddie Mueller was going in and out of the house, installing my new central air-conditioning. Every chance he had, he thanked me for the winter work.

One night Ellie brought me dinner from the winery. We shared the meal as we enjoyed my white, lit, Christmas tree. Ellie declined to decorate her home for Christmas because she had done so much decorating at the winery.

When Harold's Hardware got in a delivery of wreaths and pine roping, I was the first customer to make a purchase. I had to admit, 6229 Main Street was looking as festive as a Christmas card!

I kept my oven going in the kitchen and my only work space was the center island in the middle of the room. I loved making cookies for everyone, and after all, it was the perfect season for doing so. Anyone who was going in and out of the house truly appreciated the treat. I found men, like Cotton, become like little boys when it comes to cookies, as well as many other things. I was sensing Cotton's wife Susie was not the homemaker we all read about.

I also touched base with Jack. We would be arriving in South Haven on the same day, and he would be taking a taxi from the airport if Carla couldn't pick him up.

I was hoping any day now to have a firm contract on my house. A family of five had put in a lower offer, but I happily accepted it, in fear I may not get another. The thought of a nice size family occupying my unhappy home actually made me happy.

It was odd not seeing any sign of Clark this week. Even though he never talked much, he was pleasant to have around. The unfinished kitchen was a bit frustrating, however I knew it would be fabulous when finished. I had to keep reminding myself, I had told him I was in no hurry when he signed on for the job.

It was hard for me to get Blade out of my mind. No one from the Sheriff's dept. had gotten back with me regarding my complaints. Even with the security system, I often lay awake, wondering what might be going on outside my house.

Every day, I made it a practice to stop and visit with Josephine's quilt in the quilt room. It seemed I would notice something new, every time. I was anxious for the Friendship Circle, especially Emma, to see it. I hated to miss their Christmas luncheon, at Ruth Ann's house, because of my leaving town. I was anxious to see her place, which looked like a giant monster of a building from the street. Lueder's Mercantile must have been quite the center piece of Borna at one time. Ellie said in 1955, it became a bowling alley owned by the Meyr brothers. Hmmm, no relation, I supposed, from the spelling. She said it's when the addition was built to the back of the building. Once it would all be restored, it would me magnificent. It would be quite an investment for Ruth Ann! Perhaps her mother had the resources to accomplish such a project.

The small villages were starting to light up for the Christmas season. The city of Borna set up a wonderful nativity scene on Ellie's front yard. It made a festive greeting coming into town. Dresden had strung lights going across the top of Main Street. I couldn't wait for the Christmas church tour because it was the main Christmas event which connected all the villages for the festive season.

I was starting to resent having to leave Borna for Christmas. Next year, I vowed to Ellie, I would have a very large Christmas party. I would invite the whole town in appreciation for their friendship.

I easily decided everyone's Christmas presents, except Ellie's. I owed her so much, but she seemed to have everything she wanted. If she, by chance, wanted a man in her life, I would go out my way to find him for her. Perhaps I would find something in South Haven.

On the day of the church tour, Ellie picked me up in her car. I bundled up for the cold weather because Ellie said some of the places on the tour were not heated. It didn't start till 3:30 in the late afternoon to capitalize on the candlelight affect. Ellie warned me there would be many choices of Christmas treats at all these locations, so we wouldn't likely have dinner.

There was no way to visit all the twenty-seven churches listed on the advertised map, so we chose to stay close to our surrounding area. As Ellie drove, she was also providing me with points of interest. I tried to make mental notes to myself.

Our first stop was Concordia Lutheran church, in Borna, which I had attended. It was celebrating 175 years. There were docents who were happy to provide verbal history along with brochures. Everything was decorated beautifully and I happily purchased my first ornament for my tree. It displayed a picture of the historic church as a remembrance. I was hoping all the churches offered an ornament. Their refreshments were offered in the side fellowship room. I could have spent the rest of the evening visiting with the nice folks and sampling each of the delights.

Ellie had to drag me away from the pleasant experience so we could go on to Dresden, where we visited Immanuel Lutheran church, which was organized in 1857, by some of the immigrants from Germany. They came up through New Orleans to settle here, the docent reported. Thanks to the Mississippi River, this region became the site Germans had identified as being the most like the Germany. These villages each had their own history. I was eager to hear more about. This church had an amazing wide and high, live cedar tree.

The smell was divine! It was mostly decorated with angel ornaments. Perhaps next year, a cedar tree would be my choice. As expected, more treats were offered. I wanted to fill my pockets!

Our next stop nearby was the Lutheran Heritage Center, which displayed a multitude of Christmas trees all decorated with its own theme. The hospitality was over the top as they eagerly told the story of each tree. Their historic displays reminded me this was the place to do more research on Dr. Paulson. What a wonderful place for the community to donate their family heirlooms and research the region's history. Before we left, we had to vote on our favorite tree. After much debate, I chose the red and white, candy cane tree.

It was totally dark while we traveled to a few more churches. Other than lights from other vehicles, we had no guidance on the curvy road. Thank goodness Ellie knew the roads like the back of her hand! Two of the churches had made trees, at the altar, by arranging rows of live Poinsettias. It was so clever and beautiful. The crèches' were also an interesting facet to their Christmas displays. Some were obviously handmade from various materials and were very old.

One very, very, tiny church was only heated by two small wood stoves. The docent said it now only held services a few times a year. The last stop was the largest church, located in Red Creek near Ellie's winery. The beautiful Catholic Church also had an impressive shrine along the side property, which I hoped to visit in the daylight. I could barely make out the Stations of the Cross lining the path to the grotto. Ellie also pointed out the historic, fenced, graveyard directly across the street from the church. We could only see some of the larger ornate tombstones shining in the moonlight. When we got inside, the ornate, gothic structure was so impressive. I walked towards the front of the altar and sat down in the front pew. I couldn't help but visit with my maker and thank him for this spiritual experience.

The evening was just what I needed to get ready for the Christmas season. Even though it was exhausting to repeatedly get in and out of the car, each visit was so endearing that it was well worth it. We did indeed pass on dinner with all the treats we consumed.

When Ellie dropped me off, she remained in my driveway till she saw me safely inside. I went up to change into my warm pajamas and came back downstairs to gaze once more at my Christmas tree. I took my newly, purchased ornament and hung it on the fireplace garland. As I sat in my loveseat, all cuddled up, I dreaded the trip home to South Haven. Tomorrow would mean packing and giving Maggie and Jack a last minute call. I shuttered at the thought of running into any of the Meyrs in the days ahead, but with Jack home, I knew it could happen. I dreaded filling Jack in on the land dispute.

CHAPTER 42

After a morning of baking, I wrapped loaves of my banana bread and Chocolate chip cookies to take with me to South Haven. I was thinking more of Jack's favorites than anyone else's. I knew I wouldn't have anything in the house, unless Carla shopped, so I thought it would be nice to have a few snacks on hand. I heard a knock at the back door. I wondered who it was because the work crew wasn't scheduled till after Christmas. When I looked out the window, I saw Clark.

"Good morning," he said stepping in to the kitchen without an invite.

"Hey!" I called out. "I wasn't expecting you, but come on in."

"I came to do a few things unless this is a bad time for you," he explained.

"No, of course, I'm glad to see you and always anxious to get more of this done," I responded.

"Your countertops are in, but I need to finish up some things first before I can have them delivered," he reported.

"Great! How was your trip?" I asked as I quickly cleared some of my things away.

"Cold and icy in some areas, so it delayed me a bit," he said taking off his coat. "Has it been quiet here, I hope?" I knew he was referring to Blade.

"I haven't heard a thing about my complaints," I said disheartened. "Do you think that's normal?"

"I don't know what to tell you, but I'm glad you haven't had any more incidents," he said getting to his work. "Are you leaving tomorrow?"

"Yes, and so far the weather for the day should be fine," I announced. "South Haven still has snow on the ground, I hear."

"I saw your tree from the window," he noted. "That's a pretty big tree for someone going away for Christmas!" I nodded and laughed.

"I love it," I said grinning. "As far as I'm concerned, I'm having my Christmas here in Borna. That church tour was really something. Things are so much more traditional around here."

"I hear ya," he said, stooping to get his tools.

"Do you have a tree in your log cabin?" I curiously asked.

"No I don't," he stated. "I have trees all around me outdoors. I did bring in some pine braches yesterday, to enjoy the holiday smell."

"Yeah, it's the best," I added. "I better let you get to work here."

I went upstairs to pack my clothes, and it was a good feeling to have Clark around again. I didn't know if it was because I felt safer or if it was something else.

All of a sudden, I heard Clark calling my name to come downstairs. He said the officer was here from the Sheriff's office. Clark had let him in the door.

I quickly came down the stairs, and we went into the living room to talk away from Clark.

"I'm sorry we didn't get back here any sooner, but we did question Mr. Schuessler and he denies your accusations, Miss Meyr," he reported looking directly in my eyes. I took a deep breath of frustration. "We did however get out of him that his client is offering him a bonus of $12,000, if he can get you to sell your place."

"Did you say $12,000?" I asked in surprise. "Who would pay him that kind of money? A realtor's commission on this house wouldn't be $12,000. Did he say who it was?"

"He said he didn't have to reveal that private information, but he did say he was from out of town," the officer said as he stood to leave. "It is a bit strange, but there isn't much I can do about an arrangement he has with a client. Without any proof of your claims, I can't do anything, but warn him."

"I understand," I said with disappointment. "Maybe your warning will make him think twice, before doing something again." The officer nodded.

Clark couldn't help but overhear what the officer told me. Before the officer left, he gave me his personal number to call if anything else occurred.

I wanted to slam the door behind him; I was so angry and frustrated. Clark looked at me like he knew what I was thinking. I folded my arms not knowing what to say.

"This place has a price, doesn't it?" Clark finally said to break the silence." I nodded and took a deep breath.

"It has James' name all over it!" I said shaking in anger. "He thinks he can get anything he wants with money. That's the way they do business."

"It still doesn't explain why he wants this place so badly," Clark noted as he stopped his work. "Perhaps you'll find out when you go back home."

"I'm not sure I can trust my behavior if I go to the court proceedings," I admitted. "Some Christmas this is going to be!"

"Well, you've still got some time to spend Christmas in Borna, so how about I treat you to dinner tonight?" he shyly asked.

"Oh, I don't know Clark," I stammered. Was he feeling sorry for me again? "I have things to do before I leave, and I'm not very good company with all of these things on my mind."

"Okay, then why don't you let me try out a few of these new appliances you've got here, and let me fix us a little dinner?" he offered. He wasn't going to take no for an answer. "I can pick up some steaks, throw a salad together and open up some Red Velvet wine you have sitting on the floor in the dining room."

"Are you serious?" I questioned feeling somewhat guilty.

"Of course," he snickered. "My family's in Florida, and I'm too busy right now to join them. You would be doing me a big favor by sharing a bite with me. I wouldn't mind trying out this red wine, I've heard you talk about. It beats having a few drinks at the winery and eating alone like I do most nights."

"Well, if you put it that way," I said agreeing to the idea.

"Did you have plans with Ellie?" he curiously asked.

"No, she's got to work tonight, but we had a celebration on our church tour," I explained to him. "I owe her so much, Clark, and I can't seem to find something really clever to give to her for Christmas."

"So if your answer is yes, I'll knock off soon after I get this piece done," he stated. "I promise I'll leave after we eat, so you'll have some time to pack." It did sound reasonable, and I thought he was sincere.

"I guess if we're going to have a decent dinner here tonight, I better whip up some of my wonderful, wheat bread," I decided with excitement.

"Are you kidding me?" he responded with a big smile. "Is there anything you can't bake? My mouth just waters hearing about it. Are you sure I won't be in your way while you cook?"

"It's pretty simple, and I've managed to all my other baking on the island, so you're fine," I conceded. What was it about a man and food?

I went directly upstairs to continue packing, and Clark went back to sanding. How sweet of him to offer dinner tonight. In his great, big, masculine body, there seemed to be a kind heart and a little boy. I thought it was interesting for him to break from his usual life style to cook here tonight. I'm sure having a little holiday cheer, with his family away, was welcomed.

When I came back downstairs, Clark was already gone. I started kneading my dough when Ellie knocked at my back door.

"Hey, just wanted to stop in to say goodbye and wish you a safe trip," she greeted me holding something behind her back. "I brought you a little present!" I washed off my hands in anticipation.

"It's too hard to gift wrap, but I knew you could really use this," Ellie divulged now showing me a lovely wine rack. It had a red bow on top of the center. "I felt sorry for you having to store your wine bottles on the floor!" We laughed.

"Oh, I wish you hadn't," I responded. "I'm still chewing on what to give you. This is a great gift, Ellie, and very useful!"

"Your friendship is quite enough," she said sweetly. "If I may ask, why are you baking bread when you're leaving town tomorrow?"

"Well, you won't believe this one," I began. "Clark has offered to fix me some dinner tonight, so this is my contribution."

"Holy Moses, Kate, when did this happen?" she asked with surprise.

"Nothing happened," I made clear. "I had an upsetting visit from the county sheriff this afternoon, and he knew how much it bothered me, so he offered to cheer me up. He wanted to take me somewhere, but I declined, so he offered to pick up a couple of steaks to grill."

"Right girl, right!" she said with sarcasm. "You've got a way with tugging at his heart! Now don't deny it! So what did the officer tell you?"

When I explained to her about Blade's $12,000 bribe, she was shocked. She agreed immediately. "Blade would fall for any bribe if he had the opportunity," she concurred. "Who else could afford to pay him but your rich brother-in-law?" I nodded in agreement.

"Please keep an eye out for me while I'm gone," I pleaded. "He knows I'll be gone, I'm sure. Who knows what he'll do. I just don't trust him. He's probably really angry, since I reported him.

"Of course, I will," Ellie reassured me. "Your handsome, dinner friend will look out for you as well, I'm sure." She gave me a sheepish grin.

"Stop it Ellie," I scolded. "Any kind of relationship for me right now is the furthest thing from my mind and his!"

CHAPTER 43

The bread was in the oven filling the house with the most amazing smell known to man. I thought about how to create a better place for a little holiday dinner, so I moved aside the love seat from the fireplace and replaced it with the game table I brought from South Haven. Placing it directly in front of the fire, it reminded me of many of the romantic restaurants where I had eaten. I put another log on the fire before getting a white cloth for the table. Seeing room for a small center piece, I went to the kitchen and filled a red glass with green pine and berries. It was simple and rather festive. I wished for my better china from home, but my plain, white-ware would have to work.

I hoped my efforts would not send any romantic signals. This table arrangement was so pleasing to me, I decided it would stay till more of my furniture arrived.

I took Carla's quilt out of the basket and finished up the twenty some inches of the binding I had yet to sew. After the quick and rewarding accomplishment, I took it upstairs with me to put in my suitcase. The Flying Geese pattern she loved turned out quite well and she would be very surprised.

I took a quick shower and put on a new sweater for the chilly evening. I avoided wearing my cologne to avoid any sign of trying to attract him.

When I heard Clark drive up, I ran downstairs to let him in. I knew to keep a good distance from him as he was now in charge of preparing the meal.

"Man, the bread smells good, Kate," he said after he took off his coat. "How do you like your steak?"

"Medium well," I revealed.

"Somehow I knew that," he nodded. "Do you have a large salad bowl?"

"Oh sure," I answered as I went to a large box sitting on the floor. He laughed. It was a nice wooden bowl with matching salad bowls.

"I'll go pour us some wine," I suggested so I could get out of his way. "The bread needs to come out in five minutes." He was so intense on his mission, I wasn't sure he heard me.

Clark was experimenting with the grill which came with my new fancy stove. I was trying to observe how he used it, since it was all new to me. The steaks began to simmer, which added another aroma to the room. I couldn't remember if at any time a man had cooked for me.

"Oh Kate, your table looks good here!" Clark said when he saw the new arrangement in the living room.

"It's all I have right now, but it beats sitting on the sunshine chairs!" I joked with a giggle. "Cotton always refers to my director's chairs as sunshine chairs because they're such a bright yellow."

"He's been a great help to you, hasn't he?" Clark commented as he pulled out a chair for me.

"Yes," I nodded. "I want to keep him employed in some way as long as I can. I know he'll be helpful when they start on the garage, plus any spring, yard work I'll need done. I also plan on Susie helping with house cleaning at some point." I got up to bring out the bread. He followed me to get the steaks.

After I placed the salad bowl on the table, I announced it was time to enjoy the feast.

"I'd like to make a toast to a safe and successful holiday!" Clark said lifting his glass of wine. We clanked glasses.

"I would like to make a toast to the first ever man to prepare a dinner for me!" I announced after I took another sip. "Merry Christmas!" We clanked our glasses again. He repeated the wish with a strange look on his face.

We'd just started eating, when Maggie called. I ignored it so we could start indulging. I told Clark I would call her later.

"Maggie is a good friend of yours, like Ellie?" Clark asked as he took a slice of the warm bread.

"Yes, a very old friend, since grade school," I explained smiling. "Of course, she's not happy about my decision to move here, but she did admit, I seemed to be a lot happier since I came to Borna."

"Oh Kate, this bread is the best!" he complimented. I could tell he was enjoying each bite before he spoke again. "Not to bring up a sore subject, but are you still going to avoid going to court?" I hated to think about it.

"I told my lawyer not to expect me," I stated. "I still have to update her on what I suspect James has been up to here in Borna."

Clark didn't respond. "This steak is so delicious, Clark!" I declared. "It is so tender and just the way I like it. I'll have to start utilizing that grill. This salad dressing is very good, too! I saw you mixing up some things. What do I taste?"

"It's a secret," he teased pouring more wine for himself.

We carried on our conversation about cooking and how I loved to bake. I knew how he kept his personal life close to his chest, so I didn't ask all the questions I was dying to know.

When we finished, I offered him my chocolate chip cookies, but he declined.

"I have a Christmas present for you in the car," Clark surprisingly announced.

"Oh, no, don't tell me that," I reacted. "Ellie just dropped off a wine rack for me, and I didn't have a gift for her or for you!"

"That's good," he said going towards the door. "I almost didn't give this up! Hold on! I'll be right back."

He rushed outdoors without his coat, and within a minute, he came back inside with a wood carving about 20 inches high. I recognized it instantly. It was a carving of my large Maple tree in the back yard. It looked just like it did now in the winter time.

"I did a sketch of this tree some time back because of its unusual shape" he revealed. "I love the twisted trunk and thought it would look good carved in rosewood. It was sort of an experiment for me. As much as I like it, it should reside here, where it really belongs!" I was speechless. I knew this had to be a time consuming creation. How could he just give this a way?

"It is so awesome, Clark," I marveled as I took it from his

hands. "This is so very generous of you. I'm very much honored to have any of your work in this house. This is so special! Is it signed somewhere?"

"It is," he nodded. "It has last year's date with my signature." He turned it over for me to see.

"Thank you so, so much," I said wanting to hug him, but didn't dare. "Until I bring in more furniture, it might look great on this mantel, where everyone can admire it." He nodded with approval.

"Well, let me help you clean up the table here," he offered carrying out a couple of plates.

"Oh, it's early, Clark," I said without thinking. It seemed like he just arrived.

"You have an early start tomorrow, and I'm sure I've delayed some of your preparation with this dinner, so I best get going."

"Can I send the rest of the bread home with you, as a token of thanks, since I didn't have a gift for you?" I proposed.

"You won't have an argument there," he said smiling. I quickly wrapped the bread in foil as he brought the salad bowls into the kitchen.

"You have a safe trip tomorrow and have a good time with that son of yours," Clark said as he put on his coat.

"I will and hope you don't work too hard," I said rather sadly. "Merry Christmas!" He grinned and waved as he walked out the door.

I stood on the deck, freezing, till he drove away. I couldn't believe this man's generosity. I closed the door and went to the living room to stare at my beautiful Maple tree. Two dear friends had given me gifts so personal in meaning. As I cleared up the dishes, I kept trying to think of some way to repay them both!

CHAPTER 44

After a restless night's sleep, a warm light woke me up. I guessed I had overslept. I looked at the clock, and it was only 5:00 am. It took me awhile to realize the warm spirit was once again glowing in this room. I laid back to absorb the loving feeling. I couldn't explain what this was all about, but there was nothing, not to like about it. I wanted to relish in it and go back to sleep, but since I intended to get up early, I took it as a wakeup call and got dressed. I had most everything ready to go. I would stop at a fast food place when I got on the interstate and pick up coffee and breakfast. It would be a good feeling getting into my car knowing I would be returning to 6229 Main Street.

Driving out of Borna at an early hour was terribly dark, since there were no street lights along the way. Very few businesses had any light shining at all. The only traffic was the fast moving lumber trucks, which were on their way with a mission. I once again passed massive open spaces of land owned by the lumberyard. Would they ever run out of trees to cut in this county, I wondered? It reminded me of Meyr Lumber and what they may be going through right now.

I finally stopped for gas and purchased a hot cup of coffee. Feeling more alert, I decided to call Maggie before I got back on the interstate.

"I'm on my way, girlfriend," I cheerfully stated.

"Terrific!" she responded in her early morning voice. "When do you think you'll be here?"

"I'm really not sure, but I'll be at the Golden Bakery tomorrow morning as we planned," I assured her. "Jack will be coming home later tonight if his flight goes as scheduled."

"I can't wait to see you, and neither can Carla," Maggie said with excitement. "We both can help you in the next couple of days, so I hope you let us!" she offered. "I wish you weren't in such a big hurry to get back to Borna."

"I've got too many workers depending on me, Maggie," I explained. "I'm also anxious to be there at the start of the New Year. Ellie is having a party at the winery, and I told her I would help if she needed me to."

"I got the message, Kate," Maggie said reluctantly. "I just can't believe this is all happening!"

"Don't worry, forever friend," I said to console her. "I've got to get back on the road, so I'll see you tomorrow morning."

Once on the interstate, it was easy for my mind to wander. I couldn't help but replay what happened last night with Clark. His gift of the carved tree was a friendly gesture I sure didn't expect. At least I meant a little something to him. I knew he was happy with his lifestyle, which took pressure off of me. I always liked having male friends. Women seem to be more about their feelings than seeing things in the bigger picture as men seemed to do. When I remembered how he accepted the leftover bread like a little boy, it made me smile. Didn't they say the way to a man's heart was through his stomach? Why wasn't that true of Clay?

About 4:00 in the afternoon, I got a call from Jack on my cell saying his flight would be delayed a bit. He said he'd be home around 10:00. He was taking a cab instead of accepting Carla's offer to pick him up.

I had another three hours to go before I would see the red lighthouse of South Haven. It always made me smile. It was truly our town's signature. I didn't want to think about permanently leaving South Haven. There was so much there to love. I should probably reinvest some money from the house in a small apartment or condo along the beach. I decided to bring up the idea with Jack tomorrow.

Being with Jack would definitely bring back memories of Clay. How would Jack react if he knew about his Dad's mistress? He never even wanted to admit his Dad had a drinking problem. Jack would have to be told about James' desire to own the house and land in Borna. He would likely pick up on friction between the Meyrs and myself when I wouldn't be attending Meyr functions over Christmas.

As I was crossing the familiar drawbridge and facing Lake Michigan in the depth of darkness, I couldn't believe I had finally arrived in South Haven! In the spring and summer the draw bridge would be lined with flower boxes of Begonias. The lights of the late night establishments and the traditional, Christmas lights were still aglow, to welcome me.

As I approached my neighborhood, I was reminded of the

beautiful, commercially decorated homes in the neighborhood. What a contrast from the simple more religious displays, I left behind in Borna. There was something almost phony and insincere about the competition the neighborhood had created for themselves over the years. When I got to my residence however, I saw total darkness, with an exception of a light inside the entry way. I was pleased that Carla had remembered to keep it on.

As I pulled into the garage it seemed I was entering a strange, yet somewhat familiar place. There sat Clay's SUV, as it were waiting for him to hop in and drive at any moment. Having Clay's car would be convenient for Jack to drive while he was home.

The house smelled stuffy, yet familiar, as I turned on more lights. When I walked into the kitchen, there was a note from Carla on the counter, where she frequently communicated with me. It said "Welcome Home," and she'd be touch base with me in the morning.

Somehow I didn't feel like a welcome home was appropriate any longer. If I had my way, I'd turn around right now and go back to Borna. Perhaps seeing Maggie, Carla, and Jack would change my feelings.

I had just finished unpacking, when I heard Jack rush in the front door.

"Hey Mom, we're home!" he said lifting me up with a big hug. He did say we're, instead of I'm, I noticed. Feeling his embrace made me realize how much I missed him.

"How was your flight?" I asked.

"Delayed, but not by much," he said looking about the room. "Wow, things are changing here! It's starting to look pretty empty!"

"You're so right!" I said nodding. "Carla has taken some

things she always liked, and I took some pieces to Borna. You better speak up soon on what you want to keep, so I can get them included in the move. If you want them sent to New York, I can do that. My house in Borna is big so I'm happy to keep some things there for you if you want me to. I can't wait for you to see it Jack." He looked at me more seriously.

"Mom, you're not running away from things are you?" he wisely asked. I didn't see this question coming.

"That's a very good question Jack," I noted. "If you would've asked me the first week I went to Borna, I would've said yes. The beauty and comfort there make me feel I can be happy once again. I don't know if you knew, but it's a huge lumber town. I think your Dad and Grandfather did business there."

"Funny, I never heard them talk about it," Jack observed. "I'm happy for you, Mom, but it's just going to be different from now on. What did the Meyrs have to say about your move?"

"I was going to explain it all to you tomorrow, but since you've asked, I'll share the latest happenings," I said as I prayed for help. Jack quickly went to get a beer and joined me on the den couch.

I tried to be as fair as I could describing James' behavior. I began by telling him how mystified I was with James' desire to get his hands on the property in Borna. When I told him what he had arranged with Blade, I knew I had hit a nerve.

"But Dad left it to you, probably thinking of me as well, don't you think?" Jack surmised.

"Absolutely Jack," I confirmed. "Your Grandfather left it to your Dad, not James. It was probably for a good reason. Your Dad was your Grandfather's favorite over James, and now I see why. James is not doing such a great job with managing the lumberyard from what I hear. It's like he wants revenge!"

"I never did care much for Uncle James," Jack admitted with a deep breath. "He never treated the employees the way Dad did. I have a couple of friends who were employed there, and they said Uncle James was not popular!"

"Well, if they were working there recently, they may not be there now, the way they're laying off folks," I reported. "James obviously feels he has the money for purchasing the Borna property despite how poorly the company is doing."

"So you're not going to show up in court?" he sadly asked.

"I don't want to see any of them right now till it's settled once and for all," I explained. "My lawyer said they're going to try to discredit your Dad. They'll talk about what an alcoholic he was, and that he didn't know what he was doing in regard to the property. They want to make a case that it should have stayed on the Meyr side of the family in the hands of James."

"It's all crazy, Mom," Jack said getting up with frustration. "There's something else going on here!"

"I'm glad you understand my circumstances," I said with a loving smile. Jack was becoming more and more mature, I observed. "We both now live in places where we want to be. Maggie and Carla are really the only family I feel I have left here in South Haven." He sadly nodded.

"Let's get to bed; I'm dead tired," he said with a yawn.
"I couldn't agree more," I said following him down the hall. I thanked God for the positive outcome to our conversation.

CHAPTER 45

When I awoke the next morning, the first thing I did was call Maggie to report the latest news I had received from the Sheriff's office about Blade. I wanted to get the unpleasant conversation out of the way before we met at the bakery. I told her I thought it was James offering the bribe. She asked if I had definite proof. I had to admit I didn't, which made me a bit uncomfortable.

It was Christmas Eve, but I reminded myself I had a lot to do with the movers coming in just 2 days. There wasn't time for celebration, but I thought it would be nice to attend my church in the evening.

I called Carla on my way to the bakery, and we agreed she would come over Christmas Day and help me cook for the three of us. She said she would bring Rocky with her knowing Jack and I would like to see him.

When I walked in the crowded bakery with its heavenly

smell, I felt a sense of being home. I found Maggie in one of our favorite booths, far in the corner of the bakery. I reached to give her a big hug. Somehow we started giggling just like when we were back in grade school together.

"I got you your favorite blueberry scone," Maggie cheerfully revealed.

"Wonderful!" I responded as I remembered its crystal, sugar coating. "Remind me when I leave, to go next door to the Blueberry Shop. I want to take back some of their goodies for my friends in Borna. I'm also making Jack his favorite blueberry muffins tomorrow morning. It's all about blueberries now!" She laughed shaking her head.

"I can't wait to see Jack," Maggie noted. "I'll try to stop by for a while tomorrow to say hello."

"He'll love it!" I added. "Carla will be with us cooking, so stop by anytime. Jack has a pretty serious girlfriend now, it seems. I'll fill you in, as I learn more. It's been really good for him."

"A boyfriend of sorts would probably be good for his Mother, too," Maggie teased.

"No way, girlfriend," I stated in denial. "That's the last thing I need right now! Don't get me wrong, I have always enjoyed having male friends."

I decided not to tell her about Clark, and how he fit that description. She would interpret it as something else. We visited about an hour before I left to visit the Blueberry Shop.

What fun it was to gather up all the unique variations of blueberry offerings. There was everything from blueberry pie filling to chocolate covered blueberries. I thought Ellie would enjoy trying the blueberry BBQ sauce and blueberry wine. I loved their blueberry pancake syrup so I bought the largest bottle they had. When I went to the counter to check out, I couldn't believe who was standing in front of me. It was Sandra, James' wife, and their daughter Emily. I couldn't ignore them.

"Why hello!" I began. "Emily, I haven't seen you for so long! How is MU?" They both turned in surprise.

"Hey, Aunt Kate," Emily said with her beaming smile. "I love it! Say, did Jack make it home?"

"Yes, and hopefully he is out of bed by now!" I joked. "He looks great, and he'd be glad to see you, I'm sure!" I could see Sandra getting very nervous on how to respond.

"Emily, would you take these things on to the car?" Sandra asked as she gave Emily her bag. "I need a word with Kate if you don't mind." Emily looked puzzled.

"Sure," she responded. "Good to see you, Aunt Kate. I guess you'll be over tomorrow!" I just smiled and looked at Sandra. She took a deep breath before she spoke.

"I know you've been through a lot, Kate, losing Clay and all, but would you please, please, rethink about keeping the property in Borna?" she pleaded. I started to speak, but she interrupted. "Clay wouldn't appreciate you being a part of the Meyr Lumber Company's demise. We all thought we knew you better than that!"

"What are you talking about?" I asked feeling my blood pressure rise.

"Don't play your typical innocence with me, Kate," she smirked. "Clay left you plenty and more, but I guess it wasn't enough for you." She gave me a stern look and walked out the door. I was speechless.

I felt myself shaking all the way to the car. I was trying not to drop my shopping bags as I opened the car door. When I got in the driver's seat, I had to sit there and digest what just happened. How could I possibly be a part of Meyr Lumber's demise? What did she mean? She should be asking her husband, not me. What kind of trouble were they in?

I decided to set aside my negative thoughts till I was finished with my errands. I stopped in at The Quilt Shop to say hello to Cornelia. She was one of the Beach Quilters, and she would be sure to fill me in on any gossip. She quickly asked if I would make my customary blueberry block for the raffle quilt. I assured her I would without hesitation. I could see there was so much new in the shop, but I didn't have to browse. I grabbed a few charming fat quarters she had just gotten in and told her I would be ordering from her web site, since there wasn't a quilt shop near Borna. Having a quilt shop nearby was something I enjoyed and would miss it very much. Cornelia was always so friendly and she established a great tourist trade. Even if you didn't need the fabric, sometimes you just had to feel and absorb the beauty. With a shop owner like Cornelia, you were always kept abreast of the latest in quilting, as well as the latest gossip in South Haven.

By the time I got home in the late afternoon, Jack was getting ready to go out.

"I told Kevin and the guys I'd meet up with them at Clementia's!" Jack said putting on his coat. "I hope you don't mind."

"Of course not. Have fun," I encouraged. "I think I'm going to church tonight, so I'll see you in the morning to share some blueberry muffins." He gave me a big smile. "Just be careful."

"I will, and I'm glad you remembered to make the muffins," he said about to go out the door. "Love you!" He blew me a kiss.

Now I was alone and had time to revisit what happened during my day. I kicked off my boots and made myself a cup of hot tea.

I unpacked some of my purchases and went to sit on my chilly, sunporch. I seemed to gravitate to this spot when I was lonely or worried about Clay. If people really felt badly for me, why wouldn't they be happy for me? I had to dismiss the negative thoughts.

Instead I decided to think about Borna, which made me smile inside. What was it like on Christmas Eve in Borna? Would all the little churches ring their bells at the same time tonight? Would they get snow? Was Ellie at the winery or was she closed for Christmas Eve? Was Clark sitting by the fire in his log cabin eating my left over wheat bread? Even though I couldn't answer these questions, the very thought of Borna brought me peace.

When I came in from the porch, I freshened up before going to church. I thought I might stop at Tello's after church and bring home one of their great pizzas. I wanted to experience all the good tastes of South Haven before I left.

When I got to church, I purposely sat in the back pew so not to be noticed. I had a lot of questions to ask God. I really needed his reassurance on this trip. The church's talented, hand bell choir was performing. I had forgotten how the sounds of Christmas brought back memories. As I gazed at the two, large artificial trees on each side of the altar, I thought of how more effective real trees would have been.

I left the church in a more festive mood, so I stopped at Tello's to get my pizza for dinner. I was pleased to see it was nearly empty. I sat at the bar to place my order to take home. The server behind the bar asked if I was Mrs. Meyr. She said she went to school with Jack and wondered if he was home for the holidays.

I nearly left the restaurant unnoticed till I saw Will Cummings sit across the side bar from me. Will worked with Clay so I had to acknowledge him.

"Kate, my goodness, how are you?" he pleasantly asked.

"Very well! I'm just picking up a pizza to take home," I answered politely. "How are Edith and the girls?"

"I assume they are fine, but I guess you didn't hear, we are now divorced," he divulged. "Believe me, otherwise I wouldn't be at the bar at Tello's on Christmas Eve!" Suddenly he knew it was a foolish thing to say with me sitting at the bar.

"I'm sorry," I said preparing to pay my bill.

"Say, can I buy you a drink?" he asked in a tone I was not expecting. "After all, it's Christmas Eve!"

"No, sorry, I have things to do when I get home." I said looking a bit embarrassed. "Thanks anyway!" Was he hitting on me?

"Well, I hear you'll be moving to Borna, Missouri," he stated while he still had my attention. "That's where the big East Perry Lumber yard is located."

"Why yes, how did you know?" I asked in surprise. "Did Clay mention Borna to you?" He shook his head.

"I'm sorry, I shouldn't have gone there," he said taking another sip of his beer. It was obvious he wasn't going to elaborate on the subject. "Hey, Kate, I'm glad you are finding some happiness. Here's my card if you ever want to just visit some time. I want you to know, a day doesn't go by I don't miss Clay. The place hasn't been the same since he was killed. I miss him!" I didn't know what to say. I just nodded.

"Here ya go, Mrs. Meyr," the girl said handing me my pizza box. "Have a Merry Christmas!"

I nodded, smiled, and wished them both a Merry Christmas.

CHAPTER 46

I awoke the next morning at 7:00. I was pleased to get some badly needed sleep. It was Christmas morning. There were so many memories on this special day, like anticipated visits from Santa in my childhood days. Clay and I, too shared many good Christmases with Jack. There were many a Christmas Eve Clay would be assembling a bike for Jack. What happened to those years? Now Jack and I were trying to find ourselves a new life! It was hard on a day like Christmas not to look back. I needed to get out of bed and look ahead. This was my last holiday in South Haven, so I wanted it to be a good one.

I looked out the window and saw that very little snow had accumulated from the night before. I turned on the fireplaces to take off the morning chill. Now it was the time to get those muffins baking. There was something wonderful about the anticipation of baking. It brought back memories of my mother assembling her baking ingredients as I waited patiently for the finished product.

I stayed in my heavy, terry cloth robe as I began my baking mission. After I got the muffins in the oven, I turned on some Christmas music to inspire my late night son to rise and shine.

Carla would be here by 11:00. I smiled at the thought of giving her the quilt, I'd made. I didn't have a Christmas tree to display her present, so I put it near the fireplace in the den. My living room was too formal to enjoy our casual Christmas. Then, I was off to shower and dress.

When I returned to the kitchen, Jack was pouring himself some coffee.

"Merry Christmas, Mom," Jack said giving me a hug.

"Same to you honey," I replied kissing him on the cheek. "Did you have a nice time last night?"

"Sure did," he said grinning. "We closed quite a few places!" He looked at me for a reaction.

"Let's go eat in the den by the fire," I suggested. "I'll bring in the muffins."

We sat there reminiscing about past Christmases and sharing simple thoughts. It wasn't long, before he mentioned Jenny. It was the second time he suggested Jenny should come to visit South Haven and meet me. I encouraged the idea. It was so special to see his face light up when he talked about her. I told him, I might hop on a plane and come to visit the two of them! The look on his face showed his approval.

Carla arrived before we were dressed. She brought Rocky, who was so happy to see us he jumped all over us. He ran around the whole house in his excitement. Carla sprang into action getting our meal for the day going. She made pre-stuffed, turkey breasts and put them in the oven on a low heat. She began giving Jack a few man chores she had saved up for him. I got busy setting the table, singing along to a Christmas carol in the background. The sights and sounds of a family Christmas brought a smile to my face.

As we waited for dinner to be ready, Maggie arrived at our front door with presents in her hands. "I can't stay long, but I had a few gifts for all of you," she happily announced.

"Great! Why don't you come in to join us," I invited. "We're about to open our gifts, while we wait for our dinner to be ready."

"I can fix a mean whiskey sour for you, Maggie," Jack offered. "I remember how much you like those!" Maggie agreed to join us, as Jack went into the kitchen to get us some beverages.

We all seemed to be talking at once as we started opening our gifts. When Carla saw her quilt, I thought she was going to cry. Everyone seemed to be very impressed with my efforts considering my circumstances.

"When in the world did you have time to make to make a quilt, for heaven's sake?" Carla asked in her excitement.

"I'm not really sure Carla, but I knew I wanted it finished," I confided. "I knew you would appreciate it." I knew I had hit the jackpot, pleasing her.

Carla wasn't the only one to get something quilted. Maggie made me four table runners. There was one for each season. What a nice thing to receive for my new home. My best buddy always could think of something clever when it came to gift giving. Jack was quite pleased with the healthy check I wrote him, as well as his new attaché case with his engraved initials.

Maggie had to be on her way, and Carla beckoned us to the dining room to enjoy our meal for Christmas day. I was trying not to remind myself about this last meal here. Without any words spoken, I knew Jack realized it as well.

The rest of the day and evening, we spent getting boxes and furniture identified for the movers. Jack did want to keep his bedroom furniture, so off to Borna it would go! Carla said she would return in the morning to clean up the place after the mover's left. Now it all became exciting to me like an adventure. Jack turned in early because of his little sleep from the night before. For me it was a late night, as I struggled to get to sleep.

CHAPTER 47

As I lay half-awake the next morning, I pictured a court scene with James stating his case about 6229 Main Street. Was I having second thoughts as to whether I should attend court today? I knew it would cause havoc rescheduling the movers, so I convinced myself I made the right decision. Right or wrong, I would know the outcome by the end of the day.

Jack and I met in the kitchen at the same time for breakfast. We both knew it would be the last day in this house. We would also be separated from each other for some time. He saw the sadness on my face.

"Mom, it's gonna be alright," Jack finally said putting his arm around me. "I can't wait to visit Borna. The pictures you sent are beautiful. Don't worry about what James is trying to do. He's barking up the wrong tree, and I think he'll be sorry."

"Thanks, honey," I nodded. "That means a lot. The movers

233

will be here soon, so guess I better get dressed. I'm just having coffee, but you might want to eat something."

I heard Carla arrive, coming in the back door. She joined us with mixed emotions on her face. She observed the serious look on our faces and reassured us she would take care of any last minute details.

I went into my bedroom to dress, trying to think clearly about my trip ahead. I sat on the side of the bed and asked for God's guidance on the new adventures Jack and I were about to make. I added a prayer for James, hoping he would find understanding in Clay's wishes. I hated having any dissention between the Meyr family and me. It wasn't supposed to be that way.

Carla came into the bedroom and saw my quiet meditation. "I'm going to miss you so much, Miss Kate," she said with tears welling in her eyes. She sat down beside me.

"Oh Carla, I feel the same, but you know I can't stay here," I said sniffling a bit.

"I know, I know," she muffled behind her Kleenex. "You've been so good to me through the years. I will never be able to thank you."

"I will continue to help you," I assured her. "I hope you'll visit me!"

"I'm not one to travel, as you know," she sadly noted. I nodded.

"I've been thinking about getting a little condo or apartment by the beach, so I have a place to stay when I come back here," I revealed. "Jack would also enjoy having such a place."

"Really?" she said with a big smile. "I could certainly keep it in shape for you," I laughed and gave her a nod.

"I'll have my realtor keep an eye out, and you might

want to do so as well," I added. "Right now, I just want to get moved."

"Yes, indeed," Carla said getting up from the bed.

My cell, lying on the bedside table, began to ring. I looked and it was my lawyer Susan.

"What is it?" I asked with concern. They couldn't possibly be finished at the court house!

"Are you sitting down?" she asked strangely.

"Actually, I'm sitting on the side of my bed," I quickly responded.

"James has dropped the case," she bluntly stated.
"What?" When?" I asked in a loud voice.

"His lawyer called me when I got to the office this morning," she informed me. "He just said James had a change of heart and wasn't going to protest."

"I can't believe it!" I said with some hesitation.

"I'm sure something happened to change his mind," Susan assumed. "Frankly, I think Carl, his attorney, knew they didn't have a case, and the loss would embarrass him. I'm sure the melancholy of the Christmas season didn't hurt either."

"This is such wonderful news, Susan," I said wanting to cry. "I'm sure there is more to the story. Do you think I should call and thank him?"

"Oh, no, Kate," she said firmly. "I'm sure you are the last person he wants to hear from right now. It is a case filed "without prejudice," meaning he can come back to sue at any time if he should find more information to support his actions. Do you want me to request payment for legal fees?"

"No, please don't," I said wanting it all to end. I thanked her with all my heart before we said goodbye.

When I hung up the phone, I saw Jack standing by the

bedroom door. He had overheard most of the conversation. He looked shocked, as if he didn't know what to say. I put my hands over my face and broke into tears. It was such a relief. He came over to me and put his arm around me.

"I think my Dad may have helped us out here," he admitted. "Thank goodness, it's all over."

Emotions had to be set aside, as the movers took over my house. I had to be in charge of my thoughts, as I watched my belongings disperse very quickly. I questioned the movers once again about the road conditions, and they assured me we would be fine.

Jack packed my car to its utmost capacity. I could hardly see out the back rear view mirror.

"Mom, you should have taken Dad's SUV," Jack suggested in earnest.

"I'm more comfortable in my car right now, and besides, he'd want you to have it. It will be here for you until you decide what to do with it. I do want to get a different vehicle when I get settled. I may decide to get one of those jeeps. What do you think about that?" Jack and Carla laughed.

Carla kept herself very busy so she wouldn't break down in tears again. As it got closer to the time to leave, I told her I may return for the closing of the house. I reminded her to keep an eye out for a little place close to the beach, which brought a smile to her face.

Saying goodbye to Jack was difficult, and yet it all seemed right. He promised he would visit Borna as soon as he could. I encouraged him to bring Jenny. We both seemed to be excited for what was ahead for both of us.

As I was about to get in the car, my realtor drove in the driveway.

"I just wanted to say goodbye Kate and thank you for your business," she began. "I also have a closing date set for the house. It will be in three weeks. If you can't make the trip, we'll fax everything to you."

"I'm not sure about the trip just yet," I said with hesitation. "This winter could be a challenge with travel. Say, do you know if the condo you once told me about, on North Lakeshore Drive, is still available? You thought it would sell quickly."

"I can check, why?" she said with a puzzled look.

"I'll need to reinvest the money from this house, so thought Jack and I might enjoy coming back to visit in a place on the beach." Her face lit up.

"Well, Miss Meyr, I can assure you, if it is sold, I will find you another one!" she offered with excitement.

"Great," I said watching them close the door of the moving van.

She was happy to hear my news and waved good-bye, to Jack and me.

The time had come for me, to get in my car and be on my way. Carla walked my way and handed me my purse with her eyes looking to the ground.

"It's freezing out here, you two!" I yelled. "I love you both, and I'll call you when I get to Borna!"

Tight hugs and kisses were now in order. I dreaded this very moment, but it was step number one to my new life without Clay. I held in my emotions and got in my car. I drove away and didn't look back.

I followed the van out of South Haven, trying to think of the route ahead. When I finally got on the Interstate, I left the van behind.

I had a good visit, I told myself. It was a very different Christmas, but I was ready for something different. God had answered my prayer concerning James, and I was very grateful. It was a good omen of my future. Twenty miles down the road, I pulled off to get gas and call Ellie.

"You got away, did you?" her cheery voice asked. Did she think I would change my mind?

"I did, Ellie," I happily answered. "I'm getting gas right now. The van is somewhere behind me. How is everything there?"

"It's a bright, sunny day, despite the bitter cold," she reported.

"I have good news!" I announced. "James dropped the lawsuit right before court time."

"Holy mackerel, Kate!" Ellie shouted. "Miracles never cease, do they?"

"I still can't believe it," I confessed. "I still wonder what changed his mind."

"Well, we'll have a lot to celebrate when you get here!" she said before we ended our conversation.

I continued on my way, trying not to gloat too much with my contentment. There was always the theory, if something good happened, something bad was soon to follow!

I kept driving with only one food stop for a hamburger and chocolate shake. I felt entitled to eat fast food, after avoiding it for so many years. Part of me still wanted to get back at Clay for him wanting me to be more like him. I hoped it would go away soon. I wanted to find my own way to becoming healthy and happy.

I arrived on the county road at dusk. It would've been nice to arrive in Borna before dark. I still wasn't used to the severe darkness in the country compared to the likes of South Haven.

Now, places I passed were familiar to me. I was feeling at peace with a sense of returning home. I wondered if I would ever tire of the natural beauty these rolling hills provide.

When I pulled into my drive behind my house, it was like I had never left. I knew the winding roads would slow down the moving van, unlike the many lumber trucks which dominated this road.

When I came in the kitchen door, I turned off the alarm and sensed the stuffy odor. I slowly walked into the other rooms and saw a thirsty, dying, Christmas tree. I put down my purse and immediately watered the tree, in hopes of saving it till New Year's Eve. I passed the game table now placed in front of the fireplace. Memories flashed in my mind about the dinner Clark and I had shared in the very spot. I turned on every light I passed to let the house know I was truly home.

I went upstairs to turn on the lights and check on things so I'd be ready for the furniture delivery. Jack's bedroom set would go in the quilt room, so I carefully folded up Josephine's quilt and laid it at the foot of my bed. Quilts belong on a bed anyway, not on the floor.

I returned downstairs to turn up the temperature in the house and glance at all my mail. The van still hadn't arrived, so I went to my car to start unloading small and personal things. To my surprise, Cotton pulled up as I opened my car door.

"Welcome home, Miss Kate!" he yelled. I don't know why he always had to use Miss before my name.

"Thanks. I can't believe I'm really home!" I responded easily, using the word home. "The moving van should be here any minute."

"Well, let me help you unload the car," he offered.

"Great," I said as I handed him some hanging bags of clothing. "Everything is labeled for a particular room."

"Alrighty then," he said with enthusiasm. "Say, Miss Kate, how did the court case go?"

"Very well!" I said shaking my head at the outcome. "He dropped the lawsuit at the last minute, which truly shocked me."

"Oh lardy, Miss Kate!" he bellowed. "That's very good news. Hey, I think we got company!"

Just then the moving van pulled into the drive. Cotton quickly moved his truck. I went into the house to start directing traffic with boxes and furniture. I was so glad my move was taking place in the dark, or the whole community would be here observing all my belongings. My cell rang with Jack's name showing up.

"Are you there yet, Mom?' Jack eagerly asked.

"Yes, honey!" I reported. "I've been here about an hour. Did your plane get off on time?"

"Yeah, I'm good and all settled," he happily said.

"There's a lot of commotion here with all the movers, so I better call you later, okay? Will you do me a favor and call Carla? She'll want to know I arrived safely."

"Sure, Mom. I'll call you this week," he promised. "Love you!"

"Great. I love you, too!" I said signing off.

When the movers and Cotton left, I closed the door with great relief. It was DONE! I found a path between the boxes to get to the stairway. It was a long day and time to turn in!

CHAPTER 48

A bright light was shining in my window the next morning. It reminded me of one of my favorite sayings, "This is the day the Lord hath made; let us rejoice and be glad in it."

I got up moving cautiously. There was no question; this move had its physical results on my body. As I showered, I hoped the hot water would cure my aches and pains. When I got out to dress, I heard my cell ringing. It was my dear neighbor and friend, Ellie.

"Welcome home!" she cheered. "I saw the van last night coming home, but I didn't think you needed my interruption. I was pretty exhausted myself and anxious to get to bed. I saw Cotton's truck there so I'm glad you had some help.

"Yes, it all went well," I reported. "It did get rather late before everyone left.

"If you have coffee made, I can bring you some of Mrs.

Grebing's coffeecake," Ellie offered, knowing how it would please me.

"Oh, it would sure hit the spot!" I said enthusiastically. "Borna is going to make me a chubby country girl, yet!" We both laughed.

I rushed downstairs to put on coffee. I couldn't take the smile off my face as I looked at all my possessions sitting here at 6229 Main Street.

When Ellie arrived, I was making a fire in the fireplace. We sat ourselves at the game table. She teased me about its new location. She was referring to my intimate dinner with Clark. I told her I liked it here, for now.

All on Ellie's mind was the planning for her New Year's Eve party, the next day. It all sounded too gay for me, but she was a good business woman and folks loved going there year after year. Clay and I always left our County Club's big affair early. Towards the end of the evening, people became other people with all the liquor consumed. She said I would be welcome to sit at a table with Mary Catherine and Betsy. I guess according to Borna's standards, it was designated as the single's table. I told her with the unpredictable weather, I would take a wait and see attitude.

As I listened to Ellie's schedule, it reminded me how everyone here in Borna had their own job and responsibilities. They all had a routine and their circle of friends. Now I would no longer be considered new or a guest. I would need my own routine.

Ellie went on her way doing errands. As I cleaned the table and stared at my unfinished kitchen, I saw Clark arrive in my drive way. I happily greeted him as I opened the kitchen door.

"How was your trip?" he asked so politely. "Good Christmas, I hope!"

"It all went well," I responded as I closed the door against the bitter cold. "Everything arrived late last night, so I have a big mess here. If anything is in your way, I'll get it moved." He nodded as he got straight to his work.

"I think I'll be fine, thank you," he said, not looking up from his tool box. "I hope to finish this cupboard today. It appears you have a lot to fill it with." I nodded and laughed.

After a few moments of silence, Clark finally asked what I'm sure he wanted to know as soon as he arrived. "It's none of my business, but how did the court case turn out?"

"He dropped it right before court time!" I bluntly said. "No one really knows why, but his lawyer simply said he had a change of heart."

"Makes you wonder why, doesn't it," Clark said with hesitation. "He didn't sound like a man who would back off, unless he used the suit as a scare tactic."

"My lawyer thinks he knew this case would not have a positive outcome, and he didn't want to be embarrassed," I explained. "He may have thought since I wasn't appearing in court, I had a pretty solid case of defense."

"I guess he knew you pretty well," Clark teased.

"That might actually be true because his wife would have never defied or embarrassed anyone in the Meyr family," I added. "Well, I'll leave you to your work. I have plenty to unpack, upstairs."

The rest of the day seemed like a blur. I was going from one box to another and rearranging furniture as if I didn't have a pain in my body. It was late afternoon before I realized I hadn't had lunch, and it was near the dinner hour.

I came downstairs and smelled the latest coat of stain Clark had put on the cupboard. He was nowhere around. He just left without saying goodbye. I was learning that was his style. The cupboard was very beautiful. I could picture my Grandmother's Havilland china displayed inside. The elegant crystal I had collected over the years would look great there as well. I'd never challenged Clay with my antique collectables because our house was designed to be modern and uncluttered just the way he like it. I looked forward to the fun of rediscovering all my treasures. Borna would be their new, happy home.

I was ready to call it a day and went to the case of Red Velvet wine sitting on the floor. I opened a bottle and grabbed some cheese and crackers. Tomorrow morning, I would make a trip to the larger grocery store in Dresden.

I sat down on my love seat by the fire and noticed snow spitting in the air as I looked out the window. The thought of going to tomorrow's New Year's Eve party was concerning me. The year was ending. I had accomplished a lot under stressful circumstances. I looked forward to getting settled in during the New Year and all the fun it would be!

CHAPTER 49

As soon as I finished my coffee the next morning, I ventured out to the grocery store. I could get carried away shopping quite easily now, since I wasn't going anywhere, anytime soon. I tried to remember when I had been in a real, grocery store. I saw a few familiar faces as I walked with my grocery cart, but no one said hello. I knew the snow was accumulating outdoors, and I wanted to get home as quickly as I could. The threat of snow was making me think twice about my evening plans.

When I arrived in my driveway, so did Cotton. He helped carry in the groceries and started cleaning snow off my sidewalks. I politely asked if he would mind putting Jack's bed together after he was finished. After I put the groceries away, I started some vegetable soup which got Cotton's attention.

"Is Clark coming by today?" Cotton asked taking me by surprise.

"I think he'd be here by now, if he was," I teased. "It is New Year's Eve and something tells me Clark could care less. Do you and Susie have plans tonight?"

"Nope. Haven't gone out on New Year's Eve since I've known Susie!" Cotton said with certainty. "There are a lot of drunkards out on a night like this, Miss Kate. If you go out, be very careful. There's a dance at Brazeau Hall, and all the taverns will be packed.

"Ellie really wants me to go by the winery and have a bite to eat, but I'm still debating," I added. "I'm a big chicken when it comes to driving in the snow."

"So you didn't get an invite from Mr. McFadden?" Cotton asked as he hoped to get more inside information.

"You're crazy, Cotton," I snorted. "There's nothing going on between Clark and me other than work." He laughed and nodded his head.

"I'll get some soup ready for you to take home," I stated changing the subject.

"Thanks, Susie will be mighty pleased, Miss Kate," he said with gratitude. "Sometime we'll have to have you over for a meal. Susie makes the best meatloaf in the whole wide world when we can afford it."

When Cotton went upstairs to work on Jack's bed, I thought of his comment about affording meatloaf. There was indeed a fair share of low income people in these villages. Cotton was a good worker and very devoted to me. I wanted to do something more for him and Susie in the future.

By 5:00, I still couldn't decide whether to go to the winery. The snow had let up, but Main Street hadn't been plowed. I could decide to hibernate tonight and feel sorry for myself, or I could decide to socialize with folks who'd been so welcoming to me. I was glad Ellie wasn't pressuring me to come.

At 7:00, I looked at my watch and thought of Maggie at the Country Club dining on an elaborate buffet as she did every year. She would be wearing an elegant gown with lots of glitter. I'm sure I'll be getting the scoop on everything.

If I went to Ellie's, I'd wear my good jeans and a heavy knit sweater. It would require little effort to go, and Ellie would be very glad to see me. I really didn't want to stay home and watch the ball drop in Times Square, so I decided to give it a try. If I landed in a ditch, I had Cotton's number to call.

I cautiously got on the main road and nervously traveled at a slow pace while everyone passed me by. By now, folks were recognizing my car and were probably making fun of me. After I pulled up the gravel hill, I sighed in relief when I found a parking spot close to the road. It would make for an easy exit.

When I walked in, I saw Trout, Ellie, and another person working behind the bar. The place was very crowded, and it took me awhile to spot Mary Catherine and Betsy. They were near the bandstand, which would not be a very good thing. The band was playing loud, country western music, which wasn't my taste, but I knew the crowd would love it. Some were dancing in any empty space they could find.

"Hey guys, thanks for saving me a seat," I greeted loudly so they could hear me.

"We made a bet you wouldn't come," said Mary Catherine. "Great you could join us. Meet Fred and Alice Hadler, Kate. They are my neighbors and also relatives!"

"Nice to meet you," I acknowledged. "I think everyone in this town is related to one another." They all nodded and laughed.

"Hey there, country girl," Ellie said, greeting me at our

table. "I brought you a glass of your favorite wine."

"Thanks, but only one," I said taking it out of her hand. "I was a nervous wreck driving here."

"Help yourself to the buffet," Ellie offered. "There's a little bit of everything over there. Kelly out did himself, tonight."

"Thanks, I will," I said looking over the crowd. So far, there was no sign of Clark. It actually put me more at ease.

I sat for a short while to enjoy my wine before eating. As I analyzed the crowd, I observed most folks in Borna socialized with their family members. Ellie said the only click in town were the folks who worked at East Perry Lumber. She claimed it was so large, it was a little town within a town. She said they weren't unfriendly, but you were always reminded of their close relationships.

I finally joined the others at the buffet and ended up with too much food on my plate. That was easy to do in this town. I once again thought of Maggie dining on lobster and shrimp.

"Hey, Kate, isn't Clark McFadden doing some work for you?" Betsy asked as she looked towards the door.

"Yes, he is," I said nodding. "I was lucky to get him. He's got quite a name for himself. Why do you ask?"

"He just came in the door," she casually noted. "I know Ellie said he gets take out from here all the time."

I didn't want to turn around and look at him. Would he expect to see me here? I wondered if he was ever with someone else. I was tempted to ask Betsy, but I didn't want her to think I was interested.

"Hey there," a man said as he tapped me on the shoulder. "Would you care to dance?"

"Oh no, sorry," I answered, without sounding too rude. He

looked disappointed as he walked away. He looked familiar. I asked Mary Catherine who he was, and she told me he worked at Harold's Hardware. I then recalled seeing him there.

After I finished eating, I noted the music seemed to be getting louder and louder. I was uncomfortable. This was not the cozy, charming winery I knew.

"Hey guys, I'm going to head home," I announced loudly to my table. "Thanks for your company and Happy New Year!"

"You're going before midnight?" Betsy asked in disbelief. I smiled and nodded.

"Exactly my point," I responded. "I am worried about the roads, and it's getting too merry in here for me!" They all laughed as they stood to say goodbye.

I was heading towards the door when Clark stepped directly in front of me.

"Leaving already?" Clark asked with his deep voice. I smiled and nodded.

"Yes, I don't do well driving in this weather," I explained. "I just came to eat a bite and be gracious to Ellie for inviting me."

"Are you okay to drive?" he asked with concern. "Do you want me to follow you home?"

"Oh no, Clark, I'll be fine if I take it easy," I responded as I brushed past him. "Thanks anyway. I'll see you back to work in the next few days, I take it?"

"Sure." he said looking a bit disappointed. "You have a Happy New Year!"

"Sure. You have a Happy New Year, too!" I cheerfully responded.

I fluttered like a school girl when I got into my car. I was touched by Clark's concern for me. I sat in the frozen car till it started to warm up. I slowly drove back down the hill and carefully made it back to 6229 Main Street...barely!

I got comfortable in my pajamas and watched the clock for the New Year to change. Happy New Year, I said to myself. I had to smile, thinking how Borna celebrated life's big and small occasions. I crawled into bed thanking God for bringing me here where I could start a new life. At midnight I could hear firecrackers going off. In South Haven, Maggie was probably being kissed by her husband as everyone sang, 'Auld Lang Syne'. I missed Maggie more than I was willing to admit. I hoped the distance would not sever our relationship in time. I was where I needed to be, safe and warm in Borna.

I quickly fell asleep, but kept waking up to the horns beeping as they drove by the house, celebrating the New Year. I thought of Cotton's warning. I got up to use the bathroom and sensed a noise coming from downstairs. It made me question whether I had turned on the security alarm before I went to bed. This was not the night to forget such a thing. I decided to make sure, so I turned on the light on the stairway and headed downstairs.

When I got to the bottom, Blade suddenly jumped out of the darkness into my view in the living room. My immediate reaction was to scream as loudly as I could, but nothing came out. I was overwhelmed at the nerve of this human being! He had a horrible grin across his face.

"What are you doing here?" I shouted in anger. "How did you get in here?" I felt my entire body shake. What was going to happen next?

"It's part of my profession, Miss Meyr," he said snickering. "I'm your realtor, or have you forgotten?"

"Oh, no, you're not, and you won't get by with breaking and entering my house, you creep," I shouted again, moving closer to him. "If you think I'm afraid of you, you have another thing coming!"

"Oh, I'm scared," he jeered. "You have one last chance with me, honey, or really bad things will begin to happen to people you seem to care about." His expression now changed to anger.

"I don't think so," I responded as I inched my way to the wall light switch on the living room wall. "You're lucky I haven't pressed charges against you yet!" He grew angrier when the light came on.

"That's because you can't prove a dang thing!" he loudly yelled. "Remember, I have more friends than you do around here. My advice to you, city girl, is to get out of town before someone really gets hurt or disappears!"

"Get out! Get out of here, now!" I yelled as loudly as I could. So far I didn't see a weapon, but rage began to consume me.

"Okay, it looks like you're the type who likes to rumble," he said coming towards me. "I like a hot woman now and then." He came closer and the thought of an attempted rape entered my mind.

He quickly grabbed me and twirled me around, forcing me to fall to the ground. It was so unexpected; I hit my head really hard on the hardwood floor. Now his heavy, smelly, body was on top of me. He took my arms and held them firmly to the ground. I could hardly breathe with his heavy weight on my chest. I bravely spit into his ugly face in desperation, hoping it would distract him. It resulted in a hard blow against my cheek. I think I saw stars. Every part of me pounded with pain. My teeth chattered in fear, and I closed my eyes for whatever came next. Dear God help me, I prayed. Was he going to beat me, rape, or kill me?

His breathing was hard, heavy, and stinky. I opened my eyes as he drew back his hand to give me another hit in the face. Before he could strike, we both heard movement in the house. It startled him, and he turned his body around to see what it was.

"You better start picking on somebody your own size!" yelled Clark charging into the living room.

He quickly pulled Blade off of me and threw him against the wall with all his might, causing a framed photo of Jack and me to come crashing to the floor. Glass went everywhere, and I was in the middle of it. Clark gave Blade a punch in the stomach and a kick in the groin, causing him to double over in breathlessness. Clark was taller and bigger, which took Blade by surprise. The look on Clark's face was full of rage.

I quickly got myself off the floor away from the glass. When I turned around, Blade pulled out a good size pocket knife and came charging towards Clark. I screamed to Clark to watch out. It caught him off guard thinking Blade was still trying to catch his breath. Was he going to use that knife on me? Clark handily defended himself, twisting Blade's wrist, causing the knife to drop out of his hand. I stumbled up the stairs to escape and call 911. My breath was heavy as I reported an intruder at my address. They had more questions, but once I gave them my address, I told them to hurry and hung up.

I returned down the stairs, nearly falling, I was so scared. I saw blood on my gown and felt something warm like blood run down on my cheeks. When I got to the living room, Clark had secured Blade's hands behind him, taking him towards the kitchen door.

"I'm taking this SOB and locking him in the car, till the Sherriff comes," Clark announced, in anger. Clark gave him a good kick in the back as they went out the kitchen door. I felt a sigh of relief. Did this really happen? Would I have been killed, had Clark not arrived?

Feeling pain, I started to assess the damage on my own body. I had cuts on my arms where I landed on the broken glass. I went to the kitchen to grab a towel. I quickly put it on the laceration on my head which was starting to throb and bleed more heavily. I was hurting all over. As I stood in front of the kitchen sink, I told myself to sit down. I was getting weak. Things were getting blurred and suddenly, I didn't have feet to stand on. I melted into a puddle of darkness.

CHAPTER 50

When I came to, Ellie was looking down on me. I was lying on my loveseat and felt a cold rag on my forehead.

"What are you doing here?" I softly asked, still somewhat foggy.

"Clark gave me a ring, and thought I better get over here," she explained. "You sure know how to party on New Year's Eve!" I couldn't laugh. Everything hurt too much.

Now I saw Clark standing over me. "Are you okay?" he asked. Looking at Clark, I wanted to get up.

"No, Kate," Ellie said putting her hand on my arm. "You just rest here for a while." She pulled one of my quilts up to me. "I thought at first you might need some stitches on your head, but I think it'll be fine. I bet you'll be black and blue for a while! Would you like to go see a doctor?"

"No, no," I said shaking my head. "Clark, did he hurt you?"

"I'm fine," Clark said looking at me with sympathy. "Blade's been picked up. He can't hurt you anymore."

"How in the world did you know he was here?" I asked Clark in pain. He took a deep breath before speaking.

"I stopped by Marv's to get my last drink before going home," he began to explain. "When I parked my car, I saw Blade's truck parked on the lot. When I got inside the place, I didn't see him anywhere, so I asked Marv if he had seen him. He said he came in to have one drink and then left. I had a quick one and said hello to a few folks before I left. When I came out to my car, his truck was still there, which I thought was odd. I drove slowly by your place and saw you had a light on which wasn't on earlier. Then in an instant, I saw some movement in your window, and it was Blade. I pulled in and saw your kitchen door was ajar. I came on in, heard you yelling, and saw Blade on top of you."

"Good God, Kate, he could have killed you!" Ellie shouted angrily.

"I don't think Blade knew who he was dealing with," Clark teased. "Miss Meyr here is quite the fighter, and I don't think he expected the resistance she was giving him." He grinned at me.

"Thanks so much, Clark," I said with my throbbing head. "I hate to think of what might have happened had you not come along."

"One of the deputies is outside wanting to talk to you," Clark revealed. "They really would like you to be checked out at a hospital. Are you sure you don't want to do that?"

"No, I'll be fine," I quickly surmised. "I'll be happy to talk to him." As I lifted my arms, I saw dried blood. I knew I looked a mess. How embarrassing!

"Oh Ellie, I must look horrible," I complained as I tried to sit up. "After tonight I will be the talk of the town for sure." They both laughed at me.

Ellie helped me sit up as I took some aspirin from her. Officer Daniels came in from the kitchen and introduced himself. He knew about my former complaints about Blade, so he didn't have too many questions. I remembered everything clearly up until I fainted in the kitchen. His visit was short and apologetic. He kept reassuring me Blade would be locked up and I was safe.

I once again refused to go to the hospital. I knew if I were in South Haven, I would have had several police cars, an ambulance and a fire truck to contend with.

Before he left, Clark asked if the two of us would be okay. He had a delivery to make, since the roads had cleared. I thanked him over and over again as he went out the door.

Ellie brought me a cup of hot tea, which tasted really good. I was glad it was just the two of us.

"Oh Ellie, this is the last thing you need to be doing today," I said helplessly.

"Hey, it's New Year's Day, the winery is closed, and Trout and the crew are cleaning up," she explained as she tried to make me feel better. I was so glad she was there!

"I can't imagine what he planned to do to me, Ellie!" I cried in my weakest voice.

"A sick man works in strange ways," she replied shaking her head. "You made him very angry from the start so I bet this just kept building up for him. He obviously wasn't smart enough to know there would be consequences. Most criminals don't."

Ellie brought me a clean gown and my bathrobe to change into. I curled up once again on the loveseat, as I had done many times before. I suppose I was mentally exhausted and I faded into sleep. Now and then, I would open my eyes to find Ellie reading in the rocking chair, next to me. The comfort of her being there helped me fall back asleep.

CHAPTER 51

I woke up early the next morning and found Ellie asleep leaning to one side in her chair. When she heard me move, she immediately jumped.

"Good heavens, Ellie, go home!" I fussed. "I'm fine, really!" I knew I was feeling much better.

"Okay, but first let me see you walking to the restroom. After that, get yourself a cup of that terrible coffee I made earlier" Ellie instructed. "If you can do it without feeling light headed, I'm out of here!" I shook my head at her persistence and smiled.

I slowly, but steadily stood, taking a deep breath for strength. My head began to throb again with my movement. I felt weak, but I hadn't eaten in quite some time. I faked a smile to prove to Ellie I was fine.

I got to the kitchen and poured my coffee as she watched. She offered to make me breakfast, but I was only willing to try some light toast for the time being. I didn't want to hurt her feelings, but the coffee was pretty bad.

After I finished eating a slice of toast, Ellie thought she should follow me up the stairs so I could shower and change. She saw Josephine's quilt at the bottom of the bed.

"You have got to show this quilt to Emma," she reminded me.

"It is on my list, but thought I would just bring it to the next Friendship Circle meeting for the others to see as well," I suggested. "When is your next meeting?"

"It's in three days, and it's going to be at my house," she stated. "It's always a bit crowded, but we still manage to have a good time."

"Maybe by the next meeting I will be unpacked and settled enough to have the meeting here," I said with enthusiasm.

Before she left, we walked around the upstairs, while she admired all the new furniture I had added from my recent move. I told her I wanted all antique furniture downstairs, since I didn't have that luxury in my former home.

"Imy goes to a lot of estate sales, so she'll be very helpful finding me what I still need. I'll just take my time, and it'll be quite fun!"

"Well, the rocking chair you purchased from her was very comfortable, I must say," Ellie noted. "Come spring, all the farm sales will be starting. I think you'll enjoy attending those. They always have a lot of quilts. Not like you need anymore." We laughed. Ellie bid me farewell.

The light breakfast had given me some strength, and I couldn't help think of Maggie. I always shared everything with her, but this incident would freak her out! She and Carla would have bad thoughts about Borna, for sure. With Blade locked up, I could put him out of my life.

I sat on the side of the bed, thinking of Clark, and how brave he was to stay and look after me. When I thought of him driving by the house to check on me, it made me smile. I shuttered at the thought of what might have been.

I went downstairs and decided to keep my mind off of things by doing something productive. No one else was expected to stop by so I decided to unpack my Grandmother's china and arrange it in the new cupboard. It would be good to revisit the beautiful pieces once again. I made a mental note to actually use the fine china as soon as I entertained here in Borna.

When I finished, I stood back to admire the arrangement. As I did many an evening, I made a fire to sit by and watch. What was it that made it so comforting?

I decided to make some angel hair pasta with olive oil, dried tomatoes, and parmesan cheese for a light dinner. A glass of red wine would be the perfect touch, but I knew my head wouldn't. I brought my dinner to the game table and thought about my much neglected journal. I hadn't written in my book since I left South Haven. There was so much happening, plus my feelings were so sad and angry, I couldn't get myself to write. There was certainly a lot to say since I arrived here. Other than Blade, there were pleasant thoughts, I could record. Perhaps this quiet time would be the time to start.

My intentions were good, but instead, I curled up on the love seat pulling my quilt around my neck. The early darkness of the evening was calming, as I watched the fire go out into the night.

CHAPTER 52

❧

I had been feeling cooped up the last few days, so I was looking forward to going to the Friendship Circle meeting, at Ellie's that night. I hadn't seen any sign of Clark for days, but true to my promise, I wasn't going to contact him about his work schedule.

I decided to make a cold, vegetarian pizza to take to Ellie's. There were always so many sweets; I thought they may enjoy something different.

As I was cleaning up my mess from the pizza, Cotton knocked at my back door. He had such a serious look on his face, which wasn't like Cotton.

"Miss Kate, why didn't you call me about Blade breaking in?" he excitedly asked when I let him in the door. "I was at Harold's, and he asked how you were doing." I looked down till he was finished explaining. "I'm sorry I haven't been here lately, but Susie's been down with the flu, and I've had to look after the little one." He finally let me respond.

I reassured him I had recovered. I went briefly through the chain of events, and I could see the anger rise in his face.

"Who are these friends Blade claims he has?" I curiously asked.

"Blade doesn't have any friends!" He shook his head. "He just knows guys like me who are looking for extra work and accept whatever pittance he decides to pay us. Nobody likes him. They'll all be glad as heck to know he got what's comin' to him."

"Well, life goes on, and you'll have more work around here soon," I reassured him. "Wayne Brewer, the contractor, said they'll start on the porch and garage as soon as the temperature is over 30 degrees. Hopefully, it will happen soon and come spring, there will be all kinds of projects for you." He nodded with a half-smile as he still was thinking of Blade.

"Well, you might want me to start, by carrying out that really dead Christmas tree, you got there!" he teased. I had to laugh. "There's some snow covered sidewalks out there, too ma'am."

"Good thinking, Cotton," I concurred. "That reminds me, I have some cash here for you since you've been doing a lot of jobs lately." I reached for my purse on the counter and pulled out three fifty dollar bills. When I gave them to him, his eyes got big.

"Oh no, Miss Kate," he said backing away. "I can't take so much, plus it's just the neighborly thing to do for you."

"It's worth it to me, Cotton, and you've been very loyal," I explained. "I know the winter months are hard on folks like you, who go from job to job. By the way, I wanted your opinion on another matter I was thinking about." I paused. "Do you think the Paulson's had a wine cellar of any kind in the basement?" The question caught him by surprise.

"Didn't appear to be so, but there's a lot of shelves down there," he reported. "Do you want one?"

"We had a wine cellar in South Haven," I answered. "My husband was quite the wine connoisseur and he loved to brag about it. After he died, I gave most of the wine collection away to my Beach quilters."

"I bet they were a happy bunch," he said laughing.

"They all love wine, and I knew I'd be moving so I felt like giving it all away," I explained. "I'm sure it was another turn in the grave for Clay." Cotton didn't know if he should laugh.

We both walked down into the basement. It seemed to always be dry and cool, but I didn't want to store much down there, till I had a better feel for it. There was a small nook with shelves, which Cotton thought could have stored wine. He offered to start planning, but I told him to put off. I kept wondering what the Paulson's did store down here. There was an unsettled feeling as I walked around. I felt a cold sadness in the air. Perhaps I shouldn't be down here!

We went upstairs, and Cotton began the task of removing the big tree, which had given me so much pleasure during the Christmas season. Before he left, Cotton thanked me once again for my generosity. I was about to head upstairs when Maggie called.

"Hey there!" I happily greeted. "I thought I'd hear from you before now! How was the New Year's Eve party?"

Maggie snickered into the phone. "Same ole, same ole," she muttered. "You didn't miss a thing. James and Sandra were not there, by the way. I'm sure they didn't want to answer any questions about you or the company. I want to hear about your big evening!"

"Uneventful," I lied. "The weather was frightful, but I did venture to the winery for a while. This city girl doesn't have a hankering for county music, as yet." She laughed. "I did get asked to dance by an elderly, bald headed man who works at the hardware store." She laughed even harder.

"You would have had a lot more offers at the club, my dear," Maggie added.

"No thanks," I said with certainty in my tone. "I'm loving the peace and quiet of this town. Tonight I'm going to the Friendship Circle meeting. It's quite a diverse group of women from this little village."

"Boy, you are livin', girlfriend," she teased. She always made me laugh. We could always find the simplest things to laugh about.

I knew Maggie would be teasing me a lot, as time would go by but I also knew she was envious of my new beginning and wanted me to be happy once again.

Everyone but Mary Catherine showed up for the Friendship Circle meeting. It smelled of coffee, fresh baked goods, and gossip. I brought Josephine's quilt with me, but at first, they were only interested in eating and sharing their Christmas memories.

I helped Ellie serve the coffee and wine. The veggie pizza seemed to be a big hit and requests were made for the recipe.

"Happy New Year!" Ellie greeted to get our attention. "It's so good to see everyone! Mary Catherine has the flu, which seems to be going around." I thought of Susie and wondered if she had the same bug. I could see how quickly the flu could spread in a small place like Borna. "Anna, I think you wanted to have the floor to tell us about something!"

"Yes," replied Anna. "We are having a chili cook-off at

Saxon Village the first Saturday in February. We want to raise money for some restoration needing to be done on some of the log cabins." The ladies nodded, as if they were aware of the problems. "There's some mighty fine chili made in these parts, so with weather permitting, we'll have lots of different chilis to taste. We'll have them placed amongst the log cabins. Some will be cooking in our big, black kettles." A couple of the women clapped in support of the idea.

"Who are the chili makers? Can anyone compete?" Peggy anxiously asked.

"Let's see," Anna paused for a bit. "It's the Men's Club from Concordia, Marv's Bar and Grocery, Chris Kassel from the machine shop, and the like. My husband is representing the Saxon Village, making his own recipe. He makes the best chili ever! I hope no one thinks it's a conflict of interest. He really wants to compete!"

"I don't know why anyone would object, Anna," Ellie jumped in to say. "I've heard his chili is wonderful. I can have Kelly at my winery make some if you need more entries."

"Great idea, Ellie," Anna agreed. "I'll count on it. We have Emma and Ruth Ann offering to make cornbread for the event. I told them they can use the outdoor oven, which would be so fitting. It'll work out great for baking such huge amounts."

"That sounds great, Anna, I can't wait to be there!" I added with excitement.

"Well, that's good Kate, because I was going to ask you to be one of the three judges!" she announced. "It means you'll eat free!" I laughed picturing myself with such a delicious job!

"Of course I'll be happy to!" I quickly responded. I suddenly felt like a true member of the community.

"Okay, any other announcements?" Ellie asked. After no response, she continued. "As some of you may know, Kate found a quilt in her house which we think may have been made by Josephine Paulson. Kate brought it with her tonight for us to see. She is hoping some of us may have some information to help her analyze the quilt." There were sounds of unexpected surprise. "I think we'll lay it open on my bed, Kate."

They all followed Ellie into her bedroom to spread out the quilt. The reactions were instantaneous. I chose to keep quiet so I could hear their remarks.

"Good heavens!" said Betsy with her hands placed on her hips.

"Why is it made in sections like this?" questioned Peggy, looking up close.

"She used all black thread! "Ruth Ann remarked. "It's pretty depressing, if you ask me!"

"I have to say, it's not the best stitching I've ever seen!" noted Ellen harshly. "I would have thought she was a better quilt maker than this!"

"She was pretty religious, no doubt," assumed Anna.

Emma just stared at it and walked around the three sides of the bed.

"Mama said more than once, how sorry she felt for Josephine," Emma began to explain. "I know she was a quilter because Mama would say she came to quilting now and then. I probably shouldn't repeat it again, but she thought Doc was nothing but a drunkard. I can't imagine what kind of life his Mrs. had!" Everyone sighed and mumbled to themselves.

"My Aunt Erna sure swore by him," described Peggy.

"I think he delivered all her babies! She said he yanked out many a tonsil in those days, too!"

"The way she stitched it all in black, says to me, she was mourning in some way," observed Ellen. "She seems to be sorry for so many things and wants forgiveness. I wouldn't put this on any bed in the house. Where on earth did you find this?"

"I found it in an upstairs cabinet, above one of the doors in the hallway," I revealed. "I don't think any of the renters knew it was there, since it wasn't easily accessible. These dates indicate a stillborn or miscarriage to me. I have a feeling she felt badly and even guilty she couldn't bear any children. I hope the Doctor didn't blame her!"

"God bless her soul," said Betsy making a cross. "Look at these two silhouettes facing opposite direction from each other. That says a lot, right there!"

The ladies kept repeating out loud what they were reading and thinking. None of the remarks were complimentary. What if the quilt wasn't made by Josephine?

"I'll stop at the Heritage Center one of these days and find out more about her and the family," I shared. "I may at some point donate it to the museum." They all stared at me.

Finally, Peggy spoke. "If I was the one confessing all these feelings, I sure wouldn't want the whole community reading about all my pain." The rest of the ladies seemed to agree.

"That's a good point, Peggy," I noted feeling guilty.

"Josephine was a private person and likely made this quilt somewhere in private," added Emma." I don't think anyone ever saw her working on anything. She pretty much kept to herself in that house."

"I told Kate, I thought she was probably working on the

quilt up in the attic," Ellie claimed. "If he drank and was busy seeing patients, where else would she go? By the way, the attic has a wonderful view of the street! She could certainly see who was coming and going!"

I was certainly outnumbered on the idea of donating the quilt. I tried to record all their comments in my mind but I really hadn't learned anything new. It made me sad to hear all the criticism. I was going to be the one to research this quilt, I told myself.

I came home feeling sorry I had exposed Josephine's quilt to the club. I went upstairs and laid it back down on the end of my bed, where it belonged.

When I said my evening prayers, I asked for Josephine's forgiveness in using poor judgement by showing her quilt. I decided to keep the quilt a secret from now on.

CHAPTER 53

January's frigid weather was the only talk in town. Cold weather was not unusual for me, and my social life was pretty uneventful these days, so the weather didn't matter. I spent most of my days unpacking and making an occasional visit to Imy's antique shop when she opened on the weekends.

I'd brought quite a few books with me, so Clark suggested he add some book shelves in my bedrooms. I knew now it was more than an occasional bakery treat encouraging him to come back again. I was a friend he felt comfortable with and the feelings were mutual.

The first week of February, Eddie and Wayne, the main contractor, showed up to begin the construction of the porch and garage. Wayne agreed Cotton could indeed help them as a gofer, but hinted he wasn't a trained carpenter and couldn't help with any construction.

I made a point to bake and cook often, as there was always someone around to help me consume whatever was available. When I told the workers I was going to be a judge at the chili cook-off, they began to tease me. They said I should have entered the contest, instead of judging it.

The Saturday cook-off was on a sunny, cold day, which seemed perfect for a good, hot bowl of chili. Everyone was bundled up in their warmest attire and young fiddle players were playing bluegrass music on a make-shift stage. Under the pavilion were red checkered tablecloths placed on picnic tables for folks to enjoy their chili. I was amazed how well it was attended. Lines of cars started pulling in onto the vacant fields. Anna would surely be pleased with the outcome.

Judging with me was the Mayor of Dresden and Oscar Meers, Ellen's husband, representing East Perry Lumber Yard. Folks started gathering around us as we went from chili pot to chili pot, tasting the different varieties. There was sweet chili, very, very spicy chili, and chili that contained other ingredients like pasta. I was encouraged to chase down the flavors with a cold beer, and it worked!

When the winner was decided with our point system, Anna put ribbons on the first, second and third place winners. Marv's chili came in first, which didn't surprise anyone. Evidently, Marv had a pretty good reputation for his chili.

When I sat down on a hay bale to listen to the music and observe the festivities, Oscar approached me.

"Say, Kate, Ellen hasn't said much, but I understand your deceased husband was one of the owners of Meyr Lumber?" I nodded before he continued. "I sure was sorry to hear he was killed in that horrific accident. I met him once, but mostly did business with his father, John."

"Oh, I didn't know," I responded. "Do they still conduct any business with you, Oscar?" He looked to the ground before answering.

"Yup, until recently," he said softly. "Your brother-in-law, if you don't mind me speaking out of school, is running Meyr Lumber into the ground. We had to stop giving them credit. I really tried to work with them because I thought so much of John. I know he worked hard to build the business."

"I'm so sorry," I said shaking my head. "I'm hearing about the layoffs, too! I hate to see what Clay, my husband, and his Dad worked so hard for just fade away. I think James is making poor choices. His Dad knew Clay was the right one to run the company, but now that he's gone, it's been up to him."

"Well, it's out of your hands, Kate, but I wondered if you knew the history here. We are all thrilled to have you in Borna, by the way. I have always been envious of Doc Paulson's piece of property."

"I'm happy to be here, as well," I said happily. "Thanks for mentioning your relationship with the Meyrs. They are a great family." He nodded and smiled as he walked away.

I felt so ashamed. I could tell Oscar was a good, decent, honest man, running a good company. I couldn't help but wonder how many people in Borna had connected the dots. I had to be related with the spelling of my last name.

Before I left, Anna thanked me for judging and then presented me with a heavy, ceramic, Saxon Village mug. She suggested I take home as much corn bread as I liked for they had plenty left.

Except for my little visit with Oscar, it was truly a fun day. I gave Ellen credit for never bringing up the lumber business with me. I missed Ellie not being there, but she had a busy day planned at the winery. I was ready to get home and snuggle up by a warm, fire.

When I got settled at home with a cup of hot tea, I wanted to call Maggie and tell her what Oscar had shared with me. Even though it was late, I anxiously gave her a call. I woke her up and she immediately asked what was wrong.

"I just wanted to talk. I'm sorry," I explained sadly.

"I'm glad your fine, Kate, but do you mind if I call you back in the morning?" she said in a groggy voice.

"Oh sure, Maggie," I said with an apology. "Talk to you tomorrow!"

I was so disappointed. This was not my friend who was always available 24 hours a day. Maggie always wanted to talk to me, whatever the hour. Was she getting used to me being gone? Was this the beginning of our friendship fracturing?

I decided to call Jack knowing he would be up late, for sure! I clicked on his number, and it went to voice mail. I left my usual, motherly message and realized I was on my own for the night. I put out the fire and went up to bed disappointed.

CHAPTER 54

That next afternoon seemed like the perfect time to visit the Lutheran Heritage Center and Museum. Any little piece to the puzzle of Josephine Paulson would be a good thing.

When I walked in, I was pleased only one other couple was in the place. I knew the museum director Sharla Lee Gordon by sight, but had not met her. She smiled and greeted me immediately, as if we had already met. Ellie had described her as a colorful soul who ran the place like a battleship. Ellie said it was the best PR move Borna ever made. I wasn't sure what it all meant, but she did appear very confident, and her clever, feminine attire reminded me of my eccentric, high school art teacher. Why did so many people around here have two names instead of one? Sharla Lee of all names! Was her mother influenced by the name of Sara Lee, the incredible pastry company?

"Can we help you today?" she asked adjusting her scarf around her pony tail.

"I'm hoping so," I said looking about the place. "I'm Kate Meyr. I recently moved into the old Dr. Paulson house on Main Street, and I'm trying to find out more information on Josephine Paulson, the doctor's wife."

"Nice to meet you Kate. I'm Sharla Lee Gordon, the Director here," she stated as she reached out her hand. "Please, just call me Sharla Lee. I remember you coming to our Christmas church tour." I nodded with a smile, but she kept talking. "You're doing a fine job on the Doc's place from what I can tell. I'm going to introduce you to Gerard, whose one of the volunteers. He is quite knowledgeable about the folks in this area, and much techier than I am!" She giggled as she led me towards him. "He has become very helpful in our new archives department."

"Thanks so much!" I responded. "It's nice to meet you Sharla Lee. Any help would be appreciated. I'd love to have a look around. My friend Ellie Meers told me about this place and says you are doing a fine job. How long has this been here? It looks so new."

"The new addition was added in 2005, which is when I came on board," she explained. "Most of our historic materials are from one man's collection. He left this area a wonderful legacy for generations to enjoy. This place has been developing as we go along. We want to make sure we address the needs of the local community so I'm pleased you're here!"

We walked into the larger gallery, and she introduced me to Gerard, who had just finished talking to the other couple. Sharla Lee told him my purpose in coming, and he responded with a nod, as if he had been asked these questions on a daily basis.

At this time, Sharla Lee excused herself to greet a group of three women who just walked in the door.

I told Gerard I was mostly interested in just knowing some basic information about Mrs. Paulson, as there didn't seem to be a photo or any mention of her. He said it wasn't unusual in those days to not have photos of the women in the families, unless it would be a wedding picture or a formal family photo for some occasion. He told me to have a seat at a table where there were two computers. He explained how many people were now coming in the center to do research without assistance. He also showed me beautiful cabinets which held additional photographs and records.

I liked Gerard right away. He had a heavy German accent and truly acted like he cared about helping me. He started asking me questions, and the only thing I could tell him was the date of their house. He quickly found their wedding date of April 16, 1902, but no photograph. One genealogy web site did have the birth record of Josephine on October 22, 1879 and listed her maiden name as Lottes. Her death was listed as May 29, 1954. I started calculating and decided she was 23 when she married and Doc was 27. Gerard commented that their ages were older than most folks who got married back then. I told him the house was built in 1915. It would be nice to know where they lived before then.

"If I may ask, why do you have such an interest in Josephine?" Gerard asked turning his head to place on his elbow.

"Because she's so invisible," I said sadly. "She's hardly remembered at all, and her husband was so prominent. People say she made herself scarce when the doctor saw his patients." He nodded like he was thinking about what I said. "I would like to know if she had siblings. I know they didn't have any children, which is probably another reason I'm not finding out much about her."

"Yes, siree," he agreed nodding his head. "I can't tell you much more without spending more time looking at past newspapers and all. I'll put you on a list with some of the other people we are researching. You have asked some very good questions, Miss Meyr. Sharla Lee is not from here, but she is pretty amazing when it comes to this county's history, and who is related to whom. Folks come in all day long asking her questions and telling their family history. We're the closest thing to a tourist center the county will ever have, you might say. We can pretty much help you find places or tell you who can help get you there." He chuckled as he boasted about his knowledge. "You might want to take a look at some of our brochures and maps from the area while you're here!"

"Oh, I will," I said accepting with gratitude. "I'll come back on my own sometime, but any help you can give me would be appreciated. I don't want to take up anymore of your time. I'd like to look around here for a bit before I leave."

"Take all the time you want, Miss Meyr," Gerard said getting up from his chair. "If you have any more questions, just holler at me. They have me goin' here and there, but I'll do what I can."

"Thanks Gerard, and you can call me Kate," I directed with a smile. "You might be seeing more of me around here." He gave a warm and friendly chuckle once again as walked away.

I started browsing at the gallery entrance and noted a large bible resting on a wooden stand. It seemed quite old and unusual. As I looked closer, Gerard immediately was back at my side to tell me it was a Nuremberg bible. He pointed out the intricate artwork throughout the book. He said the donor tried to donate the bible to many other museums, but was always turned down. She showed it to Sharla Lee, and she wasted no time to tell her how thrilled the center would be to have such a prize." As he continued, his eyes were lit up, "Well, it was a pretty good move, because the donor was so thrilled at our acceptance, she gives us a generous donation every single year!" He chuckled again with the East Perry pride I saw so often. "You never know where a kind heart can lead, do we ma'am?" You could tell Gerard had that kind of heart.

"That's a wonderful story and such a blessing for the center," I noted. "I have a feeling I'll find much here to explore, since I'm new to the area."

"Sharla Lee's pretty darn good at turning over the exhibits, too," Gerard bragged. "I don't know how she keeps coming up with such interesting themes. Why the other month we had an old tool collection like I've never seen before. It drew a dandy crowd!"

"Has she ever had a quilt exhibit?" I curiously asked, visualizing the possibilities.

"Oh, my yes, we've had quilts!" he said with excitement. "We have a lot of quilters in this area, so it's always well attended. Are you a quilter yourself, Miss Meyr. I mean, Kate?" he smiled.

"Yes, I am," I was proud to say.

Sharla Lee interrupted us by asking Gerard to bring something from the storage room, so we said goodbye. I looked about the place for another fifteen minutes, before I decided to leave. Walking to my car, I felt the visit was very productive, fun, and interesting. I knew the county was quite lucky to have such good spokesmen who loved East Perry County.

CHAPTER 55

Clark was going to be gone two weeks, and I missed him. My house saw plenty of activity with workers coming and going, but he was different. Clark's friendship had taken on a whole new meaning since he saved my life from Blade. If either of us would ever move away, the bond would continue for a long, long time.

Cotton was kept busy chopping more fire wood. He also gave me good advice on how and where I might want to plant a kitchen garden. He laughed when I referred to it in those terms. I told him I wanted a raised garden, but he tried to convince me I had plenty of good soil here on the property. I persisted and told him Harold had kits one could buy for such a project. I wanted several small beds instead of one big one. Once I pictured something in my mind, it was set in stone, and he knew it. He reluctantly agreed to help me with my plan when the time was right.

The time was drawing closer to make a decision to travel to Michigan for the closing of my house. I missed Carla and Maggie, plus my realtor was putting the pressure on me to visit some condos on the beach. I kept watching the weather in South Haven and the snow storms were coming on a regular basis. Driving there would not be a good idea, which meant I'd have to fly out of St. Louis.

All I seem to do was think of spring and how wonderful 6229 Main Street could be. I already recognized dormant lilac bushes, azaleas, and hydrangeas. I had a nice variety of trees. The Red Buds were my favorite, and this part of Missouri had a lot of them. I knew I had many outdoor surprises ahead of me, not to mention the woods behind me. I loved wild flowers, but I was clueless as to what their names were. I was anxious to also explore and see if there was more than one tombstone on the property.

I had to admit, some days I felt somewhat depressed. I was used to things happening much faster in South Haven. There was part of me who loved the slow pace here, but it was extremely slower in the dead of winter. Ellie wanted me to visit the winery more often, but that wasn't a habit I wanted to pursue.

On these somber days, I let my mind go back to Clay's death, his betrayal, and Blade's attack. I had to get past my hidden anger somehow. Borna couldn't cover all of my past shadows. There were many unanswered questions I had left in South Haven. I thought of Will Cummings. I bet he could tell me a lot about Clay's secret life and the troubles at Meyr Lumber. The way he talked at Tello's, it appeared he could tell me anything I wanted to know. However, I was reluctant to call him. I didn't want to give him the wrong impression about my motives. He was newly divorced and pretty vulnerable.

Somehow the idea of buying a beach condo wasn't high on my bucket list. Perhaps it was because first I wanted to finish what I had started here in Borna. I was surprised Maggie, Carla, and Jack were not pressuring me more to do so. Maybe they were beginning to move down different paths as well.

It had been a long, cold day with way too much thinking. As I sat by the fire in deep thought, I knew I should be fixing me something to eat. I had decided not to eat, when there was a knock at the back door.

"Clark, come in!" I responded in surprise. I immediately thought about my sloppy appearance.

"Am I coming at a bad time," he hesitantly asked. I shook my head and smiled.

"Not at all," I encouraged. "I've had a long day, as you probably can judge from my appearance. I was about to pour myself a glass of wine. Would you like to join me?"

"Sure, why not," he said as he removed his hat. "I was on my way home from Springfield, and thought I better check in with my employer here and see if I had to rescue her in any way!" We both laughed.

"Don't forget it! You never know around here," I joked as I poured us some wine. "I wondered when you might return." "I know I've been neglecting you here a bit, but I'm glad to see you've had some deliveries out there, and some things are moving forward," he noted. "I take it you're using Wayne as your contractor?

I nodded. "Harold and Eddie gave him high marks and are used to working with him," I reported. "I'm insisting they give Cotton work when they can!"

"Well, if he's not busy, I can use some help cutting wood out at my place," Clark offered.

"Oh, he'll be thrilled!" I said as we walked into the living room.

"Have you eaten dinner?" I asked in our period of silence.

"Not really. I was going to pick up something at the winery to take home," he said casually.

"Well, I have some left over stew I made yesterday, and some frozen corn bread from the chili cook off, if that'll do," I offered with a tempting smile.

"Sounds fantastic," he said patting his middle section. We got up and walked into the kitchen.

"Hey, you sure didn't waste any time filling up these cabinets, did you?" he teased. "I'll try to finish up this section as soon as I can, so you can get me out of here."

"I'm not complaining! You've done a great job!" I praised. I was now watching him caress the wood he had used on the cabinets. He never hid his love for wood.

"I'm thinking about heading north to attend the closing on my house," I blurted out.

"Haven't you been noticing the weather they're having these days?" he asked with concern.

I nodded with a sad face. "I just feel I left things unsettled," I confessed. "I ran away, I'm afraid."

"You mean in regard to your husband, or what?" Clark's face took on a serious look.

"Yes, in a way," I nodded. "I'm also concerned his company is about to go under." Clark suddenly looked surprised. "I was so embarrassed the other day at the chili cook-off when Oscar, from East Perry Lumber, told me their credit was no longer good.

He said Meyr Lumber owed them a great deal of money."

"Really? Well, I'm surprised he shared the information with you. What did he expect you to do about it?"

"That was sort of my reaction, too," I said taking another sip of wine. "He knows I'm completely out of the company, but I'm still a Meyr. I hate I'll be thought of as a connection to their debt."

"That's nonsense," Clark assured me as we sat down at the game table like we had before. "Oscar is a good man from what I hear. I'm sure he understands you had no part of their bad business habits." Clark surprised me by changing the topic. "What do you like to do for fun?" Clark asked. "What did you do for fun in Michigan?"

I had to think. "Well, I enjoyed spending time with my beach quilting friends, most of all with Maggie," I quickly recalled. "I didn't play golf or play bridge, like the other socialites in my circle. I loved the beach, and antique shopping with Maggie. Clay kept me pretty busy with things pertaining to the company's charities and social life. What about you?"

"I guess I love my work, which is fun sometimes I suppose," he said with hesitation. "I like the fact I'm in charge of my time to do what I want, when I want."

"Well, that's for sure!" I said sarcastically as I went to get more bread in the kitchen. He laughed.

We continued our meal with very light and comfortable conversation. He seemed more at ease with me each time we were together. He told me how successful his work was becoming nationwide, and that he turned down many requests. He had a gallery in Springfield he was fond of and tried to keep them supplied. He seemed to be happy sharing his professional side, but I still was kept at bay on his personal side.

I was relieved somehow, because I, too wasn't ready to share too much of my past. I felt he trusted me as a friend, and I didn't want to spoil what friendship we were building.

My grandfather clock in the entry hall struck 10:00, and we both couldn't believe how the time had flown by. Clark looked at his watch and commented how lucky I was the clock had survived the long move from South Haven. I told him hearing the sound of it was like being home, wherever that may be.

"Well, it's time I get on home, Miss Meyr," he said getting up. "This was a real unexpected treat!"

"I was glad to have the company," I said blushing. "I'm sorry I wasn't dressed for company." He didn't respond.

"I'll be back soon. Thanks so much for dinner," he concluded as he got on his coat. "Now let me know if you decide to skip town." I nodded with a big smile. "Take care then."

I closed the door thinking what a different kind of man he was. He was an artist. Perhaps that made him unique. He was certainly set in his ways. That probably explained why none of the local women were able to strike his fancy. I felt lucky somehow.

CHAPTER 56

Maggie called as I was making coffee the next morning. "Good morning, girlfriend!" I happily answered. "What's up?"

"Well, I thought I'd be a good friend and offer you a place to stay, if you're coming home for the closing," she offered. "You better think about jumping on a plane, however. We just got another five inches of snow last night."

"Oh no!" I gasped. "I am seriously thinking about not attempting it, Maggie. I'm not sure it makes much difference. However, my realtor is anxious to show me a condo coming up for sale, and I'd really like to meet with Will Cummings."

"What on earth for?" she asked with shock. "He's not your type!" I busted laughing.
"You got that right!" I said between chuckles. "I want to talk to him about the company. When I ran into him at Tello's, he indicated he knew what might be going on there."

ANN HAZELWOOD

"Why do you care about the company at this point, Kate?" Maggie asked seriously. "You're out of that scene!"

"Well, not really. I've learned here in Borna that Meyr Lumber owes East Perry Lumber a lot of money and now refuses to give them anymore credit. It makes me feel terrible! As angry as I am with Clay right now, I know he would turn over in his grave if he knew the damage James has done!"

"Yeah, it sounds bad," Maggie said with some sympathy. "Why don't you just give Will a call? There's no need to see him in person, unless you just want to."

"We'll see!" I said feeling unsettled. "So what's new there?"

"Well, I guess you haven't heard about Cornelia wanting to get out of the quilt shop business," she noted. "It's causing a bit of a stir, and of course we don't want to drive thirty miles to the next quilt shop if that happens."

"Why would she want to sell?" I asked feeling surprised at the news.

"The rumor seems to be she's having an affair and wants to move away," she explained. "Her employees disagree and say it's for financial reasons. When I asked her, she said she would just continue if she didn't have a buyer. What else can she say? She's been there for so long, and I thought she was doing very well!"

"Oh, I hate to think of her closing!" I sadly responded. "Maybe you should buy it!"

"Oh Kate, someone's at the door," Maggie interrupted. "I need to go. Just let me know what you decide to do!"

"Sure," I said listening to her hang up without an "I love ya," like she always said.

I hung up feeling empty. I didn't think she honestly cared

if I came back for the closing or not. Poor Cornelia! Who knows what's really going on her life that she can't share with her customers.

I went straight to the weather channel on TV and the graphics for South Haven were grim. I could call Will I supposed. I couldn't see myself going to the trouble and stress of the trip so I decided to call my realtor and Carla.

Both of the calls went to voice mail. I left a simple message about the bad weather being the reason for me not coming. I was glad I didn't have to hear their voices and explain further.

I was feeling mentally exhausted so I went upstairs to get dressed. I did feel better now that I had made the decision not to go to South Haven. As I was putting on my jeans, I noticed something different in the room which I couldn't quite explain. I finished dressing and went to make my bed. Suddenly, I realized Josephine's quilt was no longer at the bottom of my bed. I knew it was there yesterday, and I knew I brought it home from Ellie's house. Did I mistakenly put it in Jake's bedroom, where it used to lay on the floor? I was trying not to panic as I went searching room to room. I was the only one here, for heaven's sake, I told myself.

I headed downstairs thinking I had better call Ellie to see if perhaps I left it at her house the night of the Friendship Circle meeting. I almost felt faint with fear. I couldn't think of the Catholic saint to pray to when something was lost. "Please God, please God, help me find it," I whispered. I took a deep breath before I clicked on Ellie's cell number. I had no idea where she would be this time of day.

"Ellie, I'm sorry to bother you! Can you talk?" I said with a shaky voice.

"Why yes, I'm getting gas right now, but what's wrong?" she asked with concern. "Is it Blade?"

"No, it's not him, but it's pretty scary!"

"What is?" she impatiently asked.

"I can't find Josephine's quilt!" I blurted out. "Please tell me I left it at your house!"

"No, for heaven's sake," she immediately responded. "You took it home with you."

"I know, I thought I did too, but it's gone. It's not anywhere!" I wanted to cry.

Ellie stopped on her way home and found me pacing the floor with worry. When she entered the door, she could tell from my face, I had not found the quilt.

"Ellie, I know this is crazy, but the only people who know about this quilt are the members of the Friendship Circle," I stated.

"Don't even go there, Kate," she warned. "None of them have been to your house, am I right?" I nodded in agreement. "Okay, so let's just try to make some sense of this. Do you still set the alarm every night?"

"Yes, like clockwork," I assured her.

"Putting it in perspective Kate, it's just a quilt," she muttered. "You aren't missing anything else, are you?"

"I don't think so, but nothing else matters!" I cried back. "It's not just any quilt!"

"Have the workers been in here?"

"No, just Cotton and Clark."

"Did anyone go upstairs?"

I started to say no, but then remembered Cotton put Jack's bed together for me. I told her she was crazy to think of him taking it.

"Well, if that's everyone, then there's only one scenario!" Ellie said holding her hands in the air.

"What? What?" I anxiously asked.

"Josephine herself!" she bluntly shouted. "She may not approve of you having it and made it disappear. Spirits do it all the time. Trout says we have such a spirit at the winery. However, he hasn't totally convinced me. He says things are moved about and disappear on a regular basis. It's an old building, so who knows who or what has gone on there in the past!"

"Oh, Ellie, are you serious?" I was dumbfounded. "You know she could be upset with me for taking her quilt to the Friendship Circle. I regretted it when I got home."

"It could be," Ellie nodded. "I know I wouldn't want my secrets and worries gossiped about within the community, especially since she was such a private person." I wanted to cry, just thinking about it.

"Well, if she wants you to have it back, it'll show up," Ellie trying to make light of it. "That quilt had a scary feeling about it, you've got to admit."

"I feel so badly," I had to sit down. "Please don't tell anyone, Ellie."

"Of course not," she said sitting down next to me for comfort. "Hey, I think you should come home with me for supper. I brought home some extra BBQ ribs that Kelly made. There's nothing like good food and a little wine to put things in perspective. Who knows, maybe she now knows you're sorry, and it'll be here when you return!" We both had to smile at the thought.

Ellie was always good at persuading me to do things, and so I agreed. Food and drink seemed to be the order of the day here in Borna.

I had to admit, just being in Ellie's house was comforting and reminded me of the first few days I visited Borna. While Ellie prepared our food, she was chatting a mile a minute, and I wasn't listening. When her remarks or questions were not answered, she knew where my mind was.

"I saw Clark's SUV at your place last night," she voiced changing the subject. "I thought you would have told me about it by now."

I smiled and nodded. "And I would have, but I was a little distracted," I explained. "He just got back in town, and he thought he should check in with me since he hadn't been working for a while. He said he'd be back in a couple of days to try to finish up some things."

"Well, he could have called you instead," she said in a teasing manner. "I'm not trying to be a nosey neighbor, but his car was there a few hours, if I'm not mistaken. I'm just sayin'!" She giggled.

"Ellie Meers, I'm going to get you back for all this nonsense!" I joked. "Okay, I did ask him to stay for dinner. He was going to pick up something at your place, but I had left over stew and corn bread so I made the offer. Sorry I took some business from you! Trust me, the more I know this guy, the more I realize he doesn't want a romantic relationship. I do think he trusts me as a good friend, however!"

"I'm sorry, but I don't believe that's true, but if the two of you are happy with your arrangement, so be it! Actually, it's quite ideal. I wish I had a male friend who wasn't a customer. I also know a man could never handle my lifestyle with running a business. Most men around here want their woman at home. It would take one strong dude to put up with me!" We laughed and clanked our glasses together.

I knew it was a unique relationship I was building with Clark. I think it was because I wasn't a native to the community, and he knew I admired his work. Besides, I was in no shape to enter a relationship with all my baggage.

CHAPTER 57

The entire next day I tried to go about my normal routine, but all I could think about was Josephine's quilt. It was a nice sunny day, so Wayne and a couple of his workers showed up to work on the garage foundation. Clark appeared to be a no-show, so I decided to get out of the house to get my mind on something else.

The first place I thought of was Imy's Antiques. I was glad to see she was open as I pulled in her parking lot. She was in the back of the shop painting a chair. Her face lit up when she saw me, knowing a probable sale would be made.

"Hey Imy, I need some really nice, comfortable, antique dining room furniture," I announced. "Have you seen any for sale or know where I might go to find something like it, without going into the city?"

"Oh, they come and go," she noted. "People would still want dining sets like that even though most folks don't entertain like they used to."

"My house definitely needs one," I stated as I started to look around. "I used to do a fair amount of entertaining in South Haven. I miss fixing a nice table and cooking for others."

"Most of the time I'm by myself, too since I'm a widow, but I still cook for my sons now and then," Imy said as she stopped painting.

"Where do you live?" I asked when another customer came in the door.

"Oh, down the road a piece, off of A road," she described as if I knew exactly where it was. "I sold off my acreage to the farm, but kept the house. It's been in my family too long to let it go. Plus I still like to tend a garden."

"I'm looking forward to doing some gardening myself!" I added. Imy ignored the potential customer who just went out the door.

"Now if I remember, you love quilts, don't you," Imy asked lifting a big box off of the floor.

"Yes indeed, I do!" as I helped her pull a quilt out of a big box.

"I bought these three quilts from a lady, just this week," Imy explained. "She was going into a nursing home. They're all quite nice. This one's a Carolina Lily. Are you familiar with this pattern?" I nodded.

"Sure, and I love the red and green combination. What are the other ones?" I couldn't help but think how much Maggie would have enjoyed this.

"Here is a really nice Crazy quilt," Imy said unfolding the velvet beauty. "Not everyone likes these, but I thought this one was rather different." We opened it up for full view, and the medallion style was rather unique like she said. She laid it aside. "This last one is an appliqued, pansy pattern. I love the black button-hole stitching on it. This one may go home with me. I love applique quilts."

"So these were all from the same family?" She nodded with a smile.

"Say, Kate, I hear you have quite an unusual quilt Mrs. Paulson might have made!" She surprised me with what I was hoping to be keep a secret. I guessed nothing was kept secret within the circle.

""Ahh yes," I finally answered her.

"What's it like?" she asked as she refolded the quilts. "Ellen said it was pretty darn depressing with black embroidery all over it."

"It's different for sure," I said helping her. "We assume she made it, but we just don't know enough about her."

"I'll ask my mom," Imy offered. "She's 93 years old now, but her mind's pretty sharp. She thought the sun rose and set on Doc Paulson."

"Do you think she would remember something about Josephine?" I figured answers would eventually come from somewhere.

"She might," Imy said as she picked up her paint brush to continue working.

"How much is the crazy quilt going to be?" I asked.

Imy paused. "I figure I need at least $300.00. I paid the most for that one." I knew I spotted a bargain.

"That's very reasonable," I said wanting her to be sure. "I'd like to buy it, but I hope you're making some money on it."

She looked surprised. "Great!" she responded as she put the

crazy quilt aside. "I'd really like to see Mrs. Paulson's quilt sometime, if you'd let me."

"Sure," I answered knowing I may never see it again myself.

I left with the crazy quilt in hand and decided to get a bite to eat at Marv's before I went home. The place was crowed as usual, but I found my way to an empty seat at the bar.

"Howdy do, Miss Meyr," Marv said with a big grin. "What can I get for you today?"

"I think I would like a bowl of your award winning chili!" I said grinning.

He leaned his head back and laughed. "And I should thank you for that prestigious honor, by the way!" he added. "We were all pretty thrilled about winning! I see you have a lot going on in the back of your place today!"

"Yeah, I'm trying to stay out of their way so they can get something done!" No secrets living on Main Street for sure, I thought.

"Say, you're the lady who put my friend Blade in the slammer," a gruff, heavy voice said from behind me.

I turned around and saw an older looking guy with a full, salt and pepper beard. I saw immediately he had only a few teeth, and his bad breath could have knocked me off my seat. He just stared at me waiting for a response.

"I don't think we've met," I finally said holding out my hand to shake. "I'm Kate Meyr, and you are?"

"Ben Hecht's my name," he nodded as he refused to take my hand. "Blade's a friend of mine. I've done a good share of work for him." Marv now handed him a beer like he knew his standing order. When he took the beer, I turned my stool around hoping he would go away.

293

"It's a damn shame what's all happened to him since he tried to help you and all!" I took a deep breath as I said a little prayer for help. I turned back to face him again.

"Yeah, it's a damn shame he had to break into my house and assault me, isn't it?" I bellowed back in his ugly face. I turned around once again facing Marv, who was obviously eves-dropping.

"Here ya go, Miss Meyr; you enjoy it, and let us know if you need anything else." He gave Ben a hard stare.

"Oh, this looks delicious!" I said as I tasted the first spoonful. I didn't turn around, but I knew he was still behind me from the horrid smell. The young couple sitting next to me was also eating chili so I struck up a mindless conversation with them ignoring Mr. Hecht.

He finally left as I finished my lunch. Blade did have friends, just as he claimed. They looked to be as creepy as he was. His jail time was leaving them without work, and I was going to be blamed.

When I went outside to leave, I saw him talking to some other guys standing by a pickup truck. There was no question I was the topic of discussion. I ignored them and got in my car to leave.

When I pulled in my drive, I walked over to Wayne who was supervising one of his workmen.

"Yes, Miss Meyr," Wayne said as he looked at me.

"It's Kate, remember!" He nodded with a smile. "Say, do you know a guy by the name of Ben Hecht?"

"Yeah, why?" he asked as he took on a serious look.

"Well, I think he could be trouble," I warned. "He tried giving me grief at Marv's when I went to get some lunch. Do I need to worry about him doing something to harm me?"

Wayne looked around and shook his head in disgust.

"That loser!" he said removing his baseball cap. "He gives me a rough time, too cause I don't hire him. I frankly think he's all talk. He didn't threaten you, did he?"

"No, no, not yet, anyway," I said with a deep sigh. "He's blaming me for putting Blade in jail. He could be scary holding that kind of grudge."

"Don't let anyone bully you, Kate!" Wayne said firmly. "If he thinks he rattled you in any way, he'll keep it up."
I nodded. "Thanks Wayne. Sorry to keep you from your work." I went back into the house feeling somewhat better. I had stood up to him, so I felt better.

I laid my purse on the kitchen counter and took my newly purchased crazy quilt upstairs to the bedroom. It still smelled a bit musty. I made a note to air it outdoors when it was warmer. I couldn't wait to examine it further so I laid it out on the Oriental rug in the hallway. It was so beautiful. The velvet medallion center displayed a bouquet of silk ribbon flowers. The other pieces had the typical handiwork of embroidery, hand painting, beading, and lots of feather stitching outlining the little pieces. I looked closely for a date of some kind, but couldn't find anything but some initials here and there. The velvet border was embellished as well, matching some of the same flowers in the bouquet. The backing was a dark green sateen which was turning blue and yellow from age. Maggie always referred to this green as being fugitive because the original color would escape. Maggie loved and owned several crazy quilts. She would have snapped this one up had she been with me. Maybe I'll save this to give to her on her birthday. I decided to leave it displayed on the floor for Ellie to see.

CHAPTER 58

When I came downstairs at dusk, I made a fire thinking everything would get better after such an unnerving day. I had stared at many a fire when I was home alone at night waiting for Clay to come home. I knew there would come a time he'd have an accident from his drinking. I just didn't think it would be fatal. Every time I made a fire, I first had to dismiss my pain from South Haven.

I fixed myself a small salad, feeling sorry for myself, on this Saturday night. I guessed I'd better get used to it. I decided I would go to church tomorrow. Goodness knows I had much to pray about. I also needed to be reminded about my many blessings.

As I did many nights, I brought my dinner in front of the TV and the fireplace. There was nothing but violence reported on the news, so I turned it off. I felt restless.

Part of me wanted to make a phone call to Will Cummings,

but it was nighttime and perhaps he would get the wrong impression by me calling him at night. I thought during the day would be better. I hardly ate a bite. Instead I paced the floor trying to get my mind off of the missing quilt. I didn't want to go to the winery, plus I had just talked to Ellie. So why not just call Will? What was the worst thing that could result from it? The day couldn't get worse, could it? My anxiety reminded me of my relationships in my teenage days. To call or not to call was the question.

I went to the kitchen to pour myself another glass of wine. Was I lonely in this house? I saw my purse sitting on the counter. I went over to see if I still had Will's number. I found his card right away, which seemed to be a sign to call. Of course I had to call him at night, I told myself. He would never feel free to discuss anything I wanted to know while he was at work.

I walked to my comfortable loveseat and dialed his number. I took a deep breath as it rang three times before there was a response. I was beginning to hope it would go to voice mail, but instead a familiar voice answered.

"Will here," he bluntly answered.

"Will, this is Kate Meyr!" I said in a business like tone.

"Well, how are you Kate?" he cheerfully asked.

"I'm fine," I quickly responded. "I'm pretty much snowed in here! I was going to try to make it home for my house closing, but the weather is just too bad."

"Yeah, it's been quite the winter!" he replied.

"Will, I'm calling to find out a little more about a conversation we touched on when I saw you at Tello's."

"Yeah?" he responded with confusion in his voice.

"If you recall, East Perry Lumber is located here in Borna,

and it would be helpful to know a little bit of the background of the two company's relationship. I recently received some disturbing information concerning Meyr's financial situation. Can you tell me how in the world things got so out of hand since Clay's death?" He paused, and I knew it was a subject he didn't want to go into.

"Oh brother," he paused. "James unfortunately doesn't have the skill set to run the place, and to make matters worse, he's been hitting the bottle a bit too much, just like your deceased did. Sorry, to bring it up Kate, but that's now the case."

"Oh, I'm sorry to hear it!" I said in shock. "You would think his brother's death would have been a severe warning. I don't remember him having a drinking problem."

"I shouldn't be saying anything about it, but it's you asking." he said in a softer tone, like he cared. "Ever since James couldn't pull off some deal with East Perry, he's been acting a lot differently, if you ask me. There are a lot of days he just doesn't come in, and I know it's from his drinking!"

"What deal?" I asked with my heart racing.

"Well, ya know, when you inherited the Borna property and decided to keep it," he innocently explained.

"Well, that's what confuses me," I cried. "Why would he add to his financial burden to buy this place?"

"Okay, Kate Meyr, I think I've already said too much here," he admitted. "How about we pick up this conversation when we can meet face to face here in South Haven?"

"I can't wait for such a visit, Will," I admitted. "I've had to accept the senseless death of my husband, and then I find out Clay was seeing someone else. Did you know who Clay was seeing when he died?" There was silence and hesitation before he answered.

"It was common knowledge Clay always had something going with this gal or that one," he finally said in a soft voice.

"What?" I said gasping. "How long had he been fooling around?" I could feel nausea coming on.

"Ever since I've been with the company," Will casually said. "Now Kate, you've got to realize this has always been a little Peyton Place around here. Sometimes rumors aren't always true. The women loved Clay, and he knew it." I wanted to pass out from the picture he was painting in my mind. "I'm sorry, Kate, but it sounds like you are finding some things out a little too late! He thought the world of you and bragged about you often. I know he would have never divorced you!"

"Oh well, I guess I should be thankful for that!" I said in disgust. I wanted to scream at him! "So is this Peyton Place one of the reasons you decided to divorce your wife?" He snickered knowing I was getting close to his own story.

"She decided to divorce me, by the way," he made clear. "I'm not proud of any of it, Kate. I can tell you more about it later. No one's perfect." That was the last thing I wanted to hear more about.

"Thanks, Will, you've been helpful," I said more calmly. "I've got to go." I hung up without hearing his response.

I couldn't stop the tears pouring down my face as I lay my head on the love seat. How could I have been such a fool and so naive? My dark thoughts of denial took me into sleep that occupied me till 4:00 in the morning. When my eyes woke up in the still darkness of the morning, I wondered for a moment if I just had a bad nightmare.

The fire was out and my head was aching from the tears and the wine I had consumed. I went to the kitchen to grab an aspirin before I very slowly made my way to my upstairs bedroom.

I took a hot shower in hopes it would relax me for a few more hours of sleep.

When I crawled into my cold bed, I pulled the covers over my head. Thank goodness I was here in Borna, instead of South Haven where the constant reminder of Clay's betrayal would always be haunting me.

I tossed and turned for what seemed like hours. I glanced at the clock as I watched the hours slowly go by. In between remembering Will's hurtful words, I prayed God would show me the way to happiness again. Hearing about James' drinking problem caused me to feel sorry for his wife Sandra, and what she might be going through right now. What was this deal James couldn't pull off? Why did I even care at this point? The sooner I put that family out of my life, the better!

CHAPTER 59

When I awoke in the morning, I made an effort to still dress for church. There wouldn't be workers around today and I was glad to be alone, for some reason.

I didn't arrive at church till the congregation starting singing the first hymn. I sat in the back row hoping not to be noticed. Somehow the words from the hymn and pastor were glazed over as I kept thinking of the hurtful words of Will Cummings and Ben Hecht.

I finally made myself focus on the church services thinking it might help me feel better. There was a new, younger pastor I hadn't seen before. His name in the bulletin said he was the Rev. Jeffery Lohman. His message sounded upbeat as he talked about life's challenges. He said forgiveness is a priceless gift, not only for the sinner, but the forgiver. I couldn't help but think of Josephine's embroidered message which read "Forgive them, for they know not what they do!"

Did I have people in my life who were hurting me, and not realizing the impact? Were their circumstances graver than mine? Were they not thinking about the consequences? Forgiving was a much deeper word in meaning than just saying "I'm sorry."

I nodded hello to some folks as I was leaving and shook Rev. Lohman's hand. I introduced myself and then proceeded out the door so I wouldn't have to make further conversation.

"Kate, Kate," someone called from behind. It was Ellen. "Good morning!" I said turning towards her. She was dressed to the nines as always. She had a sweet little veiled hat on her head, which I hadn't seen people wear in ages. It was so her, I thought.

"I'm so glad Oscar and I saw you this morning," Ellen began. "We had talked about inviting you to Sunday dinner sometime. When I saw you, I thought why not today? Are you free?" I had to get used to most of the folks in Borna referring to lunch as dinner.

"Why yes, I have no plans, but it isn't necessary!" I said blushing.

"I have a large roast in the oven, which is way too much for the two of us, so it would be our pleasure if you could join us," Ellen gushed. Oscar just stood there smiling, leaving his wife in control, as I'm sure he always did.

"I told Ellen when you first came to Borna, she should extend an invitation to you, so please join us," Oscar encouraged. "Alright then," I nodded. "I'll have to follow you, since I don't know where you live."

"We're right down the road a piece," described Ellen like that would be sufficient directions.

I got in my car and wondered what I had gotten myself into. I certainly couldn't refuse an invitation from one of the pillars of the community. They were right. It was just down the road a piece. I had passed their lovely ranch home coming into Borna and admired it. I also noted the well-attended landscaping, even though it was the dead of winter. Ellie told me Ellen was quite the gardener.

I entered a beautiful, pastel decorated home which embraced Ellen's love for florals. Oscar continued to entertain me with small talk as Ellen prepared the table.

"Would you like to try some of my homemade wine, Kate?" Oscar asked proudly. "I occasionally try my hand at it, and the family seems to enjoy it at least." He chuckled.

"Why sure, if you'll join me," I said graciously. "Your home is beautiful, Oscar."

"That's Ellen's department, but we are fortunate to have good carpenters available through the company. I used to enjoy working with wood myself, years ago, but haven't done anything in a long time. Maybe when I retire, I'll do a few things." Ellen gave him a big smile of approval.

"That would be wonderful," I said nodding. "That was what Clay's Dad always said." Oscar's look changed to be more serious. I regretted making the comparison.

"You've been fortunate to employ Clark McFadden, I hear!" Oscar noted as he handed me a glass of wine. "He's the best there is!"

"I've been very pleased," I bragged. "Of course I have become the fill in spot between his really important jobs." He smiled and nodded.

"Everything is ready, you two!" Ellen called from the dining room.

The dining room was huge and graced with a very long dining room table. The elegant china and crystal table setting made me wonder if they always dined in this style.

"Oscar, would you lead us in grace?" Ellen asked sweetly. He followed by saying a simple table prayer, which was a nice, pleasant touch. It reminded me of the table prayer we said at home before I married.

"So Kate, I heard you had to cancel your trip back to South Haven because of the bad weather!" Ellen said as she passed me a bowl of green beans.

"Yes, it's been pretty brutal there," I claimed as I filled my salad plate. "My realtor will just fax the sales contract to me this week, so it's not a problem."

"I've been to South Haven and visited their lumber facility there," Oscar noted. "It was about seven years ago when John was still alive. I met your deceased husband very briefly." I didn't know what to say, so I just nodded.

"This is so delicious, Ellen," I complimented.

"Well, I heard you were quite the cook, Kate!" Ellen replied. I had to smile.

"I'm more of a baker, I think," I confessed. "South Haven is known for its blueberries, so my specialty is blueberry muffins! I'll have to bring you some by sometime!"

"I could go for that!" Oscar said happily. "So are you home sick at all, Kate?"

"I do love the beach, so I'm sure this summer I will miss it," I said smiling. "I've got my realtor looking for a little place near the beach, for my son and me to visit now and then."

"Yes, I don't know if I told you that Kate has a son in New York, Oscar," Ellen recalled.

"So what does he do?" Oscar asked with interest. "I take

it he'll not be joining the family business as yet?"

"No, he loves New York and is employed in advertising," I explained after another swallow of water. There was a pause, so decided to be brave and ask some of my gnawing questions.

"You know Oscar, I felt very unsettled hearing about your misfortune with Meyr Lumber," I began. "I know I didn't have anything to do with their business practices, but I wish you could help me understand something." Oscar barely looked up from his plate, and Ellen was stone silent.

"What's that, Kate?" he finally asked looking up at me.

"Why am I somehow to blame in this whole business scenario? An employee from Meyr told me some deal didn't go through for James, but he wouldn't say what! You can say it is none of my business, but buying this Borna property has caused me quite a bit of stress. How can Meyr's business troubles be my fault? I've had revolting things left on my doorstep, a break in, and a physical attack. Now Blade's so called friends are saying insinuating things to me. I don't feel exactly safe here, right now!" That last comment got their attention.

"Oh dear," Ellen said sympathetically. They both shook their heads in disbelief. Oscar took a deep breath.

"I can't imagine you haven't been told about my generous offer to James," Oscar now pulling his chair back from the table.

"What offer?" I questioned impatiently.

"Well, when I was forced to cut off their credit, I really felt badly about doing so, for John's sake of course. I know how hard he worked to make the business a success. I tried to think of a way to be helpful." Ellen appeared to be as clueless as I was. We waited to hear more. "Your place had been sitting empty for quite a long time. It broke my heart to see renters in and out of there. No one seemed to be interested in buying it, so I told James if he wanted to sign over the house and acreage, I would erase their debt. To be honest, I just assumed the property stayed in his family with him."

"It did stay in the family with Clay and me," I explained. "John left the property to Clay and when he passed away, Clay left it only to me not James." Oscar and Ellen just stared as they tried to absorb what I was telling them. "Clay and his Dad always knew James was not prepared to run the company. I originally came here to sell the property. As I'm sure Ellen told you, I fell in love with the house and wanted to restore it, to get a better price. In time, I then decided Borna would be a new start for me, so I decided to move here." They were speechless. "Blade was not happy when I changed my mind about selling, but I never had a contract with him."

"So when you didn't sign with him, James hired Blade to get it listed so he could buy it. Am I right?" Oscar asked.

"Yes, I heard he offered Blade $12,000 as a bonus," I revealed. Oscar looked shocked. Ellen still remained silent shaking her head.

"James was dealing with the wrong guy for sure!" Oscar said in disbelief.

"Oh honey," Ellen interrupted. "I didn't know any of this! I'm sorry."

"Believe me, Kate, I wouldn't have made such an offer had I known a little more about the situation," Oscar stated boldly. "It really worked out for the best anyway. I have a feeling had the deal gone through, it wouldn't have been the end of their troubles. James is going to put the place under, if he's not careful.

Word spreads pretty quickly in this industry." It was a dirty picture, but now I understood.

"Thanks so much for making this all clearer, Oscar," I said exhausted.

"I'm sorry to hear Blade's guys are giving you some static!" Oscar said in disgust.

"I can handle it!" I wearily said. "There are too many nice folks like you in Borna. They know I'm not going anywhere, so I'm sure in time, this will all die down."

"My goodness, Kate, what did your brother-in-law have to say about Blade breaking into your place?" Ellen asked with such concern.

"I don't know," I said in wonder. "He didn't hear about it from me. If he did hear it, I haven't received an apology."

"Well, if that doesn't beat all!" Oscar responded feeling badly for me.

We continued to chat through a heavenly dessert of raspberries and angel food cake. It was a meal I would never forget, in more ways than one. I felt a sense of relief now that I knew why James wanted the property so much. Ellen and Oscar were down to earth folks trying to do the right thing. I thanked them for a wonderful meal and interesting visit. I promised as soon as I had dining room furniture, I would have them to dinner.

CHAPTER 60

I left them feeling grateful for their hospitality and being so forthright with me. Clay would never believe in a million years, what I had just been told.

When I pulled into my drive, Ellie's car was slowly passing by, and she honked her horn for my attention.

"Are you going to be home for a while?" she asked loudly from her car window. "I want to see that crazy quilt you bought before it disappears!" She laughed, which put a smile on my face.

"Sure. Come on over!" I yelled back.

Ellie would fall over when I told her what I learned from Oscar. I put on some coffee for us, despite the fact I just had a couple of cups at Ellen's house. I was stuffed, which told me tonight's dinner would not be necessary.

When I walked in the door, Jack was calling on my cell phone.

"Don't you ever check your cell messages, Mom?" Jack asked in frustration. "Today is Sunday ya know!" It was his reminder that we tried to touch base with each other on Sundays.

"I'm sorry, Jack. What did I miss?" I asked feeling badly. "I've had a lot going on."

"Well, I finally called Carla to see if you had made it home for the closing, and she said you cancelled because of the weather."

"That's right. I'll just sign the contract when they fax it to me." I reported. "The weather just wasn't cooperating. Is everything okay with you?"

"Yes, and no," he said in a disgusting tone. "Jenny's been all in a huff lately, so don't know what to make of that!"

"What do you think it's about?" I questioned sympathetically.

"I can't go into it now, but she sure has been a pain lately!" he moaned.

"I'm sorry, Jack. I know how much you think of her." I consoled. "I really do want to meet her some time!"

"That isn't looking good right now, and I'm running out of patience," he complained.

"Continue to be patient and let her know how much you care," I advised. "That's very important."

"I know, I know, Mom," he mumbled. "I probably shouldn't have said anything."

"You can call me anytime, honey, and I'll say a prayer. That's what I do best!" I heard him sigh.

"Yeah, Mom, yeah," he always responded when I would mention praying. I wondered if my son ever prayed.

"I love you, honey. Try not to worry," I tried to assure him.

We both hung up feeling sad. The last thing I wanted to hear was that my son was unhappy. It sure wasn't the time to fill him in on the news I learned today.

I thought of Maggie and how she would react from my news. What would she say when I told her about Will's remarks about Clay's unfaithfulness?

After I threw my keys on the kitchen counter, I wanted to collapse and take a nap. I had so much to digest. I quickly jotted down a reminder on my kitchen paper pad to send Ellen and Oscar a thank you note for today's lunch.

The person I really felt like talking to about the latest developments was Clark. He always reacted sensibly and calmly to things. He would not be amused when I told him about Ben Hecht harassing me. Perhaps he would show up tomorrow, even with the dismal weather forecast. I wished we had the kind of relationship where I could pick up the phone and call him. Forget about it, I told myself.

I took a cup of coffee with me to the living room, where I wanted to build a fire before Ellie arrived. I looked out the window and saw her walking towards my house. What would I do without my Borna friend Ellie and this comforting fireplace?

"You're going to need that fire from what I hear on the weather forecast," Ellie announced as she came in the door. "They just called off school for tomorrow."

"Let it snow, let it snow, let it snow!" I said without a care in the world. "I'm just glad I'm not in Michigan, and by the way, they almost never call off school because of snow."

"Well, what brought this attitude on?" she asked taking off her coat. "Did you go to church?"

"I did," I happily reported. "I also got a Sunday dinner

invitation from Oscar and Ellen!"

"Well whoop do da!" Ellie responded. "How did you swing that Miss Socialite?" I laughed as I got comfortable in the loveseat. Ellie always preferred sitting in my rocking chair.

I began giving her every detail of my impression of Ellen's table, the meal, and then what Oscar had revealed about offering James a deal which involved 6229 Main Street. She couldn't believe her ears. She kept interrupting me with questions along the way.

When she had digested the news from Oscar, I told her about my encounter with Ben Hecht. She knew who I meant, but said she never saw him come into her winery. Ellie warned me once again about Blade's shady friends.

"I have another confession to make," I divulged.

"Holy cow, Kate, I can't keep up with you!" Ellie teased.

"Last night I was feeling unsettled and decided to call Will Cummings," I revealed as Ellie looked at me strangely. "He was an employee of Clay's, and I ran into him at a pizza place when I was home. He indicated to me then, he knew quite a bit of inside news from the lumber company. I also think he thought he had a chance of picking me up on the side." I had to laugh, as did Ellie.

"Oh really. Well, I'm all ears!" Ellie responded with more laughter.

"Since I decided not to go home for the closing, I decided to call him!" I said curling my legs underneath me to get comfortable. "Unfortunately, I didn't learn anything about the company, but I did learn that as long as he knew Clay, he always had a woman on the side! He said Clay was quite the lady's man! How do you like those apples?"

"He actually told you straight on?" she asked in disbelief.

"What a so and so! Do you believe him?"

"It hit me hard, even though I knew one "babe" existed from his cell phone," I revealed in anger. "What is demoralizing is that I was so naive! I was always lecturing him about going to AA and giving up drinking, but the thought of adultery never crossed my radar screen." Ellie had her mouth open in shock. "You think you know someone, but you really don't!" By now I was shaking again.

"Well, Kate, I didn't know your husband, Clay, but if you ask me, he got what was coming to him!" Ellie said in disgust. "I know that sounds a bit harsh, since he died and all."

"I know he was bad, but he wasn't always like that!" I said as tears pooled in my eyes. I didn't know if the tears were from feeling sorry for myself or how pitiful Clay had become.

"Of course, Kate, I just feel so badly for you," she said as she put her hand on my arm. "You are certainly not the only one who has been hit broadside with deceit! At least you are here now to start a new life without his family and his employees."

"I certainly don't want Jack to know any of this!" I stated as I sniffled. "He idolized his Dad." Ellie nodded in agreement.

We poured ourselves more coffee, and we talked and talked till dusk, putting more logs on the fire.

"How about some food, Kate?" Ellie finally said as she got up and checked the time.

"Not for me, thank you," I responded. "I had a huge lunch, remember? I do want you to see that crazy quilt before you leave!"

We both went up the stairs, and when we got to hallway, there was no quilt lying on the rug in the hall. I went numb.

"Oh no! The quilt isn't here on the floor where I left it!" I yelled in horror.

"Okay, Kate, are you jerking my chain?" Ellie asked with her hands on her hips. "I think you're losing more than quilts here!"

I immediately went into my bedroom, and there, at the bottom of my bed, laid the crazy quilt. It was folded just like I had folded Josephine's quilt.

"Oh heavens, here it is, Ellie!" I said grabbing it in my hand. "I don't know how it got here! I certainly didn't put it here! Ellie looked at me shaking her head in disbelief. "I'm serious!"

"Well, girl, you've got a lot of stress going on here these days," she said in pity. She picked up the quilt to examine it. "Wow, this is really beautiful," she declared. "It'll be interesting if you can pick up any local information on it."

We laid the quilt open, on the bed, so she could see it more closely. I told her Maggie was a real expert on crazy quilts, and I would likely give it to her as a birthday present. I insisted we fold it back up the way we found it. It made me nervous, thinking quilts were moving about in my house.

"I was thinking, Kate, maybe Josephine's quilt is back up in the cabinet above the door where we found it," Ellie suggested. "Have you looked there? She definitely has a presence in this house, whether you want to believe it or not!"

"Sorry, I already checked, and it's not there!" I reported with certainty.

When we went back downstairs, I thought about some spirit living within this house. Why I wasn't more afraid was a mystery to me.

When Ellie left in the dark to go home, she flashed her porch light once, signaling she was home safe.

CHAPTER 61

It was a new week with high expectations, I told myself while making coffee the next morning. My mind was on Clark, hoping he would show up today. We were so close to having his work finished.

I saw Cotton's pickup truck pull into the drive. He had become a part of my Borna family, and I was always happy to see him.

"How ya doin', Kate?" he asked with a big smile, when I opened the door.

"Good to see you!" I greeted. "What's up with you today?"

"Ya know, there's a storm comin' our way," he warned. "Do you have plenty of wood or need anything else before it happens?"

"I think I'm good, but tomorrow I may need some shoveling done, if you're out and about," I said as I automatically poured him a cup of coffee.

"Oh thanks, Kate," he said as he anxiously took my offer. "I hope to be helping Wayne today."

"That's great," I responded feeling happy that Wayne had included him for some work. "Tell whoever shows up, I'm about to put blueberry muffins in the oven!"

"You bet!" he said giving me a wave as he went out the door.

When I needed to think or to get my mind going on something else, I had the urge to bake. Maggie always said it was a way for me to keep the beast away.

My cell phone rang, and it was my realtor telling me to turn on my fax. She said she'd be sending the pages of the sales contract. She told me the new owners were anxious to move in right away, which I felt was good news.

"Did Carla get everything out of the house?" I quickly asked.

"She did, and we're good to go!" she relayed. "Say, are you still interested in a beach house?"

"I think so, but it's hard to think of going through the hassle right now," I confessed. "I'm just getting settled here!"

"I'll keep emailing you prospects then, if you don't mind," she suggested. "There might be something to tempt you. This winter won't last forever!"

"That's fine, and thanks for all your help!" I said before I hung up.

It was time for the muffins out of the oven, and I filled a basketful to take to the workers. Just before I went out the door, Clark arrived.

"It looks like my timing is pretty good!" Clark said rubbing his stomach.

"I think you must have smelled these muffins across town," I chuckled. "Please take one. Do you need coffee?"

"Well, another cup wouldn't hurt!" he said leaning against the counter. "I thought I'd finish up today putting the last of the hardware on. Until you get the sunroom up and framed, it looks like I'm done here for a while."

I nodded feeling sad about it all. "It all looks beautiful, Clark," I complimented. "I'm enjoying all the new shelves in the other rooms, too."

"Man, these muffins are good!" he praised. "Say, have you been okay?" That was an unexpected question.

"I'd like to say all is well, but it's been an interesting week, to say the least, Clark," I announced looking down.

"You don't have to talk about it. It's none of my business. I just thought I'd ask." Clark stated.

I smiled. "Let's go in by the fire," I suggested.

I began by telling him the news I had learned at Oscar and Ellen's house. He was quite surprised, but didn't comment. Then I told him about my run in with Ben Hecht. He grimaced but didn't say anything. When I told him about calling Will Cummings and hearing about Clay's unfaithfulness, his expression changed.

"That's all pretty heavy stuff Kate," he finally said shaking his head. "If it makes you feel better, I'll take care of Ben. Frankly, it sounds like it worked out for the best with no deal being made on this property. I bet if you ever did decide to sell, Oscar's company would probably be interested."

"You have a point there," I nodded. "It is a bit haunting however, that I had the power to clear Meyr Lumber's debt. I could possibly entertain the idea, if my husband truly loved me.

"That's crazy Kate," Clark said animated. "I think things worked out the way they were supposed to! Too bad Clay didn't realize his short cummings before his accident."

"I know, I know," I sadly said. I felt like I wanted to run away from it all. "I didn't mean to burden you with all of this."

"Nonsense! Say, how about getting out of the house to-night?" Clark said out of the blue.

"Tonight in the horrid storm?" I asked chuckling at the thought.

"If the prediction wasn't so bad, we could drive into the city and have a nice dinner, but I have another idea." He seemed to be excited about the suggestion.

"Really?" chuckling once again at how surprising this guy could be.

"How about I cook us dinner tonight at my place?" he asked as if a light bulb had just gone off. "If we get snowed in, you can stay in my extra bedroom," he boldly offered.

"I'm not sure this is very wise on many levels!" I was forced to say.

"What are you afraid of?" he asked staring right into my eyes.

"This is a very small town, Clark," I said with hesitation.

"Kate Meyr, I thought you were a free spirit from South Haven, Michigan!" he stated. "You weather a lot bigger storms there than we do here in Borna! Are you telling me you're afraid to venture away from Main Street with your trusted handy man?" I had to laugh, since he put it like that. "As soon as I finish here, I'll pick up some things before I head home. It will be an adventure my friend! You need to escape from all this drama." He was truly getting excited, but I had a feeling this could lead to more drama. Did I dare accept his offer?

"Okay, you're on!" I said giving in.

He laughed as he walked towards the kitchen door. "I'll come back for you in my truck at 6:00. Now let me get back to work, woman!" He went outdoors to his truck to get his tools.

"Fine, it'll be fine," I said smiling to myself. What had I just agreed to?

CHAPTER 62

As the day went on, I was questioning my decision to go to Clay's cabin on this horrid night. Finally, I was distracted by the faxing of my house contract, which had to be signed and returned. When I pressed send, I realized I had just severed complete ties to my South Haven home. The good news was a happy, young family would now bring life to a lifeless house.

It was around 1:00 when I noticed the outdoor activity had stopped because the snow was starting to fall quite heavily. Clark decided to leave as well. He reminded me of my 6:00 pick up, as if I were a little child. After he left, I realized he might not be coming around here again till spring, since he finished up the last minute details. Even my blueberry muffins couldn't make that happen.

I was tempted to call Ellie and tell her my evening plans, but worried she might advise me against going, or think

Clark's intentions meant something else. I cancelled the idea.

When I wasn't baking, my favorite pastime, I chose to play in my sewing room. I had neglected it completely during the move, not giving it any priority at all. The new shelving Clark built was awesome, but I'd brought very little fabric with me. Carla and Maggie were thrilled to lighten my load by taking yardage off my hands. I planned for Cotton to hang one of my quilts on the one blank wall. I needed to decide which one. There was something so comforting in sorting and feeling my fabric. I sorted by color, since my stash was so much smaller. I loved having the fabric with me, whether it made it into a quilt or not!

I finally showered and dressed. How could I dress warmly and yet be attractive in some way? Was this actually a date? Dinner at a cabin in the woods, with a possible sleep over, sounded more like a romantic couple's evening than one of just friendship. It was a nice gesture on his part, after he heard all my stories of woe! Once again, he was likely feeling sorry for me. I was about to go downstairs when Maggie called.

"So did you get the contract signed today?" Maggie anxiously asked.

"Yes, about a couple of hours ago!" I divulged.

"Happy for you, but sad for me!" she whined. "More snow today, and my best friend is far away and can't join me for coffee!"

"If it makes you feel any better, it's snowing like crazy here as well," I complained. "I did make muffins for the workers this morning before it snowed so hard. I just finished doing some organizing in my sewing room and thought of you.

I'm afraid organizing my sewing room has been low on my bucket list with what's all happening here."

"I'm jealous, I admit," Maggie confessed. "I don't know if I can wait till spring to visit you. I miss you so much!"

"So nice to hear, my friend," trying to picture her in my mind. "You don't have to wait till spring, but if you're going to drive, I would wait!"

Before we hung up, I decided to tell her the news I learned at Oscar and Ellen's Sunday dinner. She was shocked at how James kept me out of the loop. She said she had lost respect for the Meyr family in general, since Clay's accident. She commented how Sandra and James were barely seen these days. I told her to be easy on Sandra, since I knew from experience what living with an alcoholic was like.

I didn't dare share my plans for the evening with her. Since I had mixed feelings on the evening myself, I thought my best buds, Maggie and Ellie, should be kept out of my plans for now.

CHAPTER 63

I paced the floor, looking out the window every few minutes for Clark. The snow was accumulating on the ground quickly. I had to admit, Borna was much more gorgeous in the snow than South Haven. Maybe it was the country churches, red barns, and rolling hillsides which emphasized the better scenery.

Clark was running late. Was it the bad roads? Did he have second thoughts about the invitation? Would he call and explain? I only recall Clark using his cell phone just once since he'd worked here. I stared out the front window in anticipation and noted the traffic had nearly stopped completely with the bad weather. I hated waiting for things. It reminded me of having a first date with too many unknowns.

Finally, Clark pulled into my drive with his black pickup truck, instead of his SUV. So when in Borna, do as the Borna folks do, I told myself. There were no country club folks to impress or care what I rode in.

I quickly opened the back door before he could knock.

"Oh Clark, what a frightful night this is turning out to be!" I greeted, as he shook off the coat's fallen snow. "We have no business on those roads!"

"Well, some us have to take care of those in need and supply a good, cooked meal," he teased. "I hope you don't mind a ride in my Black Beauty, as I call her. Silver doesn't do as well in these road conditions."

"Silver is your SUV, I take it?" He nodded and smiled.

"Bundle up good, it's pretty windy," Clark described. "It's causing some snow drifts along the road. Say, don't you have an overnight bag?"

"You're serious about me staying, aren't you?" I blushed.

"You bet! We'll be safe for the night and enjoy a great meal, or we can stay here with no food, and I'd have to sleep in Jack's room!"

I laughed. "Okay, I get it," I said giving in. "I'll just be a second."

I went upstairs with butterflies in my stomach. I grabbed my pajamas, robe, and toothbrush. Maybe I could just sleep in what I was wearing, but I threw the pajamas in the bag anyway.

After we cleaned off the windshield, we took off like two little kids on an adventure. Now and then Clark would scare me by purposely sliding a bit on the road. When we got on the gravel road to his house, I couldn't believe the beautiful snow scenes along the way. When I saw his cabin, snuggled in the forest with smoke coming out of the chimney, I felt I was in a storybook.

Thankful to arrive safely, we walked into a warm, terrific

smelling cabin. Over the front door was a carved sign that read, "Clark's Cabin." He told me a friend of his had made it for him.

After we shed our coats, Clark instructed me to pour us a glass of red wine, as he put another log on the fire. His stone fireplace nearly took up one entire wall. I was sure it was more of his handy work.

"Are you hungry?" Clark asked as he stirred a large pot on the stove.

"I'm famished!" I replied looking inside the pot.

"I made my own Brunswick stew recipe for our first course," he announced. "If you've never had it, you're in for a real treat. They used to make this years ago with rabbit, but I made it with chicken, knowing you'd feel more comfortable. They both are good." I had to snicker. "I froze you some to take home, if you like it. The recipe makes a lot!"

"Oh my goodness. This is just the first course?" I asked in wonder. "I've never had Brunswick stew!"

"It's a traditional family stew, which my family makes at least once a year. We used to have it on the night of Christmas Eve." I smiled as I pictured the scene. "I also made a Caesar salad with my own dressing, followed by brisket with roasted vegetables. I started the brisket yesterday!"

"Clark, this is enough food to feed a truck load of people!" I claimed loudly. He laughed. "Are you expecting more guests?" He shook his head and laughed.

"I know, but this is great man food, I can eat on all week," he explained as he started fixing our bowls of stew. "That's how I cook. It's nice to come home to good food when I've worked all day. Eat as little or as much as you want. I should have had you bake us some bread."

"Now you are making me feel bad," I joked. "I would have loved to have done so, but you told me not to bring a thing!"

"I'm kidding, Miss Kate," he said winking.

I could tell Clark was truly thrilled to have me to dinner. I'm sure he rarely had company. I realized I would be doubling my weight soon, if I kept going to Sunday dinners and hanging around this guy!

I took small servings of the many courses, which Clark was amused by. I told him I felt badly for not contributing to the meal, but he told me it was his way of paying me back for lots of blueberry muffins.

Clark was more talkative than I'd ever seen him. After a few swallows of my wine, I had the nerve to ask him if he had ever been married. He paused as if he really didn't want to tell me.

"Once when I was very young," he said reflecting. "We didn't make it two years!" He paused, but I waited to hear more. "We got married because she got pregnant."

"Oh, so you have a child?" I questioned in surprise. He shook his head.

"No, she miscarried in her second month, and our marriage went downhill from there," he described. "The marriage shouldn't have happened in the first place, but our parents insisted on it." I kept quiet to take it all in. This was a sad story. "I left town after the divorce and went to art school in St. Louis."

"You did? Where did you grow up?" I asked excitedly. I found this most interesting!

"A little town in Illinois I'm sure you never heard of," he briefly revealed. "I was glad to leave there, and I was fortunate my folks could afford to send me, as well as my brother, to good schools."

"You have a brother?" I asked as he nodded. Well, this was interesting! What else should I ask?

"Hey, I think it's time to taste my dessert!" He announced clearing some of the dished off the table.

"Dessert!" I moaned. "You have got to be kidding!" He proceeded to dish it up like I agreed to have some.

"I have to warm it up a bit," he said as he put a dish in the microwave. "I made my Mother's recipe for bread pudding."

"Oh, I love bread pudding, but I am so stuffed. This food fest is adding bricks onto my body."

"More man food," he teased with a smile as he filled two small dishes.

"I think I need your recipe for the stew, Clark," I complimented. "It was so good. That's all we should have had tonight."

"Well, I can't tell you how long it's been since I've had anyone here for a meal. Your visit was a good excuse to cook all my favorite things!" I smiled with approval as he brought the pudding to the table.

I took a bite of the soft and crispy pudding that was garnished with a light lemon sauce. It was divine, but I couldn't eat another bite.

We both continued chatting as we cleared the table and filled the dish washer. We touched on topics from his art work to the progress on my construction. He was so easy to talk to. We finally walked into his living room to sit on two separate love seats, which faced each other. As I gazed around the room, it was like being in a small gallery with a masculine touch. I assumed Clark had made most of the wooden furniture. The entire cabin had accents of healthy, green plants about the place, which enhanced the look of the outdoors.

"Cotton told me you have plans for a garden this spring," Clark revealed as he got comfortable.

"Yes, a kitchen garden, I call it," I said with a big smile. "I want a couple of small raised beds to grow a few things. Cotton teases me about not putting the plants right into the good ground."

"That's great, but what else do you have planned for the future?" He asked catching me off guard. "Borna's a pretty small town. Maybe you could open a little bakery, since you like to bake so much."

"No thanks," I said getting up from the couch. "I like baking when it's for my friends and family, but I wouldn't want it to be a job. I do enjoy meeting new people. I haven't been able to visit other places here in the surrounding area with the horrible winter we've had. I don't know what I would have done without Ellie next door. She didn't know me from Adam, and she let me stay with her and started introducing me to folks. I guess I thought there would be a B&B or something for me to stay in, but there wasn't!"

"Yeah, it's a problem when people around here have guests like for a wedding in town," Clark said putting another log on the fire. "It's a good thing most folks around here are pretty hospitable to host them."

"Someone should open a place to stay," I stated. "I would have loved to have had that experience, instead of going home with a perfect stranger."

"Well, maybe someone should do that!" Clark said staring at me with a funny grin. "It needs to be somebody with a big place, who also likes people, and who doesn't mind making blueberry muffins now and then!"

"Clark McFadden, you are out of your mind!" I yelled turning towards him.

"Did I hit a nerve?" he asked chuckling. "The newness could quickly wear off here in Borna, and I'm just suggesting you may want to engage yourself in a small venture. Doc's house would be a great guest house! By the way, that sun porch you're building could accommodate a lot more folks than its one resident."

"Oh really! Well, you seem to have given this quite a bit of thought," I teased with annoyance.

"You'd be a great hostess! I'm just sayin'!" I wasn't sure how to respond. Was he joking or serious?

"I didn't come here in hopes of ever starting a business!" I said defensively. "What I had planned to invest in would be a place in South Haven, like a beach house. Then I could have the best of both worlds."

"I don't see why you couldn't do both," he said with his hands up. "The beauty of a business like a guest house is you decide when you want to work and play." I wanted to dismiss the thought. I already had too much on my mind.

"Do you want me to get any sleep tonight? You're freaking me out!" I complained.

He laughed. "I'm sorry," he finally surrendered. I think we both knew we had to change the subject. "Hey, it's almost midnight!" Clark said jumping to his feet. "Let me show you something really beautiful!" He took an afghan off his chair and motioned for me to follow him. He opened the back kitchen door letting in a big swish of cold air. "Be still and quiet." He put his fingers to my mouth and placed the afghan over my shoulders for warmth.

Just then, like he had orchestrated it, three deer came walking out from the woods behind Clark's cabin.

"They venture out almost every night about this time," he whispered. "They're looking for their food."

"You feed them?" I asked in the same whisper. He nodded. "Aren't they special? They look like a family."

"Yes, they are," Clark whispered with pride.

"You're a sweet person to feed them," I whispered softly.

"I can be sweet some time," Clark said looking right into
my face, which was less than an inch from his.

Without hesitation, I gently raised my head and kissed
him gently on the lips. I couldn't believe how my natural instincts had taken over. It was so easy to respond to him. He
paused as if he were truly surprised. Now what?

"I think I'm supposed to be the first one to do that, so let's
try it again shall we?" he asked pulling me closer to him.

His lips planted a much more serious kiss on me. Who
knew he could kiss as well as any James Bond! I hadn't been
kissed like this in many, many years. I couldn't resist the pas-
sion of the moment and returned my pleasure. What was
happening here?

"Hmmm, I'm going to have to be sweeter more often," he
blushed as he closed the door.

After that kiss, I no longer needed the warmth of the
afghan. We ignored our encounter as Clark went into the
kitchen to get us a hot cup of coffee. We both sat down on
the floor in front of the fire. We stared at the fire in silence.
He wasn't the only one who didn't know what to say. I guess
it was now a real date now, thanks to me.

"This hits the spot!" I complimented as I took a sip of the
coffee.

"I can make a good cup of coffee when I have to," he said
with a big grin.

I didn't want him to think I had any more romantic ideas
so I suggested we turn in for the evening. I got up from the

floor and thanked him again for such a delicious meal.

"I hope my extra room suits you," he said joining me. "I haven't had sheets on that bed since Rock was here."

"Who's Rock?"

"My brother," he said simply. "I'll have you know, I went to a lot of trouble for my boss's visit." We laughed. Was he putting me back into an employer mode from a romantic one?

"Thanks Clark. I'm sure it'll be fine. I'd hate to think what the roads would have been like trying to go home to-night. Good night then. See you when the sun comes up!" He smiled and nodded.

As I slowly put on my gown, I replayed our experience in my mind. You can't un-ring a bell, so whatever it was, it was. I certainly didn't have any other intentions, and don't think he did either. I felt giddy knowing I could surprise him with my gesture. I think I surprised myself! There wasn't a lock on the door, but I felt very safe. I laid my robe at the end of the bed in case I had to get up unexpectedly.

I snuggled between the heavy covers and was pleasantly surprised how comfortable it was. Clark was quite the host! I wondered what made him suggest I might open a bakery or a guest house. I pondered his sensitivity with the deer think-ing how touched I was by it. I would always remember the scene and the reaction it caused. It was the icing on the cake of very pleasant evening.

CHAPTER 64

I smelled coffee; really good coffee. I rolled over to check the clock, and it was only 6:00. It was strange waking up in a strange place. I must have gone to sleep instantly.

I quickly dressed and went out to the kitchen finding it empty. I heard noise outside of the cabin, and it was Clark sweeping snow off his struck. I poured myself a cup of coffee and took advantage of the moment to check out Clark's cabin. His place wasn't large, but it was extremely neat and tasteful. His artistic talent showed in his decor and accessories. I was suddenly interrupted by my cell phone ringing.

"What's up, Ellie?" I responded.

"That was some storm, wasn't it?' she complained. "I'm concerned about freezing pipes at the winery so thought I better make a trip to see about them. Trout's out of town, or I'd send him. I called to see if you needed anything while I'm out. I didn't think you'd be venturing out today. Should I bring us some lunch?"

"No, I'm good," I said with hesitation.

"You sound strange, did I wake you?" Ellie asked with concern. "It is pretty early, isn't it?"

"No. Actually I'm out at Clark's cabin. He invited me out here for dinner last night, and it was too treacherous to drive me back home."

"Clark's place? What have I been missing?" she shouted in my ear. "You spent the night there? What is going on?"

"It's not like you think, Miss Ellie Meers." I stated. Good luck, Kate Meyr, I said to myself.

"Oh man, you got a lot of explaining to do," she demanded. "I better let you go then. You are full of surprises girl, but this one is the best! I can't wait to hear more!" We were both laughing when I hung up.

Clark came in from the cold and insisted on making us some omelets, despite me not having an appetite. I couldn't possibly turn him down. He was like a little kid trying to entertain his guest. We chatted mostly about the weather, but then he brought up my long range plans once again.

"I find it interesting you're so concerned about what I may or may not do in the future." I said after taking another sip of coffee. He paused to think about his response.

"I don't want you to become bored and move away, I guess," he finally revealed. "It's really that simple." How sweet I thought.

"I see," I said while thinking about my response. "It's nice that you are concerned, and I appreciate it very much."

"You're a pretty ambitious gal from what I've observed, and when you finish the Doc's house, you'll likely want a new challenge." I was amused at his observation. "I guess I'm wondering where it will take you."

"Actually, you're probably right, thinking about the bigger picture here, but right now, I still feel like a tourist in this town. I still have a lot to explore!"

"Well, if I've given you something to think about, then I'm glad I brought up the subject," he admitted. He was grinning.

"This guest house is worth exploring, I suppose. I'm not sure I'm ready or have the time. I'll have to see what's involved as far as regulations in this town. There may be a darn good reason why no one has pursued such a place."

"Or the fact that Borna's never had one, you may be the one making up the rules." He theorized. I remained silent.

I got up from the table so we could change the subject. "What are you working on these days?" I asked walking towards his studio area.

"Several things in the early stages, I'm afraid," He answered with reservation. "I do need to stop at Harold's to pick up some things, after I take you home."

"So you don't want to show me anything in progress?" I asked in a teasing manner. He shook his head. I got the hint.

"Not my style or practice, I'm afraid." He got our coats, and that was the end of the conversation.

CHAPTER 65

It was a treacherous drive coming back into town. Our conversation was light. I felt comfortable with Clark, as if he were my best friend or brother. The memory of his kiss told me there was a possibility of it becoming something else.

When we arrived at my house, I quickly jumped out of the truck with my overnight pack and frozen bag of Brunswick stew. I told him to drive on and thanked him for a fun evening. He looked a bit stunned, perhaps expecting an invitation to come in. When our eyes met, he returned a wave as I walked towards the door. Was he expecting another kiss as a thank you? I couldn't let that happen.

It was noon time, and I knew I'd be getting a visit from Ellie sometime in the afternoon. I would have to convince her that Clark and I did not have a romantic relationship, nor did I want any rumor to that affect to begin.

I went upstairs to shower and change, noting the crazy

quilt was still resting at the end of my bed. I now started to believe Josephine had the power to move things where and when she wanted. I stood in the shower for a lengthy time, thinking about my most interesting evening. What impressed me most about Clark was he seemed to have an interest in what I might want to do in the future. That was so different than what I had experience with Clay. It was always about him and how I could enhance his career. He never asked or seemed to care about what I might want to do. Did he think I was incapable? It would be interesting to know if his lady friends were independent and successful. I thought about calling Maggie to share my night's experience, but I knew she wouldn't have understood. She'd warn me about being vulnerable at this stage of my life. I wasn't hearing much from her lately. She hadn't brought up making a visit, like she always did. I would have to work at keeping her as my friend. The long distance was not going to be helpful.

Before I went downstairs, I walked around the second floor to see how I could possibly have guest rooms and not disrupt my personal privacy. The hall had an entrance to the attic, so perhaps that spacious area could accommodate a suite of some kind. Curiosity got the best of me, and I went up the stairs to envision the possibilities. The colder air hit me hard, as I remembered the attic was not heated.

When I got to the top, I was totally surprised by what I saw lying on the attic floor. It was Josephine's embroidered quilt! It gave me more chills when I thought about her spirit bringing it here. Was this her way of keeping her quilt away from folks like the Friendship Circle? Did she make the quilt up here, as Ellie thought she might have? Why did it appear now?

I sat down on the top step to calm myself. Finally, I spoke aloud, in case she would hear me. "Oh, Josephine, if you can hear me, I am so sorry you had to take the quilt away from me. I will leave it here from now on, so your secrets are safe with me. If you are still looking for forgiveness, as you indicated on your quilt, I know that God has forgiven you. I'm sorry you suffered so much pain as you made this quilt. I'm here in your house to give you peace and respect. I want to honor all the good you've done. Please understand I mean no harm, and I just know we can both be happy here." I sat very still reflecting on my words. Somehow I felt better and headed back down the stairs.

When I got back in the hallway, I still couldn't believe the quilt has been returned! I continued down to the first floor, where I looked for my cell to call Ellie immediately.

"Where are you now?" I asked her panting.

"I'm still here at the winery," she stated. "I thought I'd get out of here earlier, but with no one here, I am able to get quite a bit done."

"You have got to stop by here on your way home, Ellie," I said in a shaky voice.

"What's wrong?" she quickly asked.

"I'm a little rattled, but I'll explain when you come. How much longer will you be?" My voice was truly quivering.

"I can leave in the next hour or so, I guess," she surmised. "How about I bring some wine and something to eat for an early dinner? We obviously have a lot to catch up on!"

"Okay, thanks," I eagerly agreed. "I'll be waiting."

I took a deep breath, and as I looked out the window, there was Cotton shoveling a path on my sidewalks with all his might. What would I do without my Borna friends? I guess it really does take a village.

While I waited impatiently for Ellie to arrive, I made a fire and then proceeded to make a small fruit plate to enjoy with Ellie's wine. I also put on a pot of coffee, as the chill just didn't seem to leave the house. I had so much on my mind to tell Ellie, but finding Josephine's quilt took priority over my visit with Clark and the notion of opening a guest house.

Finally, Ellie arrived, and she rushed in with the gusty wind. It seemed there was always a breeze or strong wind on this property. It would be a good thing for my sunporch.

"Burr, burr, burr," she said shivering.

"Go in by the fire," I instructed as I took her bag.

"I think this is the worst winter Borna's had!" Ellie complained. "I'm darn lucky I didn't slide in the ditch coming home." She saw me pacing. I ignored her complaints.

"Wine or coffee?" I offered with my arms wrapped about me.

"Wine of course, silly. The coffee smells good, but wine will go better with the snacks I brought."

I proceeded to pour us each a glass of wine. Ellie noticed my hands were shaking, and it wasn't from the cold.

"Okay, spill it. What's going on?" Ellie asked as she uncovered a small plate of cheese.

"I went up into the attic, and guess what I found?" Ellie shrugged her shoulders in wonder. "Josephine's quilt was sitting on the floor."

"Seriously?" Ellie waited to hear more.

"I didn't put it there, don't you see!" I yelled with frustration.

"Okay, I get it! She is definitely in this house. I told you she was probably up there when she made the quilt. So did you leave it there?"

"Why yes, forever and ever!" I exaggerated. "If that's where she wants it, that's where it will be!"

"So are you frightened to be here now?" Ellie asked with some hesitation.

"I probably should be, but I'm not," I said poking one of the fire logs. "I actually had a talk with her before I went downstairs." Ellie looked at me like I was crazy. "Yes, I talked to her. I said I had no intention of disrespecting her, so I apologized. In fact, my intention was to honor her."

"Now you're creeping me out a little bit!" Ellie shared. "So, mystery solved. I'm glad you feel comfortable about it. So, my dear, what I really want to hear about is this so called sleep over!" We both now laughed. "You talk about it like it was just a high school activity."

"I know you're hoping for some romantic tale, but honestly it wasn't like that," I explained. Ellie shook her head like she didn't believe me. "He fixed a ton of food. I had Brunswick stew for the first time in my life. It was delicious! I have some in the freezer, so I'll share it with you. He evidently cooks a lot at one time, and then eats off of it for days!"
"I don't care about the food, Kate," she reminded. I had to snicker.

"He thought it practical for me to pack an overnight bag with the bad weather and all," I began to explain. "He was right. We almost didn't make it to his cabin. Frankly, I probably should have declined the invitation, but it sounded pretty good at the time. I really wanted to get out of the house. I have too much time to think of the past, and it's not healthy."

Ellie nodded. "Makes perfectly sense to me, girlfriend!" she smiled and shook her head. "Going to a sleep over is a much healthier activity." We both laughed. It did sound rather childish.

"Let's make it clear, Clark and I only have a nice friendship," I said seriously. "Who knows what might happen in the future, but I'm not ready to get into a relationship. I will say I owe him a great deal for saving my life!"

It was Ellie's turn to poke the fire. "You have a good point there," Ellie said after she placed the poker back in its stand. "I'm grateful for that, too! I would hate to see you get involved foolishly, but it's obvious he's quite fond of you. I want to see you happy and settled here. You have been through a lot of changes, plus Blade's harassment, for no good reason."

"I know, and without you and others around here, I would have never decided to stay here!" I said getting emotional. "Let me ask you something." She listened closely. "Are you expecting me to leave town when I get this house finished?" I asked surprising her with the question. "You think I'll eventually go back to South Haven, don't you?"

"Well, the thought has entered my mind," she admitted. "I hope you don't, but what brought all this on?"

"Clark asked me last night what my long range plans were. He seemed to be surprised I would stick around after the house was finished. He thought I would eventually become bored here in Borna."

"It's a natural question for him to ask, I suppose," Ellie admitted. "He would definitely feel a loss if you moved away!"

"Well, he's given it some thought because he suggested some ideas I might pursue if I decide to stay. One idea really gotten my attention."

"Like what?" Ellie immediately asked.

"We both agreed that Borna could use a guest house," I divulged. "There's nowhere to stay within twenty miles. I can't believe no one has considered such a venue."

"Borna isn't exactly a tourist town, Kate," she defended.

"That's what I told Clark, but he said there's a need for the locals to be able to accommodate their out of town guests. Not everyone is as trusting and hospitable as you Ellie. I would have slept in my car had you not offered your house."

"So what are you thinking?" she asked grinning ear to ear.

"I think it's worth looking into, don't you?" I suggested. Ellie was all ears. "Clark explained how it didn't have to tie me down, which is a big concern of mine. He said it would only take a limited number of rooms to provide such a service. I am mostly concerned about my privacy being invaded, which is what took me to the attic today."

"The attic?" Ellie asked in wonder.

"Well, I thought it might have potential to become a suite up there, with all that space. Do you think Josephine would entertain the idea of strangers coming to the house?"

Ellie sat quietly thinking. "Well, she was certainly used to folks coming and going all those years when Doc had his practice here," Ellie finally said. "It would be worth exploring, and you have already aced the location for sure! Location, location, location they say is so important for any business."

We both couldn't stop talking about the possibility. Ellie certainly had a pulse on the community, so any observation from her was important. We batted the pros and cons of the idea as we munched on a variety of goodies. I was proud of keeping my magical kiss from Clark contained in my bag of secrets. We had more important things to discuss.

CHAPTER 66

The following week finally gave us sunshine to start melting all the snow. I was counting the days till spring, my favorite season.

Jack's weekly call on Sunday encouraged me to still pursue a beach house in South Haven. The more I thought about it, the more it seemed like a good idea. There were certainly things about South Haven I missed, like good restaurants, shopping, concerts and great quilting friends. Michigan was great to visit in the summer to avoid the severe humidity I knew Missouri was known for. I told him I would encourage the realtor to keep looking.

It was nice to see a week of carpenters and electricians hustling about on the garage and sunporch. Ever since Clark noted how large the sunporch was for entertaining guests, that was all I could envision. There was no sign of him these days, but I knew he'd be checking on the progress, so he could add his finishing touches. Who knew how many times he may have driven by to check on things?

Ellie told me the city hall, where I could get information about zoning and business regulations, was just down the street. I had totally missed seeing it, but knew I'd have to visit them soon to find out any particulars if I opened a guest house. I'm sure once I asked anyone about anything, the rumors in Borna would start flying. There were many questions still haunting me about the possibility, but if I wanted to open in the summer, I'd have to make a decision soon. I was a visual person, so I had to picture in my mind how the lay out would be. Where would I plant gardens and create an inviting outdoor environment for the guests to enjoy? Which rooms would I designate for them? The big question lurking was would Josephine approve? I would also have to choose an inviting name and make sure I got Borna's approval. I didn't need some of Blade's friends starting rumors I had plans for a house of ill repute. Ellie teased me about the thought, and I wasn't naïve enough to know there wouldn't be some opposition to a plan for a guest house.

It was a good feeling to know I had the support of two of my most favorite friends in Borna, Ellie and Clark. While making plans for my future, I was mellowing in my anger about the past. I was still struggling with forgiving Clay for all he had done to me. Perhaps Josephine was feeling the same way and had expressed her anger and guilt in her quilt! Maybe we both needed to forget and forgive and move on with life.

I did have to give Clay credit for leaving me the Borna property. What would he really think of me living here and opening a guest house? I wanted to believe Clay was sorry for many things and really loved me, but with his sudden death, I would never know. He certainly would want me to be happy, I think. That's what Jack and Carla had told me. I certainly came to Borna as a frozen woman and now I was starting to thaw. The process was a little painful, but necessary. Responding to Clark's kiss was also a reminder, I was a woman with feelings and my natural instincts had not been permanently damaged. That made me smile.

CHAPTER 67

Another week had passed, and there were early remind-ers that spring was not far away. I always thought of spring as a season of hope. I truly expected it to be one for me.

As I was putting on my robe to start my day, my eye caught something else reflected in my mirror. Josephine's quilt was now lying on the edge of my bed once again. How could I have missed it when I awoke? I couldn't help but smile. "Welcome back!" I said caressing the top of the old quilt as if it were an old friend.

I came down the stairs in my robe and gazed out the win-dow of my front door to see Ellie turning into my driveway. I hurried toward the back door to let her in. I loved her unex-pected visits!

"Good morning!" she said glancing at my attire. "There's a lot going on out there! Did you just get up? I can't imagine sleeping late with all this noise! It even woke me up at my house!"

I smiled at the thought. "I know, I can't believe I slept so long," I said yawning. "That's unusual for me. Come in and have some coffee. "

"You sleeping in is a good sign you're finally settling in!" she said cheerfully. "I'm on my way to the winery and thought I'd extend an invitation to come to our fish fry tonight. With lent approaching, we're going to be frying catfish on Fridays."

"Catfish? Seriously?" I asked. Ellie laughed. "Can that be good?"

"The whole community thinks so!" she responded. "I take it you've never tasted it?" I shook my head. "If you're gonna live around here, you're going to have to try it sooner or later!"

"Let me get you some coffee," I said getting out some cups. "I have some news to share." I poured our coffee as she eagerly waited to hear what I had to say.

When we both sat down at the table, I described to her what I found at the end of my bed. I was surprised she barely reacted. She nodded as if it was no big deal. By now I was betting Ellie thought I was a complete fruit cake.

She was hesitant in her response. "I think she's forgiven you for exposing her quilt," Ellie said calmly as she sipped her coffee. "She is making friends with you, and that's a good thing, especially if you're going to live in this house." I smiled in agreement.

"That's what I would like to think, Ellie," I shared taking my first sip of coffee.

"I'm really getting excited about the prospect of you making this a guest house," Ellie said looking around the place.

"Remember you mentioned Susie would be a good house-keeper for you some day. I'd look into it! You have a lot of resources here, Kate. Those blueberry muffins of yours would attract folks from everywhere, once the word gets out." I had to laugh at that thought. "Peggy just said to me the other day, she wished there was a place to have small dinner parties and showers other than church halls and taverns. As a professional interior decorator, you could make this place gorgeous!"

"Oh Ellie, stop," I said shaking my head. "This is just an exciting thought right now. I do want to please and honor Josephine with this house. If she's not happy with my decision, this will not be a happy place!"

"What's not for her to like?" she said throwing her hands up. "You are giving her respect and recognition, which she has never received."

"Then do you think she'd approve of me naming this place, 'Josephine's Guest House'?" I boldly asked Ellie.

"Oh, Kate, yes, the name is perfect!" Ellie cheered. "You could even put a plaque in her memory on the front of the house. It's a brilliant idea!"

"I thought so, too and my large attic certainly has possibilities." Our excitement seemed to fill the room. "Do you think she'll continue to move quilts around?" We chuckled.

"That could be an added attraction we haven't thought of, Kate." Ellie teased. "A lot of folks love a supernatural experience, if it's a pleasant one. I think she may enjoy the whole experience, since the house is all about her!" I never thought of that possibility.

"Oh Ellie, we think too much alike, and that's very dangerous! What would I do without you?"

"You'd already be back in South Haven, that's what!" she teased. "If you would have slept in your car the first night, you'd have signed the realtor's contract the next morning and headed back to South Haven!" We laughed knowing she had made an accurate observation. "Things happen for a good reason, Kate!"

"I think you're right, Ellie. I'll be eternally grateful for your hospitality and helping me turn the corner towards my new future. Let's make a toast to Josephine."

As we raised our cups of coffee, Ellie shouted: "To Josephine's Guest House!"

THE END

More Books from AQS

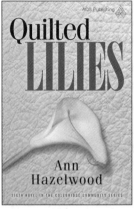

#1697

#7274

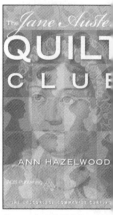

#1542

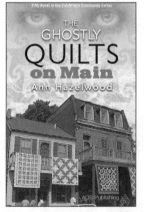

#1643

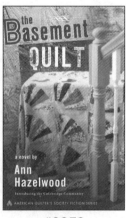

#8853

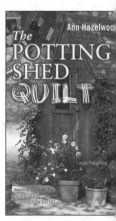

#1256

Look for these books nationally.

1-800-626-5420

Call or Visit our website at
www.AmericanQuilter.com